END OF THE HALLOWED

BY JUSTIN FERRANTE

TABLE OF CONTENTS (1)

TABLE OF CONTENTS (2)

CHAPTER 1 - THE END OF THE HALLOWED

The Hallowed: A select few that remain, untouched by the human greed that consumes all portions of every aspect of society.

The internet that was once used for the communications of the everyman had been reduced to artificial bots selling items made by "entrepreneurs" in their mothers' basements. The buyers? Other bots that used shoppers' wallets before confirming the purchase.

The workplace had never truly been a place of fun, but there used to be a sense of security in having a job. The writers were replaced with generative programs that scanned and vomited cheap imitations of the human soul. Sentences with nothing behind them. Words with no purpose.

Video was generated using prompts and cleaned up with minimal edits. Slop was produced en masse in order to grab any remaining attention that existed.

Humans rarely practiced medicine anymore. Insurance no longer covered it, even without agents. A robot would direct one to have a procedure completed by a robot.

Those who used to fill these spaces with warm hearts and full smiles were no longer welcome. They needed food. They needed breaks. They needed to breathe. *They were inefficient.*

Those that were "no longer needed" roamed the streets. They didn't have a way to provide an income, and with the limited amount of jobs left to be completed by humans, there was no choice. Many had no homes and became bitter, fighting for survival. These many felt invisible. But some found ways to do small jobs and still live somewhat normally, even if under what used to be considered poor conditions.

But humanity's hatred could not be quelled. The divisions between the "haves" and the "have-nots" had risen to an enormous degree. The seething rage behind the skin of each person made kindness a rare anomaly, and fighting a more common occurrence.

Through the past decade, the humans who owned everything resented the existence of those whose lives they plundered, as to them, they were an eyesore in the way of their greatness. To those who had everything taken, those in power were equal to the devil in comedic amounts of evil. There was one who observed in life, a few who did not conform to either side. They observed a select few that genuinely fought for the good of humanity as a whole. These were, in their eyes, "the hallowed." The select remained of good people in the world. But as conditions changed, even they couldn't hold on to their morals any longer.

That was the end of that group. The end of all those people who held on. All had been consumed by bitterness, or the hopelessness prevalent in the world.

At the end of their rope, and at the end of the hallowed, this person would come to be known as...

"GODSEND!!!"

At sharply 4:36 PM, Thursday 25th of May 2051, a security guard at an upper class department store hit the panic button under a desk. Before him lay the bodies of a freshly neutralized elderly couple.

"GO, GO, GO!" one of the attackers in a ski-mask shouted. A dozen or so more people ran into the store, armed. They ran through multiple sections, smashing and grabbing any expensive items that they could.

A humanoid robot started to panic, "BREAK IN ALERRT! BREAK IN ALERT!" This was one of the attendants of the store, used for helping people find where specific items were.

One of the thieves ran up to it and smashed a metal bat right into its head. It sounded as if it was continuing to make the alarm with a muffled speaker, but continued bats from the assailant muted it permanently.

"Damn clanker," the thief spat, jumping over the remains of the robot.

At the same time, a hovering aircraft remained pinned in the sky above the store. Cameras were pointed at the front of the store with the windows smashed.

"Such a coordinated robbery effort has never hit this chain before. It's rather sad to see this happen in *this* neighborhood. I guess there's a first time for everything," the news commentator spoke over footage of the outside of the location.

Inside was still pure chaos. Parents held their children's cries with their hands before the presence of shotguns. Those in the way and those who had resisted had already drawn their final breath. The bloodbath seemed indiscriminate, and only to eliminate obstacles.

The wealth disparity had grown so vast that in populated areas, one luxury good from a store such as this could supply ammunition and arms for a few dozen people. These people knew that even just stealing a few things would have made their raid worth the effort.

But the entire raid came to a halt when they heard the following over the store's loudspeaker.

"EVERYONE DROP TO YOUR KNEES, NOW! OR WE'RE GOING TO HAVE TO SEND IN THE DRONES!" a police captain's voice boomed over the loudspeaker. The bystanders in the store ducked down even further.

"WE'D GET CAUGHT IN THE CROSSFIRE!" one woman shrieked, despite a gun pointed at her by one of the thieves.

They all knew what this meant. Recently, the police had been testing a fleet of drones that would use their best guess and artificial intelligence in order to wipe out those breaking the law, bringing a quick end to a conflict. However, they were notorious for creating extra casualties. The rich had funded them regardless, stressed for their own safety and the belief that it would never be them in that situation.

Before anything else could happen, the entire building shook. The lights flickered.

"What was that?!" one of the thieves shouted to the other.

Another shake came directly afterward, and this time it was accompanied with a portion of the roof caving in. With the cave in came a single humanoid.

"THERE'LL BE NO NEED, OFFICER..."

The woman on the floor at gunpoint looked up. All she, and her captor, could see through the dust was one digital green bar, floating in front of what looked like a head. As the dust settled more and more, the woman could make out something grotesque. She could not tell if it were human or a robot, but it resembled a human, being bipedal with arms.

The person or *thing* looked to be made of entirely tiny pieces of metal that moved around like fluid. While still resembling a person, it had claws rather than hands. It didn't look solid, but more like a fluid of small chunks of metal being suspended together by a human shape of gravity. All of the appendages were overly long and tall, with spikes coming out of the shoulders and back, looking like a knight in armor. The head had four rounded spikes, guiding the shape of the back of its head. The lone glow of the singular green bar, acting like eyes, prevailed through its face. The dark gray figure floated above her.

The woman felt terror, looking into this imitation of humanity. Her assailant quickly pointed his weapon at the towering amalgamation of fleshy metal.

"THE HELL DO YOU WANT?!" the man shouted, aiming at the monster's face.

"**I WILL REBIRTH THE HALLOWED...**" the amalgamation spoke while reaching out its right claw, "**...BY ENDING ALL ELSE**."

In less than a second, the metal person-shaped *thing* sent out tranquilizer bullets in fourteen directions at once. Most of the thieves instantly fell to the ground, including the one right next to the woman.

"A godsend..." she looked down at her lifeless assailant, "You're a godsend..." she repeated as she looked back up at the metallic humanoid. The digital green bar floated around to the bottom of its face, now looking like an eerie grin on an eyeless face.

"**THOSE OVERCOME WITH GREED WILL BE PUNISHED. THOSE WHO MURDER WILL BE PUNISHED**," the "Godsend" spoke. It then turned its head to one last remaining thief with a ski mask. It was a younger woman with a baseball bat, the one that had destroyed the robot. But she hadn't killed anyone.

In an imperceivable moment, the metallic humanoid "Godsend" grabbed the girl and flew out of the store. To her, it was as if she teleported hundreds of feet in the air.

"AHHHHH!" she shouted at the top of her lungs as she was dragged through the atmosphere by the metallic humanoid. The metal figure used the machines in its body to fly off quickly toward another spot in the city, miles away.

Within another imperceivable moment, they were now in an alleyway behind an apartment building. She was disarmed completely, and without her ski mask.

"What? What the?!" she suddenly stood in an unfamiliar area. The metallic humanoid stood behind her, walking away.

"**IT ISN'T TOO LATE FOR YOU, CHANGE YOUR WAYS NOW**," it told her, dropping a stack of cash at her feet. She immediately picked it up and counted it. As she finished counting, she saw the metallic humanoid starting to walk away.

"WAIT!" she shouted as it turned back to her, "Why me?"

"**YOU HAD A WEAPON ON YOU. I KNEW ABOUT THE PISTOL BELOW YOUR WAISTBAND. YOU NEVER USED IT, OR EVEN THOUGHT ABOUT REACHING FOR IT. YOU ARE NOT A MURDERER. SO BE KIND TO YOUR NEIGHBORS**."

The "Godsend" took it and broke it. With that, the fluid metal monster made another leap that was akin to teleportation. The lone woman counted her money again, pondering what in the world just occurred before her.

6

"That sounded like a voice filter. Like a male voice? It was too glitchy and computer sounding though. Who was he?" she questioned, walking out of the alleyway.

Meanwhile, the metallic humanoid flew to another spot out of the public eye, but not far. When it landed, it flew between two buildings with no people around.

"**WELL, NOW I KNOW IT WORKS. I REALLY HAD TO TRY THAT AT THE SPUR OF THE MOMENT**!" the person said as the small chunks of metal all started to move out of the way, as if letting the person beneath out of a suit all the micro-robots formed. The person then held what was once a powerful metal suit as a small disc, in the palm of their hand.

"**WITH THIS POWER, IT NO LONGER HAS TO BE**...

...the end of the hallowed."

Between buildings, the one who interfered in the department store raid shoved their disc, which transformed into the fluid metal armor, into a bag they brought. They took off quickly, running into a nearby building where they would slide quietly into a group of people. The building was a local church, and the group of people patiently waited for a new alcoholics anonymous group to start.

The group of people all seemed distrustful of each other, not wanting to talk. They all awkwardly sat in an odd silence outside of room 109 on the first floor of the church. Most of them scrolled on their own devices, whether or not they were smartphones or smart glasses. But the silence was disrupted as the door to the room was opened.

"Are you guys all here for the A.A. meeting?" the balding, skinny hispanic man asked, pushing his glasses back toward his eyes. Some people outside didn't respond, others already knew the drill and started to walk in. A few nodded in silence to the man.

"Well, come in if you are," the man opened the second of the double doors, letting the others in. They went through to a room with a single large window, a whiteboard on the wall, cream white walls, and grey carpet. Eight seats were arranged in a circle, and the hispanic man took his seat as the leader of the group. Three people had already taken their places around the pastor. The four others awkwardly seated themselves, as if this were new to them.

"I just want to start by saying *all* of you are welcome here, and I am sorry for the odd question at the door. We just haven't had a group larger than five for ages," the pastor clarified his previous question, and continued,

"My name is Alan Rivera, feel free to call me Pastor Alan, or Pastor Rivera, or just Alan. Shepherd Mid-City is a church, but first and foremost, an alcoholics anonymous. We often talk about God... or spirituality, but if you aren't about that then don't let it bother you."

The seven besides Alan were eyeing each other, gauging each others' reaction. Nobody seemed uncomfortable with the idea. The one who picked up on this, Pastor Alan himself, was really the one starting to get uncomfortable.

"Quite a layer of ice we have, huh? Haha," He awkwardly laughed, "Let's get to introducing each other then. Would the newcomers raise their hand for introductions, if they want to?"

Two people raised their hands. One was a Korean-American man in baggy clothing and clean shoes. The other was a pale man with an androgynous bob-cut and black jeans. Pastor Alan gestured to the pale man, indicating he started with his introduction.

"Hi... everyone. My name is Milo Dupont," Milo spoke robotically, trying to mask his nervousness, "I, uh, well, I'm not really sober yet. But... that is why I'm here."

He nodded, then he hurried to sit down. He just hoped he didn't say anything incorrectly.

"Yeah, thank you for that, Milo. We don't have to get into talking about sobriety until we get into the tokens portion. However, that was honest of you to tell us all. Now you also had your hand up earlier, right?" Pastor Alan gestured to the other man in the gray sweatshirt and pants with a more Asian skin-tone. He quickly stood up, hands still in his jacket pockets.

"What up. Name's Owen. Owen Park. I... well I just realized how bad it was when I saw my bills. It was taking a good chunk of change. You know the drill, that's why I'm here," Owen explained about himself.

"Thank you, Owen. Also honest of you. That being said, is that it for newcomers?" Pastor Alan asked. He was met with silence, and took that as a cue to move on. He continued, "Alright, well, I believe neither of you mind if we start with an opening prayer?"

Both Owen and Milo shook their heads to indicate they didn't mind.

"Dear God, thank You for allowing us to come together and grow as a group today. Thank you for allowing our group to grow and for more people to come to a place where they can strive for sobriety. In Your name I pray, Amen."

The tension in the room died down as Pastor Alan finished up the prayer. People brought their heads back with their eyes open now.

"Now! Let's move on," Pastor Alan stood up, and walked over to one of the men on his right, "I wanna start off tokens by saying congrat—"

The young, blonde dude quickly grabbed the token from out of Pastor Alan's hands. He smirked, cutting him off.

"Thank you, thank you! I knew I would get to this point with just a *little* help!" the blonde guy cut off Pastor Alan.

"*Yes*, Calvin *Becker*," Pastor Alan responded, "Congratulations. But maybe don't cut me off while I'm giving you your token."

"Yeah, yeah," Calvin threw the coin up and down in his hand. Pastor Alan rolled his eyes.

"I'll also give out the 'Starting the Journey' tokens for coming here," Pastor Alan said, pulling out three tokens.

He handed one to Owen, one to Milo, and he held out a third to one of the ladies sitting on the other side of the circle. She quickly snatched it from his hands, turning her head away from him.

"What was that all about?" Calvin whispered to another guy next to him.

"Why would I care?" He asked.

"Let's refrain from talking outside of our group," Pastor Alan immediately turned upon hearing whispering.

"Look what you did," the man angrily averted his eyes from Calvin, crossing his arms.

"Alright, Declan. Not now. Let's get into this week's reading. People can share afterwards, if they feel comfortable," Pastor Alan tried to alleviate the situation.

Pastor Alan sat back down, opening up a book titled "Living in Sobriety." He told the newcomers a synopsis of the first three chapters, and began chapter four. There was little interference from the participants of the meeting, and it was mostly just them listening to the reading. Calvin got up, and made himself some coffee about halfway through the meeting. The newcomers watched, wondering if that was okay. There was no backlash, so Owen ended up doing the same thing after.

"...and that does it for chapter four," Pastor Alan finished up, "Before we get into anything else, did anybody feel like they found anything applicable for their lives in the text?"

At first, there was silence. But after a few awkward moments, one of the women by the Pastor's side raised her hand. Pastor Alan gestured to her to go.

"Well, I know at least for me, having someone else be your accountability partner has helped in the past. It's just... well for me, I usually have someone who isn't going through the same thing. So internally, I just started to get bitter. My mind would be like, 'Well you don't know how it feels. Don't boss me around.' I know that isn't healthy," the woman explained, "But I think maybe being accountability partners for the same issue at the same time would help me out greatly, like you were saying at the beginning of the chapter."

"Thank you for being honest, Amara," Pastor Alan interjected, "Those frustrated feelings can be a source of temptation when trying to distance ourselves from relapsing. If we distance ourselves from the instructions of others, like downplaying their advice, there ends up being subconscious justification going on in the back of the mind. If we truly believe they don't get it, or don't understand us, it gives the brain an excuse to keep going, or to ignore that advice. So finding ways to cope with that is definitely a must for accountability partners."

At that time, another one of the women in the room raised her hand. She was another young adult in her late twenties, wearing glasses over her light, Asian-American skin tone.

"Yes, go ahead... Margot, right?" Pastor Alan asked as he gestured for her to share her thoughts. She wore a gray tank top and black cargo pants. Her black hair was neck-length. The combat boots were a stand-out as well.

"I haven't really thought of having an accountability partner in the first place, so maybe that's something I should do," Margot admitted.

"I would highly suggest it. I personally have seen some of the quickest results with accountability partners in the past," Pastor Alan told her, "Anybody else have anything?"

Silence.

"Well, I hope you're all okay with me cutting a little bit of open discussion time today. My old fridge broke, but I have a friend who's giving me his old one. I just have to rent a truck to get it to my house. So just for today, I'll skip to the ending prayer and you all can feel free to stick around and talk on the patio, okay?" he told everyone.

Just like that, he went through the ending prayer and all the participants were out on the patio. Pastor Alan was out and on his way. The one girl who never spoke in the meeting was attempting to leave, when Calvin called out to her.

"Hey, you never spoke up! What's your name?" Calvin loudly asked her back as she walked the opposite way. She froze, turning around.

"Pretty sure my friends made a mistake making me come here. I can handle this on my own," she spat back at Calvin. Her condescending attitude matched her punk appearance despite the blonde hair, with her graphic tee and black skirt. She was caked in makeup, too.

"It's not that easy, girl. Trust me, if I could have done it alone, I would've," the taller, bearded man named Declan yapped back at her.

"It's Hazel. Don't call me 'girl,' beardo," Hazel shot back at him, making him visibly annoyed. So Hazel turned around and left. Declan stayed silent, cooling himself off.

"I was just going to say, she really didn't say anything. She was new this week, too. Guess she was forced to come here," Amara speculated aloud.

"But seriously, the group grew more than double over the past two weeks. Wonder what this says about society at large," Calvin pointed out.

"Oh, so she was new? I guess I should have known from the token," Owen realized, seeing as she was the only one besides himself and Milo to get the starting token.

"Holy crap!" Milo shouted as an explosion sound came from his phone.

"What's going on?" Declan asked intimidatingly. Milo turned his phone and the others watched the video play out.

The group all saw a video of a department store in the middle of a robbery. But in the middle of the video, a metallic humanoid crashed through the ceiling and saved the day.

"Based on the footage, the people in the comments are calling him 'Godsend.' Those comments also refer to him as a hero, saving the ordinary citizens in the building. Or perhaps it is something different, as some speculate it's a government experiment. Other comments have been calling it a humanoid drone. Who or what exactly is this mysterious vigilante?" the news anchor explained after the in-person footage of the event.

"Crazy world we live in, right? You never know what the government is gonna do next," Declan sneered, turning away from the video.

"That thing is a drone? I thought drones looked more like flying discs," Margot commented.

"You both think it's a drone? That's definitely a person. No way public funding could build something like *that*. Unless it's someone from the military gone rogue," Amara added.

"Who's to say it's from here?" Calvin thought aloud, "Could be someone from abroad. With speed like that, it's impossible to tell."

The few gathered continued to watch as Milo still held out his phone.

"None of the cameras were able to gather any information on Godsend. It seems the technology used to create this metal monster also scrambles any radar. Even the police are dumbfounded, unsure of how something like that could come and go so quickly. Some even think that Godsend is truly supernatural," the news anchor continued to mouth off.

"Well I'm not robbing any stores. Just look like whatever it is, it's just doing the cops' jobs. Not my problem," Declan looked the other way, starting to leave.

"Their job? Is it the police's job to decide what justice is?" Margot asked aloud. A few of the others looked at her as if she were crazy.

"Duh—"

"Of course not—"

Owen and Milo both spoke immediately, both cutting each other off. The two paused, looking at each other.

"Why wouldn't the police put down people like that?! They were murdering innocent people to try and make a buck!" Owen immediately got defensive.

"Well... I just don't think that— I don't think that it's in their jurisdiction. I think the laws around what they can do have changed a lot—" Milo presented his side of the argument.

"Guys, calm down. All of you," Amara stepped in, "Part of the reason I drank was to forget my folks' political ramblings. Here we are after AA arguing about the news. Is that any way to meet people? Who cares about what's going on out there? We're here to support each other."

The group realized this. Maybe it was the fact there were new people to the group, or maybe there was an unease over society as a whole at the moment. But all those present outside of the church knew that they had horrible histories in connecting with others. Of course, this would lead to strife.

"Who cares about this so-called-hero Godsend? We're here for ourselves. We need work. We keep mistaking our hero as the liquor store across the street," Amara continued to rant.

"I get it Amara," Calvin's usual chipper tone suddenly went somber, "I don't need a reminder." He walked away, not looking back but waving his hand. As he left the building, the echoes of his last words rang through, "See you next week."

The new people stood in shock, while Amara and Declan both looked blank-faced.

"Does he change up often like that?" Owen asked, hands in his pockets.

"Yeah, maybe. Something like that. But with that, I'm also gonna head out. If you all decide to stay, let's talk more next week," Declan used that as an excuse to head out himself.

"Well then."

"Guess that's time then."

"See you next week!"

"Take care guys."

The group all parted ways, taking different means of transportation back home. From buses, to cars, to bikes, and more, each person went about their way differently. They all lived differently, and saw the world differently. But one of them was no different from the "hero" they saw.

The one who left early from the meeting pouted, hating that one bearded man who spoke ill of her. This, of course, is Hazel Schulz. She didn't feel like going to that alcoholics anonymous meeting, but instead was urged to by peers. She believed herself to be better than their perception.

"Where does that Alan guy get off? Seriously? Even people that don't know they need help need it? Sounds exactly like what Becca would say..." Hazel complained under her breath as she walked down the street. She looked up to see a Southeastern Pennsylvania Transportation Authority sign outside of the train stop. She waited there for the next train.

Roughly half an hour later, the door to her apartment slammed open. She returned with an attitude. To her dismay, her roommate was sitting on the couch right in front of her.

"Yo, Hazel. So how'd it go?" her roommate, Becca, smirked. Her face was brewing with the confidence that she was a changed person.

"Shut it, Becca. I don't wanna talk about whatever *that* was. It was an embarrassment to even be there," Hazel complained, putting her bag down and heading toward her room.

"You really got *nothing* from that?" Becca asked, genuinely curious why Hazel was so oppositional.

"Everyone there was older than me! There were old dudes there who had, like, families and stuff. I can't believe you and Emma convinced me to go to that thing. Just because I drink a bit too much doesn't mean I belong in a damn AA meeting!" Hazel shouted, venting her frustrations to Becca. The air between them was electric. Becca didn't realize it was going to upset Hazel this much. It started to make sense from her perspective after her ranting. However, she said one thing that stuck with Becca.

"So you admit you drink a bit much?" Becca asked in response, clinging on to the one thing that might convince Hazel otherwise.

"Well, I mean—" Hazel trailed off, realizing what she said and desperately trying to find an excuse.

"You said it. Not me. You *do* drink a bit much and you know it! When Emma and I were trying to get you to go to that meeting you refused to say you even drink *often*," Becca took this chance to lay it on thick, "But we see you, Hazel. We want what's best for you. We've both seen you come home at two in the morning most of the days of the week. We've seen you downing shots on the couch just so you can go to bed. We've seen how you wake up with yesterday's makeup still on and how you can't get out of bed until noon. It's a problem! Even your parents know—"

Click.

The door opened. Emma, the third roommate, appeared in the doorway. She started to overhear what Becca was yelling about, and understood what was going on. But as she opened the door, she saw Hazel about to burst into tears.

"Stop there, Becca," Emma demanded. But it was too late. She had pressed a button.

"Do *not* bring them up," Hazel demanded, seething through her held-in tears. She quickly grabbed the bag she just put down, and started a sprint into the other room.

"Hazel!" Emma shouted to try and get her attention. It was to no avail. Hazel quickly locked herself in her room.

"I'm sorry. She just... I don't know. Seeing how she couldn't tell what was wrong got me so riled up," Becca apologized, seeing the disdain on Emma's face.

"Well we're the ones who made her go to alcoholics anonymous. She's already gonna be mad at us if she didn't feel some kind of belonging there, or something," Emma put simply.

"Well she *went*. That's something. But it sounds like she only met older dudes with families there or something. It doesn't seem like it's for her. At least that's what she told me," Becca informed her.

"I stood outside for a minute. I got the gist. And I know you just want the best for her, but bringing up how she got basically disowned isn't gonna help," Emma argued.

"Yeah, yeah, I realize that now. I mean, if your parents kick you out over that kinda stuff, don't you know that it's a *problem* at that point?" Becca questioned.

"Yeah, but that's not the point. The point is that it hurts, so it's easier to live in denial. Just to focus and devote yourself to... anything else," Emma speculated. The two sorted out what had gone wrong.

At that same moment, Hazel was in her room curled up in the fetal position. She refused to sob, but she felt as if everyone was against her. Almost out of instinct, she grabbed the bottle of vodka hidden under her bed. But when she looked that way, she noticed a token laying on the ground. It must've fallen out of her pocket earlier, but under her arm was the welcome token from Pastor Alan.

That made her stop for a moment. Even if she hated that group, and felt uncomfortably awkward there, why did she still go? Despite claiming that her roommates forced her to go, she knew that nobody held her hand all the way there. Remembering that she was the one that decided to take the train there, she let go of the bottle.

She got up, throwing her bag into her closet. She picked up the bottle of vodka, and a few other secret shooters that she was keeping secret. Holding them all in her arms as if she were cradling them, she kicked open the door to her bedroom. Becca and Emma immediately turned around to see the commotion, watching as she quickly came out. She quickly walked over to them, looking down and not making eye contact.

"Take these from me," Hazel demanded, putting out her arms full of booze. The others couldn't see her face, but saw mascara drooping down her cheeks.

"You had more in your—?"

"Shush. Just take them," Emma cut Becca off, grabbing some of the bottles from her. Becca watched as Emma went over to the sink, pouring them out and recycling the glass. Becca sighed, following and doing the same. Hazel stayed still, unsure of how to approach the situation.

"Hey," Becca broke the silence, "I'm seriously sorry. I probably took that too far."

"No, Becca... you're right. I just... ah, man," Hazel sniffled over her words, "It's like, just a lot easier to blame someone else. Or something else. Just make it so I'm not the problem. You know?"

"She should know. I gave her a talking to right after making you retreat to your room. I guess it ended up being a good thing, though. You really could have chosen to keep diverting the problem there," Emma gave her two cents.

"Ugh," Hazel sighed deeply again, "Sometimes I just hate myself. I'm the one who dug this whole... mess."

"That's not what this is about, Hazel," Becca quickly corrected her, "You just got back from a *recovery* meeting. Remember that. So just know, this problem extends past you, but you're doing what you can to fix it."

"Yeah, and just because you didn't like this group doesn't mean we can't find you another one, or maybe even a different method? Maybe an online meet with face calls?" Emma tried to alleviate the situation more. Hazel shook her head, calmed down, and slowed her heart rate.

"No. It's that stupid token the guy there gave me that reminded me I shouldn't be drinking, or trying to escape. I just kept trying to blame something else, or saying that I wasn't a problem. I should go back, and I should probably... say sorry," Hazel admitted. The two roommates looked at each other as if she was crazy. The two never knew Hazel to be so blunt about apologizing.

"Are you sure?" Emma asked. Hazel nodded.

"I can't just have a sour attitude every time I'm told maybe I'm wrong," Hazel admitted. Emma smiled, grinning a mischievous grin.

"HEY!" Becca shouted as Emma grabbed the two of them, making them do a group hug.

"Aw, Hazel. You're finally growing up. So sad to see our iconic trash talker have a look in the mirror. But hey, good on ya!" Emma laughed.

"HUH?!" Hazel angrily retorted, still kept still in the group hug.

"Seriously, Hazel," Becca spoke up, "It's brave of you to face the change head-on." The three of them continued to embrace.

"Would you guys forgive me if I hid *more*...?" Hazel quietly asked.

"What?" Emma asked, finally letting Hazel and Becca go. Hazel suddenly turned.

"Nothing!" she tried to course-correct.

"Do you have *more* alcohol in the closet or something?" Becca asked, sounding disappointed. Hazel took a moment to respond.

"I do NOT! But if I did, would you still forgive me?" Hazel asked.

"Knowing you, you might. Maybe we'll do a search," Emma joked around. The three of them laughed it out, glad that they could reach a conclusion. All felt harmonious between roommates again in the apartment of Hazel Schulz. She would continue going to Pastor Alan's group.

In the shadows, Godsend remained.

After the fight, Hazel and her roommates needed to pick up some things for the apartment. Something for dinner, and snacks for the week.

The three walked down the snack aisle, looking for extra stuff to have out during their binge watching sessions.

"Now what kinda chips should we have?" Becca asked, kneeling down to a few different flavors.

"Barbeque. For sure," Emma adamantly stated her opinion. Hazel looked back at her like she was mad.

"Uhh, you mean sea salt? The best kind?" Hazel fought back. But right after she said that, she noticed a familiar face. Down the aisle was someone in a gray hoodie, picking up some dipping sauce. Hazel was sure it was Owen Park. Who knew she'd see someone from AA so soon?

"I'm not taking orders from an alcoholic law student," Emma joked, grabbing the barbeque chips off the shelf.

"EMMA! TOO SOON!" Becca shot back at her. But she then noticed Hazel hadn't even heard the comment. Hazel was too focused, looking at Owen down the aisle. She tried to get her attention, "Hazel, what's up?"

"Huh?!" Hazel suddenly snapped out of it, looking at her two roommates who seemed curious.

"Do you know him or something?" Emma asked, darting her eyes over to Owen.

"Don't look! He's from my *group!*" Hazel whisper-shouted at her friends, turning her head away.

At this point, Owen slightly turned his head. He noticed that it was the girl that was all angry at the AA meeting he went to. *Oh, look, it's little miss can-do-it-herself,* he thought. He wasn't sure if she was just embarrassed or something, so he just decided to walk into the next aisle over. He pretended he didn't even notice her.

BZZZT! His phone went off with a notification as he went into the next aisle. He looked down, reading the notification. It was a text.

"**PASTOR ALAN**: *Hey Owen, just checking in. How have you been doing since the AA meeting the other day? Hope you're having a good week.*"

Owen rolled his eyes. But, on second thought, the meeting had been helpful for him. Even having that dumb token was another reason to feel like he shouldn't fail now.

"I should probably go thank him..." Owen admitted to himself, grabbing his stuff and hurrying to the checkout.

Outside, Owen walked between two distinct areas. The clean streets of Philadelphia had lights illuminating rows of gleaming outlet stores. Well-dressed shoppers strolled by, their laughter echoing off the pristine facades. Many were just absorbed in their digital worlds, looking in the direction of each other without seeing each other.

Just a street away, however, the scene dissolved into stark contrast. Dilapidated buildings leaned precariously, casting long shadows over the broken pavement. Stern security guards stood watch at a heavily guarded checkpoint, their presence a clear message: only "their kind" were permitted to cross.

"Can't believe we voted on this shit," Owen scoffed, walking by the checkpoint, "Income checkpoints."

"YOU!" a security guard shouted. Own immediately thought it was him the guard was talking to. But as his eyes darted in that direction, he noticed another person. A

24

hooded man was attempting to sneak in from over the gate.

"Good luck, buddy," Owen saluted.

"DON'T MAKE ME MEET YOU WITH LETHAL ACTION!" the guard shouted. Owen heard the perpetrator's body hit the ground with a loud thud as he walked in the other direction. He shrugged.

Now, back at Shepherd Mid-City Church, Owen cautiously knocked on the outside door of the pastor's office. It opened immediately after.

"Owen! Glad you could come see me!" Pastor Alan opened up, wearing a Hawaiian shirt and his usual overly-warm grin.

"I just had some time... are you always here?" Owen asked.

"What do you think I do for a living, Owen? This is essentially my second home," Pastor Alan teased, gesturing for Owen to come inside. The office was small and cluttered, stacks of papers and well-worn books and Bibles overflowing from shelves. A single window looked out onto the street. Owen stepped in hesitantly.

"Please, have a seat," Pastor Alan said, clearing some papers from a chair.

Owen sat down, the vinyl cool beneath him. An awkward silence hung in the air for a moment.

"So," Pastor Alan began, leaning forward with a gentle smile, "how have you been feeling since the meeting the other day?"

Owen shrugged, looking down at his hands. "I don't know... better, I guess. That token thing... it's stupid, but it's like... another reason not to mess up." He fumbled with the small coin in his pocket.

"It's not stupid if it helps," Pastor Alan said softly,

"Sometimes we need those little reminders."

Owen nodded slightly. "Yeah, I guess," he hesitated. "Thanks... for the meeting. And the token." The words felt foreign coming out of his mouth.

"You're very welcome, Owen. That's what we're all there for." Pastor Alan paused. "What did you think of the others in the group?"

"Not the type of people I thought would be involved with AA. Then again, what exactly *are* the 'type' of people? Even *I'm* not the type... I think," Owen speculated aloud. "Oh yeah," he continued, "I saw that one girl who didn't say anything—"

"Owen," Pastor Alan cut him off, "I don't mind if you guys are all friends with each other, but I like to try and keep our personal lives separate. Well, besides you."

"Clearly," Owen laughed, "Just because you're good friends with my Uncle Ken, huh? Didn't know if you remembered..."

"Right," Pastor Alan smiled, bridging back nostalgia for Owen. His family was from Philadelphia, and he had roots here. It reminded him of times when he was younger, and things were simpler. But the mood suddenly shifted.

"So who are you, really?" Pastor Alan's usual chipper tone was gone. He sounded dead serious.

"What... do you mean by that? It's me, Owen, duh," Owen tried to laugh it off. The atmosphere grew tense. Pastor Alan leaned forward.

"Owen, you know he cares. Your uncle, that is. He's a good man, and he worries about you."

"Yeah, well, I'm doing better, Pastor. Really. The meeting helped, talking to people who... get it, I guess." Owen avoided eye contact, focusing on a loose thread on the arm of the chair. He wasn't sure why this mood shift had occurred, but he suddenly felt like he was in a job interview.

"That's good to hear," Pastor Alan continued, his voice softer now, but still probing. "But lately... there's been talk. Things happening in the city. Unbelievable things."

"Unbelievable things? Oh there's been nothing but unbelievable things since the last election. What could be more unbelievable?" Owen desperately tried to make the atmosphere lighter.

"You haven't heard?" Pastor Alan seemed surprised. "The robbery at that department store the other day? And... the figure that stopped it?"

Owen's heart rate continued to rise, uncertain why Pastor Alan still felt like he was investigating him. He tried to keep his expression neutral.

"Vaguely. Something about a vigilante, right? We were talking about it outside. The news was reporting on a kind of... robot dude," Owen played dumb.

"Vigilante is one word for it," Pastor Alan said slowly. "Others are calling it... Godsend." He watched Owen's face carefully for any flicker of recognition or surprise.

Owen shrugged again, trying to appear nonchalant. "Sounds like a comic book. Glad someone stopped those robbers, though. People are getting desperate these days."

"Indeed," Pastor Alan agreed. "But this... Godsend. The descriptions are... unusual. Metallic, almost fluid. Incredibly fast. Did your uncle mention anything?"

"Uncle Ken? No. He's been busy with work, I think." Owen kept his answers short, hoping to steer the conversation away from this strange topic.

Pastor Alan shifted in his chair. "You know, Owen,

27

your uncle mentioned you've been... tinkering. With technology. Said you were always a bright kid, good with your hands."

"Oh I get it now," Owen shook his head, "Or at least I think I do. Why on God's green earth do you think *I* would be Godsend?"

The pastor seemed relieved. Owen hit it right on the money.

"Well, your uncle did say you were really good with technology..." Pastor Alan mentioned.

"I'm good with technology in the *'look at my gaming setup'* way. I helped uncle Ken set up his phone, that's all. Making a freaking *Iron-Man* suit? Yeah, not in a million years. Why would you even think it could possibly be me?" Owen responded, putting any rumor to rest.

"Okay, I figured it wasn't you, but I had to check at least a little!" Pastor Alan complained, going back to his usual self, "Some scary police officer showed up, saying that they think Godsend attends this church or something! It was too much for me to handle!"

"Godsend... attends this church? They confirmed it was a human in that suit?!" Owen loudly questioned.

"I didn't wanna ask questions. Dealing with the police gives me too much anxiety. All I know is that they said they believe that if Godsend were a person, the last audio recording of their glitchy voice-filter was captured on the way *here*. On the same day as the AA meeting, too. I figured, maybe it was someone in the meeting?" Pastor Alan blurted out.

That was a lot to handle at once. Godsend, in the group?

"Why would Godsend be a drunk? Or emotionally unstable?" Owen asked aloud. After remembering how they crashed into the situation without permission, he continued, "Actually, I could see it."

"It's weird, but it almost makes sense, doesn't it?" Pastor Alan asked, but realized how much he was saying aloud, "Well... before you answer that, I should probably check myself. I'm really not supposed to be telling you this, but I just couldn't help it. I figured, since I knew your family, you'd be the *least* likely."

"I appreciate that, Pastor. Really. But I'm just trying to get my life back on track. AA, maybe find a job soon. No time for superheroics." Owen stood up, feeling the need to escape the confined space of the office. "Thanks again for everything. I should probably get going."

Pastor Alan stood as well, his expression still thoughtful. "Owen... if you ever need to talk about anything... *anything* at all... you know you can come to me, right?"

"Not just if I figure out who Godsend is?" Owen asked, about to leave.

"It really isn't your responsibility, Owen. I'm talking more... helping you avoid any substance abuse," Pastor Alan was upfront with him, "Let's forget about the whole Godsend thing for now. It isn't even for sure."

"I'll make sure to let you know," Owen told him, quickly vanishing from the place.

Drops of rain still slithered off of the cold, metal badges of the police. They hadn't brought an umbrella that day, and as they walked into the mall, they were still drenched.

"Damn weather app..." one of the officers complained, "No matter how advanced technology gets, it's still wrong sometimes."

As they strolled into one of the populated food court areas, people around the officers became visibly uncomfortable. As their power grew, so did the potential consequences of interacting with them. The group of four ignored it.

"You remember the call. Sounded like a 'Karen.' Persian man, skinny, facial hair, and black hoodie. Matches perfectly what a racist would think," another cop scoffed, pushing her hair out of her face.

"C'mon now. We need to treat this like it's a threat, just in case. She said she saw a weapon," another cop yapped back.

Sirens. It was too late for speculation. Most of the mall around them didn't even flinch when the alarms started to blare.

"Did another middle schooler pull the fire alarm?" a nearby man speculated. The cops nodded to each other, running to a vantage point to see over the balcony of the food court and down to the first floor.

There, they saw him. The very person that the woman was talking about on the phone was in the middle of robbing a jewelry counter. The cop who complained winced.

"Guess this is real," another cop sighed, pulling out a pistol. The other two near him pulled out a rifle each.

"EVERYBODY GET OUT! WE HAVE A—"

BOOM! The man already shot back. No fear in his eyes. The police ducked and ran the other way. The man, eyes cold and unwavering, squeezed off another shot, shattering a display case nearby. Shards of glass rained down as shoppers shrieked and dove for cover. The police, regrouping, returned fire, their rifles barking in the echoing mall.

"STAY DOWN!" a police officer yelled, pulling a terrified woman behind a potted plant, "He's got a clear shot from there!"

The shooter ran behind the fallen plants. He reloaded quickly, a grim on his face.

"He's trying to draw us out! Don't take the bait, stick to cover!" one of the officers, a burly man named Officer Miller, shouted.

A bullet whizzed past his head, embedding itself in the wall behind him. Miller ducked lower, his hand tightening on his pistol.

Another officer, the younger woman who called the caller a 'Karen,' attempted to flank the robber, creeping along the wall of a nearby shoe store. But the robber's eyes, quick and predatory, caught her movement. He spun, firing a precise shot that grazed her arm. She cried out, stumbling back into cover, clutching her bleeding limb.

All around looked above themselves. The glass ceiling had been obliterated. The shards had been turned to dust. Rain poured in, drenching the whole group. The robber, and the cops all looked in awe as the metallic angel descended into their vision from above.

"We're going to need backup," the younger female cop spoke into her hidden wrist communication device, "*Silver Prophet* is here."

Godsend had returned. The metallic humanoid hovered above the group. All civilians in the mall had retreated. Some started to film the occurrence.

"**GREED**-" Godsend beamed down on the people below, "**GREED HAS DESTROYED THE HUMAN EXPERIENCE**."

"It talks..." Officer Miller nervously spoke under his breath, unable to move at the terrifying sight.

"GODSEND!" the robber shouted, dropping his weapon, "I AM ONE OF YOUR PEOPLE. I AM ONE OF THE HALLOWED! THE SYSTEMS IN PLACE ROBBED ME OF EVERYTHING! I JUST WANT TO PROVIDE—"

CRASH. Godsend shot a shockwave through one of their fingers, throwing the robber back against the wall with sheer force.

"**THE POLICE**..." Godsend continued, "...**HAVE INDEED BEEN USED. USED BY THOSE CORRUPTED IN THEIR GREED**."

They paused. The man had hope in his eyes.

"**HOWEVER, YOUR THEFT IS STILL UNJUSTIFIED. TAKING FROM THOSE WHO DID NOT WRONG YOU WILL ONLY CONTINUE THE CYCLE OF HATRED**," Godsend beamed at the man, "**YOU ARE NOT... THE HALLOWED**." Another shockwave sent the man into paralysis. He fell to the ground as the green beam across Godsend's face swirled in circles.

The police started to fire at Godsend. The bullets bounced off of the fluid metal suit.

"You probably get off, thinking that you *embody* justice, BUDDY!" Officer Miller shouted, "But exercising unchecked power is just going to make you go crazy!"

"**THOSE... BEHIND THE STAGE PLAY OF THE WORLD. THEY CONTROL YOU. YOU ARE NOT THE HALLOWED**." Godsend returned. They gathered what looked to be energy into their limbs, and shot directly up, back into the sky in a digital green bolt.

The officers sank to their knees. The rain continued to pour in.

"Cuff the robber. We're taking him in. Whether or not our *Silver Prophet* intervened, we have a job to do," Miller told the rest.

"BUT—!"

"I SAID..." Miller raised his voice at the female officer who tried to interject, "...Cuff him. Publicly, nothing much besides a robbery happened here. But between us, we have to collect all the possible footage and recordings we've got."

The officers saluted, and got to work. The ambulance showed up soon after, hoisting the man into medical care before his detainment. Despite not saying anything, officer Miller felt the most defeat of anybody there.

"Godsend..." he muttered to himself, leaving the scene of the crime and heading back to his patrol car, "I thought I had an idea of who you were. Showing up here throws off everything," he slammed his door behind him, frustrated.

Back at the police station, officer Miller entered his office visibly frustrated. However, someone was waiting for him there.

"You don't have to sit in my chair like that," Officer Miller said, annoyed. The other man, in a tan coat, turned his chair to face him. He wore a tan hat as well, his face covered in darkness.

"Code *Silver Prophet*. It was too late to call it discreetly. I heard he was already there before anybody suspected anything," the man in the chair said.

"Get up man, we can discuss but stop acting all shady," Officer Miller shooed him off the chair. He rose, sighing as if his act had been ruined.

"Okay seriously, Miller, what happened with Godsend? He really just appeared, said nobody there was 'the hallowed' and left?" the man in the coat asked.

"Basically. It's thrown me off, Hadley. How do we know Godsend is from that church group, anyway?" Miller asked the man in the coat, whose name was Hadley.

"Every method we've tried to track this guy with— has failed. Something in the mechanics of the suit blurs video enough that nobody can make out the details of the suit. We tried to use satellite imagery, infrared, you name it. The strangest of all is *how* we don't know what this is. Whether it be a suit or a drone, something this powerful had to have *billions* of dollars go into it. So *why* then can't the CIA track it? They could tell me my social security number before they even knew my first name— but suddenly this 'Godsend' appears and they shrug their shoulders?! It pisses me off to no end!" Hadley ranted, getting progressively angrier.

"You somehow avoided my question..." Miller got annoyed, prompting him again.

"Right. The last audio we have is a civilian video taken right outside of the church there. It was live too, so there's no way it was AI generated," Hadley pulled up a hologram on his watch. He swiped through the air until it displayed what looked like a live video coming from a civilian phone.

They were live-streaming on social media, talking to random people on the street right by Shepherd Mid-City Church. But in the background, for just a moment, was a glitchy voice—

"**Well, now I know it works. I really had to try that at the spur of the moment**!"

"There!" Hadley pointed out, pausing the video, "And we've deduced that this is Godsend... by the... voice filter. Duh."

"And the voice is getting quieter rapidly, but clearly. So they were walking directly away from the camera—"

"—To where the church is. That's what I came up with. But both you and I deduced that they seemed to be some sort of vigilante, like the news said. But..." Hadley, cutting off Miller, couldn't conclude what to say next.

"It appeared as if he worked with the police on the first go-around. But this time, he basically told us to screw off. Or did he unintentionally work with the police the first time?"

"Or is Godsend more than one person?" Hadley added to the speculation. The two of them were stumped. Pulling up files for each person, nobody fit the description.

"**HAZEL SCHULZ**? No, she's in college. Living with roommates. Her family is wealthy, but it doesn't seem like they would give her access to something like that.

"**MILO DUPONT**? Looks like he's struggling just to get a job. Lots of resumes sent out this month. Would you *need* a job with a suit like that?"

"**OWEN PARK**? Living on his own, used to be a streamer. He played video games a lot. Now he's in AA meetings. It says he's unemployed. But the pastor could vouch for him."

"**MARGOT DAVIS**? A single woman in her 20s, working as a waitress. Her mom was a widow, now she's dead. The parents used to own a sailboat business."

"**DECLAN VOLKOV**? I'd say he's the most likely. He's only a second generation citizen. His family is from Russia. However, they have no history, and he's a chef. There's no history of crime, and the parents are still alive and live nearby."

"**AMARA TAYLOR**? Her father is a cop, kinda like us. Her mom is an accountant." Hadley stated.

"Yeah, Hadley, but we're detectives. We might be working as cops right now, but if we don't figure out who this guy is, the head of the CIA ain't gonna be happy," Miller reprimanded him, "That only leaves him, Hadley. We might have to investigate him."

Hadley turned to face the wall, looking serious. But then he laughed, "Calvin?" Hadley slapped his knee, "Oh Calvin couldn't hurt a fly. My younger brother might talk smack, but he's just insecure."

"He's the one most well-connected with rich people. Your family isn't exactly *poor*. He's been living alone for nearly a decade, and has quite the inheritance. Not *billions* of course, but—"

"You really think **CALVIN** could be *GODSEND*?" Hadley beamed at Miller, "That boy could care less about justice and all that, he didn't really take after his *detective* brother after all."

"We can't pretend he couldn't be, Hadley *Becker*."

Thursday had come again for Shepherd Mid-City. Pastor Alan sat alone inside room 109, cleaning the coffee machine. He hummed to himself quietly, wearing yet another Hawaiian shirt.

"It's about time," Alan cheered to himself, walking to the doors. Upon opening, he heard the chatter come to a halt. The same seven as last week had returned. Most notably, was the reappearance of the runaway.

"Come on in, take a seat!" the pastor gestured inside. Quietly, people arranged themselves back into a circle, Owen lagging behind the rest.

"They were just chatting about current events, Pastor. Nothing relevant for our case," Owen whispered to Alan before sitting himself down. The pastor did not react. But the room did indeed come to a standstill. Declan was the last to sit, holding a coffee.

"How was this past week?" Pastor Alan asked aloud, met with silence. Declan sipped his coffee. "Tired from something, Declan?"

"Early morning shift. Short ribs gotta be served, and they aren't really quick," he explained, setting down an already-empty coffee cup.

"Short ribs?" Alan asked.

"C'mon Alan. I've told you I'm a chef," Declan seemed a little more cooperative than usual.

"Well I'm glad you could make it anyway. Anybody else have something interesting going on? All I did this week was mow the church lawn, hah!" Pastor Alan fibbed.

"I— I'm sorry," Hazel spoke up, "This... isn't on topic or anything. But I'd just like to say sorry. For... last week. Didn't wanna make anybody feel bad about themselves."

37

"I think you're good," Margot interjected, "Seeing how young you are, I get that it might be embarrassing to come here. Even I feel young coming here. But I am pushing thirty, I guess."

"Hah, listen to her. 'Pushing thirty.' Oh how you'll realize..." Owen laughed aloud.

"I'm twenty-five, though," Hazel cleared up.

"You're *twenty-five?* Jeez, I thought you were nineteen or something. But hey, all are welcome!" Calvin couldn't help but blurt aloud.

"HEY!" she shouted back.

"Alright, alright. I'm losing you guys. You're all talking over each other. Milo? Amara? Thoughts?" Pastor Alan redirected the conversion.

"Not much to report. You?" Amara immediately deflected, gesturing to Milo.

"Ah, I dunno. Just... still looking for a job," Milo quietly explained. "It's a tough world out there, Milo. Keep at it," Pastor Alan encouraged. "Anyone else have any progress updates, or anything they want to share about their week? Calvin, how's that token treating you?" Pastor Alan asked, turning to the blonde man.

Calvin tossed the coin up and down. "Still here, still sober. It's... well, it's a constant reminder, I guess. In a good way."

"Glad to hear it. And Hazel, anything you'd like to share since your apology?" Pastor Alan asked gently.

Hazel fidgeted with the hem of her shirt. "It's... harder than I thought. But my roommates are being really supportive. And... I didn't drink anything all week. So, small victories, I guess."

"That's not a small victory, Hazel, that's a huge step!" Pastor Alan exclaimed, his face alight with pride,

"That's what this is all about. Taking those steps, even when they're hard."

"Have you got another reading for this week, pastor?" Margot asked.

"Of course. Oh, that reminds me! The intro prayer... Alright everyone, let's move into our opening prayer. If you're comfortable, please bow your heads."

The room quieted, and heads bowed.

"Dear God, we thank You for bringing us all together again today. We thank You for the courage to face our challenges, for the support we find in each other, and for the strength to take each day as it comes. We pray for continued progress on our journeys, and for open hearts and minds to receive the guidance we need. In Your name we pray, Amen."

Pastor Alan examined their behavior while he read the weekly excerpt aloud. Nothing seemed out of the ordinary, other than some spacing out due to being presumably tired. He figured the subject matter wasn't related to anything like 'Godsend,' so he shifted gears after the reading.

"Now!" Pastor Alan finished up, "I figured before wrapping up, if you all wouldn't mind, we could share some personal stories?"

"On what topic?" Amara perked up, after listening more intently to the reading.

"I'm glad you asked, Amara. I don't mean to be... too on the nose. I understand what all of us have struggled with. But, for you personally, was there ever another time you just couldn't stop yourself from doing something?" Pastor Alan asked the group, only to be met with confused looks. "I mean like, if you saw a cat get stuck in a tree, did you run to save it without thinking? You couldn't stop even if you were told to?"

"Ah. That makes more sense. I was wondering why you'd wanna hear about every time I reached for the nearest Vodka," Calvin laughed to himself.

"Not that. I just mean— well, it doesn't even *need* to be positive. Just whatever comes to mind. I think it'll just help me understand you all better," Pastor Alan clarified.

The others all looked at each other. It seemed that nothing initially came to mind. Or had Alan been *too* on the nose about Godsend?

"Lemme see..." Owen spoke up, nodding to the pastor. Owen caught on to what the pastor was doing. "When I was in my college days, I couldn't help but shout at games. I was one of *those* guys who would play every night. Mainly multiplayer first person shooters. But I would get so angry. I just couldn't stop myself after we lost totally unfairly. I was *pissed*, and I'd throw the controller too."

"Really?" Amara asked, "You... don't seem like the angry type."

"Maybe not now. It was because at some point, I really had to ask myself *why*. Why was I even doing that? Why would I play things for 'relaxing' when they would just make me angry?" Owen questioned aloud. He tightened his grip. "Perhaps the issue that drove me here isn't too different."

The other all looked at each other. After one person put themselves out there, it was hard to not feel compelled to share as well.

"I guess... I can't really help but argue with my parents," Hazel piped up, "It was still going on last week. I'm not even sure *when* our relationship took such a turn. But, it's hard to even just *talk* to them. They always say

40

something outrageous and then it immediately turns into a fight. Not that I'm free of guilt either."

"Thank you for sharing, Hazel. You too, Owen. If anybody else wants to, now would be the time," Pastor Alan left the floor open for anybody. At first it seemed like nobody wanted to speak up. But then—

"I always feel like I need to set people straight..." Calvin muttered to himself.

"What was that Calvin? You don't have to share if you don't want to, I just didn't catch that," Pastor Alan only wanted to hear more.

"I just— well you know. I see what's happening with the government. How can we ignore the fact that we've just all accepted mass surveillance? I fight with people online who just suck up to billionaires. I wonder why I even do it. It doesn't really do anything for me, so I should probably just knock it off." Calvin looked equally angry as he did tired. He knew his online comments weren't doing anything to change the world he lived in.

"That's rich, coming from you. You're on the other side of it all—" Declan was cut off.

"Save it for after the group, Declan. Right now, people are free to share what they feel," Pastor Alan interrupted. But Calvin ignored him, getting up and pointing at Declan.

"But you never know how close you are to losing it all, and ending up like *them*. Do you even know what a millionaire is to a billionaire? NOTHING!" he shouted as Amara and Pastor Alan stood in front of him.

"Don't do this. Not here," Amara told him, "If there's one thing I can't help myself from doing, it's stopping this. I don't want to see you overly emotional. I don't wanna see you have to give up those tokens, either." She sat down.

41

"Well, thank you, Amara," Pastor Alan said, "I figure I should let you guys talk this one out. I think I'll wrap up for today, and we can go back to this topic later. Then if anybody else wants to share, they can."

The group de-escalated. Pastor Alan prayed once more to end the meeting, and they all went outside to talk on the patio. Owen, however, went to use the restroom. When he came back, he went to see the pastor instead of leaving.

"I went out briefly. Looks like Calvin calmed down and is making jokes now. Sounded like he didn't wanna talk about what his story was about," Owen informed the pastor.

"Do you think it's possible that Calvin is Godsend? If Declan is right about him being wealthy, wouldn't his family have a way to create that suit?" Pastor Alan speculated.

"Is that not too obvious? If anything, what Declan said matches more with Godsend's recent appearance at the mall. Amara hopped in to stop the fight, too," Owen talked about his other ideas.

"But just because they *feel* that way doesn't give them the ability to enact it. The police seemed semi-certain it was one of them, but maybe it was just someone else in the area?" Pastor Alan asked Owen for his opinion.

"I don't know them well enough. I don't want to pry here, but the police could be right. Especially with the motivations I heard tonight. But you're right, motivation alone doesn't make having a crazy suit like that suddenly possible," Owen thought aloud.

"Guess we'll have to figure out more, and see what happens in the next coming week. There is a planned protest against a controversial piece of legisla—"

"You mean the Commoners Safety Act, don't you?" Owen asked. "I thought Godsend might appear at that protest as well. We'll have to see if he's a man of the people."

"That we will," Pastor Alan nodded.

Anger roared into the atmosphere. The people weren't just going to sit there and take it anymore. Those with signs ignored the humid heat of June and shouted chants to those driving by. Signs held up displayed a red strike over "Commoners Safety Act."

Pastor Alan, going to clean up his office, saw the crowd outside the church on the street corner.

"It's already happening?" he asked himself. He knew the *danger* that came with associating himself with *those people*. He moved along, locking the church doors behind him. The protesters continued behind him.

"PRESIDENT HULLS WILL BE WATCHING YOU!" one of the protesters shouted.

"DOESN'T PRIVATE EQUITY OWN ENOUGH?!" another shouted.

A pickup truck with blacked out windows drove up to the street corner. The driver's window lowered, barely revealing a man in the seat.

"How can y'all be out here protesting against safety for the common folk like you and me?" he asked.

"The name is a *lie* man. They're going to take away consumer protection laws for privacy! Every microphone and camera around could be hard coded to share all of its data with the government and private firms!" a protester shouted back at him.

"So you're scared because *you're* the one doing illegal things," the man angrily snapped back at him.

"What?! No, man— are you serious?!" the protestor questioned in disbelief.

44

"President Hulls is doing so much to make this country better and people like *you* have to go and ruin it," the man snarkily spat out the window, driving off.

All the protestors started shouting at his vehicle as he drove down the other street. The man who was spat on let his arms droop to his sides. He dropped his sign to the ground.

"What's the point?" he asked aloud.

"What do you mean? Don't let one jerk throw you off! We might not get the attention of the news, but someone will! And we'll call the hell out of our senators!" the woman by him tried to get his spirits up. He took a moment, chuckling to himself.

"It isn't one jerk. It's us versus a few dozen billionaires, and we're all losing. They divide, they conquer, they win. They could advocate for everyone cutting off their ears and somehow people would still defend them." The man sank in his posture. The woman had no response.

A nearby hologram screen in a store played the news. The big text read: "Commoners Safety Act passes the Senate."

"We have confirmation that this new act, introduced with many different facets, has passed both the house and the senate. This marks another historic, yet controversial win for the party, as polling shows that approval only polling at about twenty-three percent across the nation," said the talking head.

Pastor Alan, also seeing the news on his phone, worried for the worst. Even though he knew what was going on, he knew he didn't have the power to change it.

"First the new laws cause those checkpoints, now my phone is essentially a CIA agent? Is this really what people want?" Pastor Alan muttered to himself.

He opened his blinds to see people all out on the corner videoing themselves. The protestors were now streaming directly to the internet, as the act still had a small chance of being shut down in the final vote.

Downtown, a lot more people gathered doing the same. Entire streets were shut down and overrun with people.

"SHUT IT DOWN!" the people shouted. They truly feared for the worse after seeing the real-life consequences of the heavy-handed administration.

The news on nearby devices continued.

"The president has expressed his excitement at the newest security act. He has openly expressed that this is a big win for the everyday American, making the country far safer than ever before for the common people," the news anchor read aloud.

"You know, Frank, he's right about that. The American people are tired of the over-abundance of crime in our country. This act aims to eliminate everyday threats of bad actors by putting together an online database of potential perpetrators. This will save many the headache of being illegally targeted," the lobbyist that was paid thousands to appear on the news explained.

A nearby protestor looked online. An angry text post from a person online read: "*First, they force income checkpoints on us. Second, they make it easier for the rich to stay rich, and harder for the poor to earn. Now, after forcing the opposition to turn to crime without a choice, there's a legal way to track us, imprison us, and murder us. Welcome to today.*"

"What is right anymore?" she, at a loss for words, threw her phone on the ground. She walked back, through the crowd of protestors. It felt like nothing could work anymore.

The devices continued to display the news all around.

"It appears the house has reached a narrow conclusion. They haven't yet announced but—"

The woman who left her phone on the ground felt helpless. There was nothing left that any of the protestors could do as they all listened to the same news. They all felt that their loss was all but inevitable.

The woman— anger welling up inside her— remembered a story buried behind the media after a week. The story of a vigilante. The story of a—

"**GODSEND!!!**" she broke out into a scream of pain, "GREED IS WINNING, SPILLING OVER OUR STREETS, GODSEND! PLEASE— DO SOMETHING!"

People nearby started to film as she broke into hysteria. A plea, a cry; the hero named Godsend. Perhaps Godsend could save it all. Others started to join her hysteria. Unfortunately, all this did was alert the police nearby.

"What are you lot doing, shouting the name of a vigilante?!" the police chief, jumping out of a cruiser, asked.

"GODSEND! YOU HAVE TO SAVE US!"

"Are you calling for *him* to destroy what the senate has decided on? I'd call that a conspiracy to commit **MURDER**!" the police chief shouted.

All hell broke loose. Police cruisers started pulling to the curb by the dozen. The protest became a riot as police tried to push them off of the streets with riot shields and tear gas. Many ran from the scene. Many were targeted, and arrested on the spot.

Despite the news being on display all around the riot, the news did not touch on the unrest.

"It appears now the Commoners Safety Act has been signed into law. This happened just now after the final, close, vote in the House of Representatives. We've yet to see how this plays out, but peace should, potentially, be kept easier now," the news anchor spoke as his face was displayed behind the police detaining the commoners.

"What are you doing? Hey! I wasn't even protest—"

"This is my right! I have the freedom of expression based on the first amendment—"

"This isn't right man, she was just talking about some vigilante. She doesn't speak for us all—"

"My wife is waiting at home, sir. I really was just about to go—"

"Do I not have the right to make my voice heard here—"

"You all have the right to remain silent." The police detained many, and drove off the rest. In the background, the news continued. The president came on screen to start a press conference. A usual business suit. Another wrinkled face with white hair and a necktie.

"Well that was a while," President Hulls started, "I can't believe they would argue over such an act. This is a great, huge victory for America today. With all of the cheaters and rats on the internet today, you never know if you're going to be targeted by someone getting your information online. We're gonna stop that now!"

Many applauded for his small little speech. Many that benefited; many that filled their pockets with his words. A small, small many containing the top percentage point of wealth, and owners of companies. All of which

48

were exempt, given free reign over information that the government had declared its own.

Pastor Alan, still in his office, looked out of the window once more. There were no more people on the sidewalk. He shrugged, figuring that the people went home after seeing the news.

"Well, hopefully it isn't too bad," he sighed, sitting down, "But... where was _he_?"

In the shadows, Godsend remained.

The living room was silent besides the projection of the news. It was a disaster. The "rioters" didn't go down without a fight. The police were ordered to use force on the citizens they were ordered to protect. It was as if war had broken out in downtown Philadelphia.

Amara looked through different streams of news, not finding anything about what was happening. But she was looking, for she knew her dad, an officer, had been called out there. Giving up on conventional news, she turned to social media. Initially, nothing popped up. But after some searching, she found some accounts live streaming.

"It's absolute chaos in downtown," said one person streaming. Citizens were throwing fireworks into brigades of police. Police surrounded groups of people with dozens of police cruisers.

Amara quickly switched apps, texting her dad. She internally begged that he was okay. But even after a few prompts, he was not responding.

The news continued. The president's men blabbed on about how amazing the act was going to be. Amara rushed to social media to see a post about injured police being rushed to the closest hospital. She did not hesitate, grabbing her car keys and rushing out the door.

With tears in her eyes, and suppressing her hyperventilation, she drove downtown. Veering through traffic as if there was nobody else in her way. At the closest street, she poorly pulled over in a dubiously-legal parking zone. Despite the riot still actively happening, she ran over the barriers and burst through the two front doors.

"IS THERE SOMEONE HERE NAMED ANDRE TAYLOR?!" Amara shouted, running to the front desk.

"Ma'am there are too many people—"

"I DON'T CARE!"

The receptionist at the front desk saw the desperation in her eyes. Nodding, they showed Amara that Andre Taylor was in room three hundred and sixteen.

"THANK YOU!" she shouted, sprinting down the hall. She flew up the stairs and burst into his room; her father's room. There, she saw him on a bed with stitches in his legs. Another man, wearing a brown coat, sat in the room. But she didn't care, she ran forward, hugging her dad.

"Amara. You came," Andre smiled. They embraced and the other man in the room stood up.

"Ah. You must be his daughter. I'll be on my way," the man in the brown coat announced.

"Hey. Thanks for being here, Hadley. Tell the boss I'll just be a few days. I'm alright," Andre told Hadley, a partner of his in the police force.

"Of course," Hadley left the two of them alone, ducking out from the room. As he was on his way, he remembered something. Amara was another one of the people suspected to be Godsend. Was her appearance here an indication that she was Godsend? After all, Godsend never showed up at the riot.

Hadley took out his phone. He knew that his brother, Calvin, was the number one suspect at the moment. He was already set to see him after his shift.

"I think I can convince them it isn't you, Calvin. It couldn't be," he muttered under his breath.

The faint glow of a screen was the sole illumination in the room Calvin sulked in. He read the caption on that screen: "Commoners Safety Act Passed Into Law." He tightened his grip, scowling at the article.

"I can't believe this shit. How did the majority of our country think it was a good idea to let *this guy* run it?" Calvin grumbled, sinking down in his seat. He grabbed his glass of water nearby, taking a swift gulp. While continuing to scroll through the article, he got a message.

"Hey. Coming over in a bit. Be there soon," was the message displayed in the top right. The sender was marked as "Hadley."

Calvin ignored it for now, pissed off that this egregious piece of legislation was allowed into law. He continued to scroll around the internet for a bit, avoiding all of the garbage articles praising the bill. All of them were clearly written by artificial intelligence, anyway. One of them, however, caught his attention. Not enough for him to actually click on it, but the title intrigued him nonetheless.

"'CSA Passed. What Can You Do?' Interesting. What *can* I do?" Calvin grinned, reading the title aloud. But he was quickly interrupted— a knock at the door. He sighed, going downstairs and opening it up.

"Hey man!" Hadley, Calvin's older brother, greeted at the front door.

"Hey. Come on in," Calvin met him there in a deadpan voice. Calvin closed the door behind Hadley and the two of them took their shoes off.

"I promise I'll make my visit quick if you want. I know you moved out years ago and I just figured I should stop by and say hi, see the apartment," Hadley made it clear he wasn't trying to impose.

"You're good. Might as well check it out," Calvin told him nonchalantly, following his brother to the kitchen. He could tell that Hadley was looking around.

But Hadley was doing more than just "looking around." He was looking at every piece of furniture and the placement of objects as a story, telling a tale of the inhabitants of the abode. *Hmm… that towel is left out. The fridge is kind of empty. There isn't much decor. Obviously he didn't put up this wallpaper either.* Hadley's initial conclusion was only that Calvin was lazy.

"What've you been up to lately? Bringing any girls around here?" Hadley nudged Calvin, suggesting something. Calvin sighed, rolling his eyes.

"Does it really look like a prime 'bachelor pad' in here?" Calvin sarcastically remarked.

"Hey, just saying. You totally could be," Hadley shrugged.

"Alright, what's going on? You never visit just for the sake of it," Calvin shouted, suddenly disrupting the peace in the room. Hadley's fingers twitched.

"Seriously, I just hadn't seen you in a while. Just wanted to check in, see how you were doing. Not that I think you're doing badly," Hadley played it cool. Calvin rolled his eyes, his breath getting tighter.

"I'm sure all is going fine for you. But who put you up to this? Your boss? Are the cops trying to investigate me?" Calvin questioned, wanting to get more out of Hadley.

"Look—"

"No, you know what, don't bother!" Calvin's breath started to hasten, "I get it. The parents have probably told you I'm not doing the best, and you probably just got a huge pay raise because of that bullshit act they just passed. Glad the cops are being paid more, but it's all at our EXPENSE!"

"Dude, calm down—"

"I AM CALM!" Calvin shouted, cutting him off again. But his breath rose so sharply, he started to gasp for air. Calvin suddenly sprinted into the other room, his brother quickly following in complete confusion. Calvin was trying to grab a glass while holding his throat.

"Just drink this!" Hadley shouted at him, handing him a water bottle from his coat. Calvin did a double take, doubting the safety of it, but drank anyway. He gasped for air as his breath stabilized. Hadley leaned against the door frame he stood by, "I heard you started going to AA. I didn't think that was like you, but neither was getting snippy out of nowhere."

"There's something wrong with me, Hadley. Not like you're one to care," Calvin sneered. Hadley didn't flinch, taking no offense. But he was fed up with looking for clues on Godsend. Hadley decided to just go for the direct approach.

"Alright. You're not Godsend, are you?" Hadley casually dropped. Calvin couldn't even respond for a moment.

"The vigilante on TV? I *wish* I could do stuff like that. Those freaks in power have ruined it for the rest of us common folk," Calvin began to rant, still panting.

"Well that answers one question. I didn't think you were Godsend either. But you know, of course the government wants to know who he is. I do, however, have another question for you. What makes you think you're part of the 'common folk?'" Hadley cut the bullshit, speaking his mind now.

"How could I not be? I'm just here, living on my own—"

"Yeah. But you have enough money. You were born in the same family as me, and guess what? You and I, we're basically set next to those people."

"Did you just say *those* people? What are you?!" Calvin backed away, disgusted, "Not like I have that money anymore either."

"I knew from mom you went gambling. You spent all of it?" Hadley scorned.

"Damn near did. What are you gonna do about it, huh? Admonish me more? Trust me, asshole, I would go back and undo it too if I could," Calvin defensively fought back. The two of them looked at each other, neither saying a word. Hadley exhaled, putting his hand to the bridge of his nose.

"Well. I can't control the world, Calvin. I'm sorry you're clearly upset about your situation. But I'm trying to cover for you. I'm here for your sake. I don't want people thinking you're a vigilante," Hadley explained.

"Is that seriously something people thought?" Calvin asked, looking up and meeting Hadley's line of sight. The two made eye contact, but nothing was said. Hadley stepped back toward the door.

"You should get a hobby, Calvin. Something to replace what you used to do for fun. Maybe hit the gym," Hadley put his coat back on.

"Yeah, sure. I'll just ignore the atrocities being committed by the government," Calvin ignored the advice as Hadley stepped out.

"It's for your own good, bud." Hadley slammed the door behind him.

Late spring brought warm days in the city of Philadelphia. The Commoner's Safety Act had passed, and despite the riots, one would be hard pressed to find any significant impact.

Well, life went on like usual for many. Some threw out their phones or sued in solidarity against the act. The majority of people forgot about it, and moved on with their lives. Including those in the AA group at Shepheard.

A meek hand pushed one of two glass doors open, walking into a well-kept and well-respected restaurant. Not inside of one of the checkpoints, and one of the last "high-class" restaurants available to the many. This hand belonged to Milo, coming in to check on the lunch specials.

"Party of how many?" the hostess asked Milo at the front door, not even making eye contact as she shuffled through menus.

"Is... is there any bar seating?" Milo nervously chuckled as he asked awkwardly. The hostess handed him a single menu.

"Right this way, sir," she prompted him to follow. He quickly found himself tucked away by the bar at the restaurant. He only wanted water as well, it was just that asking for bar seating was less embarrassing than asking for a single seat.

"If not a drink, what can I get for 'ya?" a waiter asked him.

"I just saw the lunch special combo with the... uhh... the— you know? The sandwich and drink?"

"The pesto turkey sandwich and soda combo?"

"Yes!"

"Alright. Coming up," the man took his menu from him, passing through a handle-less swing door. Through the door, Declan barely saw what was through. He was at his job and looked up for just a moment. He saw Milo's awkward expression in between swings as the door slowly went back to its closed position.

Without warning, it burst back open.

"WHAT ARE *YOU* DOING AT THE *BAR?!*" Declan demanded, jumping out of the doorway to question Milo.

"It's not what it looks like, see!" Milo yelled back, holding up his glass of water and pointing at it desperately.

"DECLAN!" a deep voice shouted from the other room, "WHY ARE YOU SHOUTING AT A CUSTOMER?"

"I know the guy!" Declan bowed his head back in for a moment. He turned back to face Milo, "My break is in fifteen. I'll question you when I get the chance." Milo just nodded.

Fifteen minutes went by quickly, and Milo explained to Declan what was going on in between bites of his sandwich. He was only at the bar because it was easier than saying "table for one" to the hostess, and had no intent to break sobriety.

"Well I had to at least come out and ask. I had no clue what the hell someone from the Shepherd AA group was doing at my restaurant. Especially at the *bar*," Declan reiterated, sitting next to Milo as he finished his sandwich.

"I didn't even know this is where you worked. It's a really weird coincidence, honestly. I didn't think twice about the bar seating either, which is probably good that being around it doesn't make me think about it," Milo thought aloud.

"Well if that's your recovery, you're sure having a lot less trouble than I did in the beginning, kid," Declan replied, taking a sip from his own glass of water.

"'*Kid?*' Really?"

"You're young enough to be my kid. But I don't have any. Kids, that is. Never had a wife, so there wasn't really a chance. But with what's going on today, not sure I'd want one either," Declan reminisced, tense about the future of the world.

"You mean the safety act?"

"Not just that. Natural disasters seem to keep popping out of nowhere too. Didn't you see the floods?" Declan asked Milo.

"Oh yeah.I think I heard something about that. I'm not super up-to-date with the news anymore," Milo commented.

"I envy you. I don't wanna be connected like I am— but, it was Texas, and South Carolina. Both of them had deadly and unforeseen floods. People speculate that it was due to funds moving to the Safety act you mentioned," Declan informed Milo.

"Why don't you just... turn it off?"

"What?"

"The news. You don't wanna be connected so, don't be."

"You're right. But Calvin rubbed off on me. He doesn't really talk about it anymore, because I was the one who told him to stop but— He used to just talk on and on about whatever the news said. It was nonstop doom and gloom from him. Yet he would still act prideful and like he could fix it somehow. Somehow that 'monitoring the situation' mentality he had infected me. I began to worry I

58

was missing something important," Declan told Milo. Milo thought silently for a moment.

"I guess I didn't see that in him. You told him to stop?"

"Yeah, it wasn't *our* problem. I don't know why headlines are so hellbent on making your life worse when you're not even feeling their effects. But yeah, I just want to be informed, I guess."

The two stopped. Declan took a look at the time. He finished his glass of water, and got up off of the chair.

"My time is up. Guess I'll see you Thursday?" Declan asked.

"Yeah. Hopefully by then, maybe we'll hear some good news."

"Heh. It'd take a miracle to cut through all the bullshit of what's going on today. I wouldn't bet on it," Declan waved before leaving, as did Milo. Milo chuckled, looking down at his drink. That water. That same substance that gave life could take so many away in a weekend. It could take a "miracle" to stop.

But maybe, Declan's idea of a miracle wasn't as outlandish as he thought. It may not have been what he originally imagined, though.

Only a few days later. A small camp in Uniontown, Pennsylvania is given a flood watch warning. A group of youth campers with three leaders are currently there. Only one of the leaders has service.

"It says something about a flood warning. It couldn't mean...?" the leader with service said to the others. Rain poured down, but not alarmingly hard.

"There have been a bunch of false readings recently. It's possible it's one of those," another responded.

"Or it could just be that we're in the same zip code of an active flood. Is it severe?" the third one asked.

"I can't load any videos. Service is spotty out here. How about we just take the kids to higher ground just in case?" the first one responded. All three agreed, and they started to take the kids uphill. But upon gathering them all together, one of them noticed that they were down a person.

"Hey! Have any of you seen Kathy?"

The earth sloshed out of the way. The ground became mud and moved without resistance just a few dozen feet away. The little ditch they moved out of quickly became a stream.

"KATHY IS DOWN AT THE BATHROOM!" one of the kids screamed, pointing to the outdoor restroom on the now-flooded trail.

"EVERYBODY RUN UP TO HIGHER GROUND! I'M GOING TO GET HER NOW!" the tallest leader shouted, running before they could be told to be stopped.

Heart racing. Thunder clapping. The rain, pounding on the ground. The leader sprinting, jumping over the small streams starting to form under their feet. The sound of screams from the restroom echoing. The earthy water, starting to fill the area.

"KATHY! IF YOU CAN HEAR ME, WADE OUT OF THERE AND COME TO THE DOOR!" the leader leaped on top of the small building. "I'LL BRING US BOTH ON THE ROOF!"

CRACK — The small building itself was unlodged. Screams came from inside as the leader realized exactly what was happening as stronger floods flew down the hill.

"ARE YOU OKAY?!" There was only continued screaming. The group leader no longer had any ideas. Both the two of them started to move faster downstream. They seemed to be out of options, and the young girl Kathy could be drowning, *and they both might die, and—*

"**NEED A HAND?**"

The leader turned, realizing that the building had stopped moving. There, the metal monster known as Godsend hovered, one hand on the small structure.

"Ye—yes..." the leader stumbled over their words. Godsend's bar of green light shone through the darkness of the rain, and hovered to the bottom of their face. It then changed shape, resembling a mouth.

"**I'LL SAVE YOU, THEN.**"

Godsend descended to the door of the bathroom structure, holding out a hand. There, they could see the girl. She shouted in shock at Godsend's appearance.

"KATHY! He's here to... help us..." the leader shouted down to her. She reluctantly took Godsend's hand.

A minute later, a camera and crew filmed as Godsend descended upon the youth group, dropping both the young girl Kathy and the leader off with the rest of the group.

A reporter stood in front of the camera, narrating the news. "It's hard to believe what we're seeing in Pennsylvania today, but *Godsend* here just saved this group from the floods here in Uniontown. Apparently two got separated and he has returned them together—"

WOOSH, Godsend vanished from the background. It was the first time in a while that they appeared.

"There he goes now," the reporter continued, "And that wasn't even the end of it. According to some hikers up the trail, he also safely removed them from the danger zone too."

The clip of Godsend went viral. As their actions grew, more became interested in what they were doing, and why. Only a week would go by before they appeared again.

A lone person looked down at their phone. One message shone back up at her as she crouched down in the corner of a room: *Storm conditions are set to continue for the next hour*. She could hear shouting from the outside.

"What are you doing?! We should have been out of here by now!" an older man yelled.

"I didn't think the hurricane was going to last all the way to our *house*!" a woman, the same age responded. She was trying to get their truck started, but water had already risen too high for it. The daughter, still curled up on the inside. A news helicopter flew by, pointing their cameras in that direction.

"Oh! It looks like a few are still stranded in the flooding areas. Hurricane Fernand has headed up further than expected, but it seems like the change in projection was done a little too last minute. Many seem unaware of the conditions forecasted for today," one of the people spoke to the video feed. Suddenly, a green streak came flying in from off camera, prompting "What was that? Oh!"

Godsend slowed down to a stop midair. They glowed with digital green energy.

"HONEY! IT'S THE METAL GUY FROM THE TV!" the woman in the truck shouted, pointing.

"Oh thank heavens. Is there any way you could help us out?" the man pleaded, looking up at Godsend. They looked around, seeing stranded animals, as well as people still in nearby buildings.

"**YOU'RE GONNA WANT TO STAND BACK FOR THIS.**"

ZAP— Godsend flew forward with the force of another hurricane. The sheer energy from the blast caused the water to fly back towards the ocean in a wave, creating a dry area around the houses. The people held on to the things around them as wind blew by their faces. Even the rain stopped for a moment.

The couple looked the way of Godsend. Their very being emanated a venting hot wind, pushing the water from coming back.

"**TAKE THEM AND GO.**"

The truck started. The strangers stranded all got in the back of their truck, and their daughter ran out and into the back seat. The camera operators caught everything.

"This week Godsend..."

"And during the hurricane, Godsend—"

"It was none other than Godsend!"

The news spoke about them over and over again. Whether it was saving people in a hurricane, from a fire, Godsend started to appear all over the news.

The detectives were all obsessing over every little detail that came from the footage. It was astonishing to them that there was still nothing that led to Godsend's identity. It frustrated Officer Miller, the first real officer to come into contact with Godsend.

"There's *no way*. Are we dealing with someone out of a comic book?! Come on, you guys. Ultraviolet reveals nothing? X-rays reveal nothing? How can they keep disappearing without a trace, even with the Commoner's Safety Act in effect?" Officer, or detective, Miller complained aloud. Hadley Becker, another detective doing double duty as an officer, was in an empty interrogation room with him. They were going over the evidence, or the lack thereof.

"We don't know anything new about who could be connected to this 'Godsend' character, but we do know new things about Godsend himself. If he is a 'he,' that is," Hadley responded. Miller raised an eyebrow.

"Hit me," he responded, knowing Miller had more to say.

"Godsend, the drone or person in a suit, is able to put out way too much power for something that small. Like you said, it seems like it's out of a comic book. It feels wrong. It feels impossible. Yet, our eyes and ears tell us otherwise. There's only one type of technology that could even *theoretically* make something like that. It was discussed as a concept for electric cars in the twenties, too," Hadley laid out on the table, picking up on Miller's suspicions and frustrations.

"Thanks for the hint, jackass. We're both detectives, you know? The real question is who actually made a *working* nuclear battery? In such a small form factor, too," Miller spat back. Hadley turned away, trying to think for a moment how exactly it would relate at all back to the alcoholics anonymous group at Shepherd Mid-City.

"Do you think it might have been stolen from our military?" Hadley prompted, engineering his questions to go in a specific direction. At this point, he didn't care who Godsend was. He needed an answer that was not his own brother, despite them not exactly getting along.

"Stolen from our military? Well, if anybody's gonna have that technology first..." Miller paused for a beat, "So what do you mean by it? None of our suspects are ex-military. Unless you have any new suggestions."

"This is going to sound off-topic, but I promise it's relevant," Haldley stated, "Do you remember how people *literally* called for Godsend on the day that new privacy act was signed?"

"You think it was someone in the government, then? Someone who supported it?"

"Not necessarily. I just worked off of the idea that our alcoholics anonymous group is our main group of suspects."

"Of which, your brother is the most likely case, if I remember correctly."

"The problem being that my brother hates that privacy act, but wasn't busy during the time. If he were Godsend, he could have gone and intervened. What exactly were the *police* going to do against *Godsend,* anyway?"

"We... are working on a plan for that scenario..." Miller gave a half-answer.

"I happen to know someone who is both connected to the military, in the group, and had a very pressing concern at the time people were calling for our *Silver Prophet,*" Hadley hit a bulls-eye while leading the conversation. Miller tilted his head forward, interested in learning what he had to say. Hadley turned his head, "The daughter of Officer Andre Taylor."

Detective Miller's eyes widened.

"A military family, dissatisfied with the current government. A cop unconnected with his own daughter who has stronger connections to her older family. The older family with *security clearance,* I should mention," Haldey went on.

"Tell me more," Miller took the bait.

A couple of group sessions had come and gone without much to note. Everyone seemed like their usual selves, barring one individual. Amara didn't show up the week of the Commoner's Safety Act riots. She came back the following week, quieter than usual. According to Declan, she "didn't act like herself."

Another alcoholics anonymous meeting had just wrapped up with everyone in session. Nearly everyone shared, being a positive week and marking a new point of sobriety in everyone's journeys. Amara was the only one who didn't.

"Amara, wait up!" Pastor Alan called out, seeing her try to slip away from the group gathering on the patio. She paused, turning slowly. Her usual lively expression was gone, replaced by a blatant blank expression.

"Everything alright, Amara? You were really quiet today," he asked, approaching her cautiously.

She offered a small, forced smile. "Just... a lot going on. Dad's doing better, at least."

"That's wonderful news. I *was* praying for him," Pastor Alan said sincerely, "But is there anything else on your mind? You know this is a safe space, no judgment here."

Amara looked around at the other members of the group, who were starting to filter out onto the patio, chatting amongst themselves. "It's just... everything. The world feels like it's falling apart. And then there's Godsend."

Pastor Alan nodded, "He's certainly been making headlines."

"Headlines that are all over the place," Amara scoffed, her voice regaining a bit of its usual pep, "One

66

minute he's a hero, the next the police are warning people about a 'vigilante.' With my dad being a cop, he's certainly been a nuisance to my life."

"How so?" Pastor Alan questioned, wondering how it might personally affect her.

"Just because my dad is obsessed, for some reason. Not in a good way either. He believes there's some sort of sinister plan behind this 'Godsend' character. Like he's just trying to gain people's trust right now. He thinks it's the police's job to arrest him," Amara explained to Pastor Alan.

"I see," Pastor Alan replied, his gaze drifting from Amara, "He certainly stirs up strong opinions." He considered her words for a moment longer. "Well, I hope your father stays safe out there. The world is a strange place right now."

Amara nodded, a flicker of something unreadable in her eyes. She mumbled a quick goodbye and walked away, sneaking by the crowd on the patio. Pastor Alan watched her go, a thoughtful expression on his face. He then turned to pay attention to the others, who were now deep in conversation.

"Can you believe it?" Calvin was saying, gesturing wildly with his hands. "Godsend is everywhere! Saving people from floods, hurricanes... and the police still act like he's public enemy number one. It's ridiculous!"

"Right?" Hazel chimed in, "The news is so skewed. All he's done is help, and they're warning people to 'be careful of this vigilante.' It's like they *want* us to be afraid of anyone they don't like."

"The news is all bullshit anyway," Declan grumbled, taking a sip of his to-go coffee, "Always has been. They only show you what they want you to see. I figured they would go the whole 'Russian-spy' route with the whole thing." Everyone suddenly quieted down. He quickly glanced around, as if worried he'd said too much.

"Russian? The hell is Russian about that guy?" Margot, who had been quietly listening, raised an eyebrow at Declan's comment.

"I mean, I guess it takes one to know one," Declan started, "But the way he said 'them' on the news once was a giveaway to me. Even through the voice filter I could hear the Russian-accented '**z**em' instead of '**th**em.'"

The group went silent. None of them knew what he was talking about.

"If what you're saying is true," Owen started, "Why *hasn't* the news run with it?"

Declan quickly got out his phone, frantically trying to find something. "I promise you I heard this. Hold on, let me try to find it." Declan quickly pulled up a clip from a news segment. "Here," he showed the others, a clip of Godsend saying "*take them and go*" from afar. He played it over again. "See? You can kinda hear them say 'take **z**em.'"

"It's a bit of a stretch," Owen thought aloud, not believing it.

"I don't know, Declan," Margot said, also not buying it. "It sounds like a distorted voice anyway. Could just be the filter messing with the pronunciation."

"Yeah," Milo piped up, finally speaking after listening intently. "But honestly, even if it was a Russian accent, who cares? We've been talking about the news for like ten minutes now. How have you guys *actually* been?"

"You can't just change the topic!" Calvin disagreed, throwing his hands up in exasperation. "They want to maintain their narrative, and a good guy who doesn't play by their rules messes with that. Ignoring it means giving them control."

Hazel, who had been quiet, spoke up again, "I just think it's funny that the police are so fixated on his identity when he's literally pulling people out of hurricanes. Like, priorities, much?"

Declan just shrugged, taking another sip of his coffee, "I dunno Calvin. I told Milo the other day that your 'news-obsessed era' was over. Looks like I might have been wrong."

"It's just— interesting! I don't know, it's like there's a truth behind all this!" Calvin continued.

"But it's got nothing to do with us. Milo's right, we sound obsessed. Not our fault, the news is totally sensationalizing it. But really, we should move on," Margot added.

The group went quiet, realizing how much they were obsessing. All of them stirred, wanting to break this new ice.

Calvin finally broke the silence. "I guess I'm just trying to stay out of trouble myself. It's hard enough getting sober without getting caught up in... the news. I guess recently I figured out I need a new hobby."

"Yeah, clearly watching news feeds twenty-four-seven isn't doing you any good," Declan jabbed. Calvin rolled his eyes.

"I'm too busy with school to help with anything," Hazel spoke up, "But you could start with, like, looking through niche hobby communities online? Last year I got super into building legacy keyboards. The switches and keycaps and stuff like that were all fun to obsess over."

"That sounds too difficult for me," Calvin immediately rejected.

"I didn't mean that *specifically*!" Hazel argued back, "I just meant, like, looking at what people do online."

"It's too much. The internet is just... a rabbit hole of arguments. I don't know. Going through forms like that, I can't help but get dragged back into political arguments," Calvin sighed, running a hand from his forehead to his hair.

A notification tone interrupted the situation. It was Declan's phone. He finished the last gulp of his coffee. "Sorry to cut this short, but I gotta head out. Early shift tomorrow."

"No worries, man. See ya," Owen said, the other nodded and they all waved before leaving. Owen then turned back to Calvin, "Ever thought about video games, Calvin? You seem like you might get into them."

"Yeah! Maybe... you could even get into the online scene. You seem like the type to get into dissecting a game's lore," Milo added.

Calvin shrugged. "Nah, not really my thing. Too much sitting around. I need something with more... action."

"Well, if you're looking for action, I go indoor rock climbing," Margot seemingly offered, adding, "The regular gym is kind of... filled with influencers these days. It's pretty friggin annoying. But climbing is great! It's kinda sporadic, but I can let you know next time I go?"

Calvin looked at her, then back at the ground, considering. He hadn't really thought about anything like that before. "Indoor rock climbing, huh? That's... actually not something I've considered before. I'd be down to try that."

More notification noises. This time coming from Hazel's phone. She laughed. "Sorry guys. My roommates are wondering where I am, sending me a bunch of nonsense."

"It's getting late anyway, we should probably all get going," Owen mentioned, looking at the time.

The group all said their goodbyes, saying they would meet again next week. But Calvin walked off with Margot to the side, wondering when she was next going rock climbing.

She started looking through a digital calendar on her phone. "Let's see here..." Calvin looked over her shoulder out of curiosity. There was nothing actually *on* her calendar. Just the stark, plain dates.

"Margot... what exactly are you *looking* for?" Calvin questioned, a bit of confusion in his voice.

She jerked the phone away, embarrassed. "I... well I just remember what happens most of the time. I just look at the dates and... think of the events. Looking at the calendar just helps me remember in what order they go. Like... rent being due." She readjusted her glasses, which had slid down her nose earlier.

"Alright?" Calvin responded, making a confused expression.

"Let's aim for next Tuesday, since I'm off work. Does that work?" Margot asked, pointing to the date on her calendar.

"Tuesday afternoon is perfect," Calvin gave her the green light. The two exchanged contacts, and she gave Calvin the address.

Internally, Calvin challenged himself to ignore the doom-and-gloom news that had been taking over his mind. At least until then.

Just a few moments before Margot and Calvin exchanged contact info, Declan had disappeared from the group. However, his statement about having an early shift was a lie. In fact, he wasn't even scheduled the next day.

The text he received read: "*To your left, down the street, on your left. This is for your friend Calvin's sake. Don't be long.*"

He immediately left, citing work. But he angrily paced down the sidewalk just far away enough to find a guy mostly covered up, wearing a brown fedora that covered his eyes.

"What do you want? How do you know Calvin?" Declan angrily questioned the man.

"Slow down now, Russian. Don't make me shift gears into thinking that *you're* Godsend now," the man replied, lifting his sight. Declan still didn't recognize him.

"What's Calvin got to do with this? He ain't my friend, but I'm not about to let you threaten him," Declan got in his face.

"I'm simply a detective. Name's Hadley," he introduced himself, omitting the fact he was Calvin's brother. "I believe that Calvin was asking people to get together. Is that correct?"

"Why should I tell you?"

"Because I believe the person you know as 'Godsend' may be trying to fake their identity as Calvin," Hadley immediately spat back in Declan's face.

"Huh? That guy couldn't do all that if he wanted to," Declan refused to back down.

"Look, I get you like to speculate, but that's gotta be an error of the voice filter. Nothing more. Because...

everything points to Amara Taylor," Hadley insisted, his voice dropping to a persuasive murmur. "Her father, Andre Taylor, is a high-ranking officer. He's got security clearance. Amara's extended family has access to military-grade tech."

Declan shoved Hadley away from him. He didn't want to hear any more.

"Are you joking? Do you sound serious to yourself? That quiet girl? Plus you're telling all of this to me? *How* did you even get my number?" Declan exploded at him. He then showed his police badge.

"Don't threaten an officer. Under the Commoner's Safety Act, we can access *any* portion of a citizen's device if we believe they're involved in something we're investigating. Understand? So don't turn this into more work than it has to be," Hadley groaned, scowling at Declan.

Declan clenched his teeth, seething but hiding his anger now. "Gotcha. Cool. I'll pretend that's just something everyone would be cool with knowing."

"I just want you to see how Amara acts in-person. I want you to respond to that number with what you observe. We're putting together a case, currently. We really do truly believe it's her," Hadley told him, "Plus, don't blab about me. Because I'll know."

Declan nodded as Hadley already had begun to turn the other way. He walked off to who-knows-where. Declan just felt like he wanted to hit something.

Still seething, he looked down at his phone. He didn't give a damn if this guy knew. He deleted the text conversation.

Meanwhile, Hadley was looking down at a device of his own. He re-read a text he received from detective Miller.

It was a screenshot of a cash bonus offered to the detective who could find the identity of Godsend.

The latest text read, "Even if it isn't her, the real one will show up. We can make *him* disappear if needed." Hadley grinned.

But Declan did not respond. He had no intention to. But to Hadley's mind, it just indicated a waiting game. Especially since Godsend didn't even show up anywhere. Even when it had reached Tuesday afternoon, there had been no public news of Godsend.

At the time, Calvin was just pulling up to the rock climbing gym. At the doors of the place, a large logo loomed over reading, "RockRunners." Exactly where Margot had said to meet up. But... she wasn't there?

Calvin pulled out his phone frantically looking to text her before realizing she had already sent him a "be there in a sec" text. So at least she was on her way.

In just a minute or two, Margot pulled up in a beat-up compact truck. Calvin wasn't really expecting her to drive a pickup, but it was probably "something reliable" in his mind.

Out popped Margot, wearing white baggy pants and a cropped black sports top. She waved. "Sorry for making you wait," she let out, quickly running to the tailgate of her truck.

"I suddenly feel underprepared," Calvin looked down at his button-up and shorts. Margot laughed, opening the back of the truck and lifting the tonneau cover. There, she had two sets of harnesses, climbing shoes, and everything else needed.

"Don't sweat it. We'll take turns. I'll belay you, but I'll free climb so there's no pressure on you," Margot explained, grabbing her equipment.

"I have no clue what that means," Calvin added. She began to explain it to him as they went in, checking the both of them in with her punch card. Calvin saw the prices on the board out of the corner of his eye. "Jeez, you sure you don't want a little help paying?"

"It's not a big deal, don't worry about *that*. What you should be worrying about is how you're gonna climb," Margot teased him. Before he could respond, she walked off back toward the counter. She spoke to one of the people who worked there right out of Calvin's earshot. The two came over to him.

"What's up now?" Calvin felt intimidated, the two putting on their gear now.

"Since you haven't been, I'm gonna have her belay me first so you can watch," Margot let him know.

"There's a lot more to keeping yourself up there than it looks!" the girl working there chimed in. Margot then tied her hair up in a ponytail like the employee had, and the two of them went over to the wall. Calvin, having just put his gear on, also went over.

"Are you sure you want to show him on *this one*?" the girl whispered to Margot.

"I'm confident in this one. Plus, it has a lot of variety to show crossovers and stuff like that. Plus…," Margot whispered back quickly, adding one thing just out of earshot. She just nodded, both of them tying their sides of the rope to their harnesses, each showing Calvin how it's done.

"Mhm…" Calvin nodded, watching. But his eyes also glanced over to the course that Margot had chosen. They were all rated on difficulty, and this was one of the highest rated ones. He internally thought, *is she seriously gonna do this one?* To him, it didn't look possible.

"Watch this Calvin. We're starting here at the bottom," Margot started, getting herself on the wall, chalk on her hands. The employee held her side of the rope, showing Calvin what she was doing as well. "The first thing we're going to want to do is get ourselves upright, body parallel to the wall. This is going to use the least amount of energy. After that, we're going to solve the course like a puzzle, moving one limb at a time."

"Gotcha," Calvin affirmed, trying to take in a lot at once. As he watched Margot scale the wall, as well as how the worker pulled the rope as she went up, he started to get it. But his mind also drifted to other things, like the fact that Margot's back muscles now looked enormous. He never pinned her as muscular at all, but as she climbed up the wall she looked like a body-builder as she flexed.

Margot continued up the wall, doing what looked impossible to Calvin. "Then, you'll want to do a crossover here. Put your left foot in this spot, and swing around," Margot exasperatedly instructed, "At this part, I'm gonna jump. You won't have to do anything this difficult."

Calvin watched as she jumped for the next two rocks. *There's no way she can do that, can she?* He thought. But then, Margot slipped. She fell, and he instinctively jerked back, afraid to watch her fall. But then she just hung there by the rope, giving a thumbs-up.

"This is why we're always here, holding the rope on this side. That way we're ready to catch them at any moment. The belay device makes this very easy as long as you're holding the rope. Want to try?" the employee asked Calvin.

"Uh, yeah sure," he immediately responded. She widened the gap between her hands, instructing him to grab the rope there as Margot got herself back on the wall.

"I can't completely let go, since you aren't certified, but I can loosen my grip and let you hold her up for just a moment. Are you ready?" she asked him. He gulped, nodding. For some reason, it felt nerve-wracking to hold up someone in such a crucial position.

But he realized, at that moment, that she had already loosened her grip. With the belay device holding the rope securely, it felt like no issue holding up another's body weight. It was almost too easy. The employee gripped harder again.

"Now you won't be scared to practice," the employee told him. He nodded. Margot got herself back on the wall, and then made the jump with what looked like ease, getting herself to the top. When her hands reached the top of the wall, that signified she was done. The employee readied her grip, and slowly let her down.

"So, are you like... a professional?" Calvin asked, utterly surprised by her ability as the employee took off back to the counter.

"Not a professional. But I'm dedicated, for sure," Margot smiled, relishing in her accomplishment. "So, are you ready to try? Wanna do the same one?"

"Let's start with something easier!" Calvin nervously spit out. Margot nodded, and the two started to walk to the other side of the rock wall. But behind the two, a group of two boys gossiped.

"Dude, you hear about that Godsend guy?" one of the teenage boys asked the other.

"Duh, I did. Why you ask?"

"Just feel like the government is getting lazy with its cover-ups. Cool that we basically have real life *Iron-Man* though."

"Dude, that thing is nothing *like* that. Did you read *any* of the comics?"

"Concept is the same though. Wonder where he is, hasn't shown up in a bit."

"I don't think he's part of the government, honestly."

"Whaaaat?"

Margot and Calvin overheard all this as they went to the other side of the room. Margot was gauging Calvin's reaction, wondering if he had anything to say on that topic. Usually he was super caught-up on the news.

"Do *you* know what's new with that character?" Margot asked Calvin, sounding like she was baiting him into something.

"Nope, haven't looked at the news since. I've just been living my own life," Calvin proudly looked back at her. She gave him a slight smile back. That was the first time he spent more than a second looking at her face. "Hey, wait, I just noticed your lack of glasses."

"Contacts are in." Margot pointed to her eyes. He was able to tell after squinting.

"You don't usually wear them?" he asked.

"They're uncomfortable, so only when I need to. And hey, stop trying to change the subject. Let's get you on that wall," Margot told Calvin, handing him one side of the rope on a course marked "easy."

The two both got in position, Calvin mirroring what Margot had just done earlier. Margot tied in, knowing that it was done by muscle memory without looking down.

"You know what to say now?" she asked.

"On belay?"

"Belay on," she grinned, getting ready to hoist him as he put his hands on the wall. He started off well, putting his hands in the east-to-reach jugs.

Calvin was able to scale up the easy one without much help, getting to the top, and getting an adrenaline rush as he was hoisted down, not initially trusting the rope.

"Just trust me, I got you!" Margot shouted up at him.

"What if the rope snaps?!" Calvin asked, still letting go of the wall anyway.

"Hell will freeze over before that happens," Margot shrugged. He eventually got down, a little exhausted from not jumping off earlier.

"I think... I think I can do a harder one," Calvin was half terrified, half excited for the next one.

"Think you're a master suddenly? I've got a next one in mind for you then." Margot met his challenge.

"Don't put me through the ringer," Calvin suddenly regretted letting her take the reins. She took him over to one that was medium difficulty. It was a bit of a leap from what he just did, but for someone of average fitness, not impossible.

"You ready?" she asked.

"If I fall, just catch me," Calvin sighed, grabbing his side of the rope and getting chalk on his hands.

He got on the wall, doing well for a medium-difficulty course. But it was clear that as he got closer to the top of the wall that he really started to struggle. He strove to grab the next rock with his right hand, and missed for the first time, stumbling back to where he was.

"Jeez..." he gasped, starting to pant heavily. He started to realize that clinging to the wall in one position like this was easily more exhausting than advancing.

"Take your mind off of it!" Margot shouted up at him, "If you think or talk about something else, you'll start to progress without thinking too hard."

"What's that supposed to mean?!" he angrily shouted back down, still facing the wall. But he sighed, trying to catch his breath. He decided to give it a shot. "I think..." he shouted, getting himself back on the wall, "...the police think that *I'm* **Godsend**."

"What?!" Margot asked in shock. Calvin hoisted himself up, continuing past the rocks he had trouble with.

"Yeah," Calvin continued while climbing, "My brother is a cop, or really more of a detective. He doesn't know that I heard, but I could overhear his call from the other room." He climbed up more, not thinking about it.

"Why you?" Margot asked, continuing to belay him up. She started to notice he didn't have so much trouble while not thinking about it.

"I don't really know the details. I can tell he's defending me, but he could care less about me. He's doing it for our family image!" Calvin shouted, hoisting himself up more.

"So you don't *want* him to defend you?" Margot asked, confused on where this was going.

"No, I appreciate it," Calvin climbed up further, "But it really feels like he just doesn't care. Like he's using all his will for the sake of appearing good. Or to get on my family's good side so they'll reward him more!"

"Sounds like he's being greedy to me," Margot commented, more focused on the fact that he was nearly there.

"Are all people like the greedy politicians in the news?" Calvin muttered, getting stuck right before the end.

"Not you!" Margot shouted at him, "Imagine being more determined than they are greedy. You can come out on top."

"To outdo *their* greed is like climbing Mount Everest." Calvin was near the top.

"Nonetheless," Margot nearly interrupted, "Reach for that wish."

Calvin mustered up all his strength. He pushed past his limits, skipping the last two stones and gunning straight for the top. There, he grabbed on. Barely hanging on, he stabilized himself and pulled himself to the top.

"See!" Margot shouted from below, "Maybe it's a little more attainable than you think."

"CAN I COME DOWN NOW?" Calvin heaved, covered in sweat with no energy left. Margot lowered him, congratulating him on making it up. He took off the harness and started to drink water, recovering his stamina.

"You did it though, good job. That would be hard for a first timer," Margot commented as she stood in front of him.

"I know you would make it look easy, so please do a different course," Calvin complained, leading to her laughter.

"You sound like you wanna get back at your brother though. That must have kept your thoughts off of falling off," Margot concluded.

"It did..." Calvin muttered, thinking back to what he said. He felt apprehensive about saying all that. "But don't talk too much, with that new safety act, I'm probably being surveilled."

"Look around," Margot pointed around the room. Their phones were a few dozen feet away in their bags. All the cameras were facing toward the front. They were free from oversight here. "Nobody's gonna get anything from here."

"Well, maybe I do wanna get back at him then." Calvin crossed his arms, not sure what to do about that. "I just... I don't wanna hurt him either. I don't want to do something rash, I just want him to look at people rather than tools he can use for his benefit. Him and every other figure in politics."

"You said he was defending you. Making sure that none of the cops thought you were Godsend, despite them... thinking so? For some reason?" Margot asked, obviously alluding to something with a playful look on her face.

"Yeah...? Where are you going with this?" Calvin wondered, not sure where she was going with those questions.

She pondered for a moment. Then, snapping her fingers, she gave her suggestion.

"What if you *were* Godsend, then?"

With a stack of papers in his hands, Hadley had everything he needed in one place. His, and Miller's, boss stood in the next room. He took a deep breath at the doorway, holding up his papers and then marching forward.

The next room was a walled-off, windowless conference room. Only his boss and one assistant awaited Hadley.

"This better be good, Hadley. Hulls doesn't want that guy on the street anymore," the CIA director spat out, referencing the President.

"Mr. Blackwood. I assure you this is worth the wait," Hadley began, "I believe I have all of the evidence in-hand to begin the prosecution of our *Silver Prophet*. And I believe... it isn't even a *guy* per se."

Director Blackwood raised an eyebrow. His assistant seemed focused on his smart device, overlooking other current events.

"Go on with it," the director demanded. Hadley took a deep breath.

"First and foremost," Hadley took out the first page of his document. The projector behind him cast a giant version of what he read off of. "The most crucial part of evidence is our recording of Godsend during their first appearance. Shortly after appearing at the department store, we picked up their voice on the way to Mid-City. Specifically, on the way to Shepard Church right before their alcoholics anonymous meeting."

"You seriously think he's an alcoholic?" Blackwood muttered under his breath, watching the clip regardless. But as more and more evidence started to point toward

Godsend and that group. None of Godsend's appearances had coincided with the group time. It was in the epicenter of each appearance. It became more credible as the time passed.

"Now I believe, between detective Miller and myself, that we have the exact culprit in our group—"

"*Silver Prophet,*" the assistant said, cutting into Hadley's words. "The code was just called on a police channel."

"You don't mean...?" Director Blackwood wondered.

"The subject in question is on the move now. In Mid-City as we speak," the assistant assured him.

"Let's put it aside for now. Pull up whatever cameras we got. Get it on the projector," Blackwood insisted. Hadley nodded, internally pissed off that he was interrupted.

A bit earlier, on one of the main streets of Mid-City, Philadelphia, a handful of cop cars were in pursuit of a single white crossover with a broken driver-side door. News covered every second of the chase.

"Philadelphia Police now in pursuit of a single suspect. Currently, he is wanted for resisting arrest and assaulting a police officer. However, he was streaming his drive of his project-car to his social media followers. The video... paints a different picture," the news-anchor explained, live for the viewers. The video showed the man getting pulled over during his drive, questioning why he was being pulled over.

"Yes sir, officer? Is there anything I can help you with today?" the man asked, his drivers license and registration already on the dashboard.

"Your headlights weren't on. You do know that rain can be considered a hazardous weather condition?

84

Headlights have to be turned on for that," the officer informed him. Despite that, the camera showed that it was only a light drizzle outside.

"I'm sorry, officer. Still calibrating the automatic headlight sensor on this car I'm working on," the man admitted. The officer took another look. First, he looked at the registration. Then his eyes glanced down at the messy car.

"I don't believe this is registered properly if this is a project car. It seems you also have something hidden. Are there any firearms or drugs in the vehicle?" the officer asked.

"No sir. This car is registered to Virginia law, sir."

"I'm gonna need to see proof that there's nothing illegal in the vehicle." The officer tried to reach inside, in an attempt to move a jacket.

"I never consented to a vehicle search, sir," the man responded in a calm tone, despite the officer overstepping his boundaries.

"I don't need your consent," the officer spat in his face, continuing regardless. His arm was still over-extended, halfway inside of the half-rolled-up window.

"C-can you call your supervisor?" the man asked, trying to get answered for what went wrong. No response. The other cops all started to surround the vehicle. "Please officer, just call in your supervisor—"

SMASH! An officer broke the drivers-side window open.

"SHOW ME YOUR HANDS, NOW!" the second officer demanded.

"Sir, for what? I seriously need you to call your supervisor—"

SMACK! The first police officer hit him. "EXIT THE VEHICLE, NOW! STOP RESISTING ARREST!" the first officer ordered.

The video showed him nearly out of commission, his nose bleeding at this point. What was he being arrested for at this point?

The man, coming to, shoved the officer out of his car as he broke one of the hinges of his driver-side door. In fear for his life, he accelerated without saying a word, ending his social media livestream.

Now, speeding around, he continued running away from the police. He couldn't stop, in fear that a simple mistake would cost him his life. But *why*? Why would a system paid for by the people attack its own? For a quota? For a profit?

"PERHAPS THE SYSTEM WAS NEVER FOR THE PEOPLE AT ALL."

His car came to a complete halt. It wouldn't move anymore. He freaked out, feeling something hit the ceiling of the vehicle. Cop cars swerved in on both sides on this main street, securing the perimeter. Civilians ran away, not wanting to be associated with the scene. The man started to pant so hard, he nearly passed out.

Just then, the metallic monstrosity descended. Godsend, having flown in onto the man's roof, hovered facing the windshield. The man, knowing this metal amalgamation from the news, increased his level of panic.

"I DIDN'T DO ANYTHING, I PROMISE!" the man screamed out the window in fear, "I JUST LEFT MY LIGHTS OFF! I JUST THOUGHT IT WAS FINE SINCE IT WAS ONLY A CLOUDY DAY!" His fear grew, thinking that Godsend was coming to aid the police.

"**I KNOW**," Godsend's booming voice responded. Godsend turned to face the cops with their weapons drawn.

"Code *Silver Prophet*. I repeat, code *Silver Prophet*," one of the police muttered into a communications device.

All the cameras turned toward Godsend. They touched down on the ground, continuing to walk toward the police officers. The green bar on their face still glowed under the slight drizzle and dark clouds.

"You've got your own arrest warrant, buddy. You want to add to your sentence?" one of the police officers threatened, all of them had weapons drawn. Godsend's green light bar flipped to the bottom of their face, turning into a wicked grin.

"**I WAS BORN TO PROTECT THE HALLOWED. TO DELIVER THE WORLD FROM GREED. DON'T BE A TOOL OF THE SINNERS. WHAT, RIGHT NOW, ARE YOU PROTECTING?**"

The officers looked at each other, weary. Some knew the whole thing was nonsense, starting from one cop trying to lazily fulfill a quota.

"The law must be upheld! Whether *you* like it or not!" a cop pointed his gun at Godsend. His hands shaking, he fired regardless. The bullet bounced off the fluid metal suit, as if it were never fired in the first place.

"**THE LAW IS A TOOL AS WELL. I SEE.**"

Godsend began floating, hovering above all of the police officers. As they curled up into a ball, electricity seemed to gather up and create shockwaves around their fluid metal body.

"WHATEVER YOU'RE DOING, STOP THIS IMMEDIATELY!" a cop shouted, firing continuously at

Godsend. Some began to join in, despite the appearance that Godsend was charging up something.

One of the cops who had just returned to work was also called to this stand-off. It was Andre Taylor, the father of Amara. Knowing how the victim was treated, he did not fire at Godsend. Rather, he was the only one to run toward a nearby building for cover.

All of the energy reached a boiling point. Godsend exploded outward, letting out an eardrum-destroying cry that sent green shockwaves of electricity outward. The force alone toppled the police cars around him. The driver who was evading the police was unharmed, the car still in the condition it was in before.

None of the police were brutally harmed, just knocked over. It was as if a small tornado had swept through the area, leaving Godsend still hovering above everything.

"**AGAINST THE PENT-UP JUSTICE, WHO FIGHTS TO END GREED, ITS TOOLS MEAN NOTHING**," Godsend's voice boomed louder than ever before. "**I AM THAT BURNING DESIRE. THE DESIRE TO CORRECT THE WRONGS OF THE WORLD. THE POWER OF THE POWERLESS. YOU SHALL NOT HARM THIS MAN**."

Godsend turned away, about to leave. But from behind, *something* crashed into the scene. A peculiar set of noises, pneumatic in nature, had Godsend assume one thing. *They've sent in an exo-suit soldier?*

As Godsend turned back, there was a lone person in front of the toppled over cops, of which Andre Taylor was left standing. But before him was an individual in a black jumpsuit. They wore goggles over their eyes to see, and had on a military exo-suit. One with a bulky battery-pack on the back and metal appendage attachments all over their body.

"You... can't just decide justice on your own!" the masked person put up their fists. But they had no voice filter. It was clearly a young woman. Godsend twitched for a second, looking directly into the masked individual's eyes.

"Amara?" Andre muttered under his breath, in disbelief that it would be his own daughter out there on the field with him. She did not turn back to him.

"**TELL ME WHY YOU DO, THEN**," Godsend demanded, sounding less sure of themselves as before.

"Police have lives too! It sucks that we need money to survive now, but just abandoning one's job could cost them their family! It isn't their fault they have a job to do!" the masked person shouted back.

"**COMPLIANCE WITH GREED CANNOT BE CONTINUED, MASKED REBEL**."

"So be it." The masked rebel used the exo-suit to boost themselves into the air, thrusting forward toward Godsend. Godsend caught their fist, but a plasma cutter came out of their mechanical glove. It appeared to do damage for a moment. Godsend, not paying attention, was looking into the masked rebel's goggles. In disbelief, they confirmed for themselves it was Amara. Godsend dropped her to the ground. She caught herself, using the exo.

"Amara!" her father, Andre, called out, "What are you doing here?!"

"I'm not gonna let this guy do whatever he wants! If he wants to be a hero, fine! But I won't let him be a nuisance!" Amara, still in her suit, looked to Godsend. Godsend, appearing motionless, suddenly vanished. The

89

man who ran from the police came out of the vehicle with his hands up.

"I... I mean no harm! Can I just go home? Please!" he shouted, nervous tears in his eyes. The police looked at each other. One of them, out of turn, went up and cuffed him.

"We'll review in the holding center." The policeman dragged the guy off. Some of the cop cars began to leave. But Andre still looked at Amara, shocked. She looked back, having no explanation. Using the exo, she jumped into a nearby alleyway.

"Should we pursue the 'masked rebel' too?" one of Andre's coworkers asked him. He shook his head.

"I'm sure the two of us will have a nice, long, chat later," he told his coworker.

As all of this unfolded, the broadcast footage was being beamed directly into the room with Hadley and Blackwood. They mostly stayed quiet as they watched the events unfold. Hadley was secretly sweating buckets after they watched the last cop car leave.

"We should be able to trace them now. On with it, Hadley, which one of them is Godsend?" Blackwood asked.

"Oh!" Hadley faked dropping all of his papers, picking them up one-by-one. But his assistant had already pressed the "next" button on the projector.

Hadley only noticed then that his paper proclaiming that Amara was Godsend was being displayed behind him.

"Hadley. I'm gonna let you leave. The two of us will pretend like this never happened. Okay?" Blackwood ordered him. He nodded and left without argument.

In the shadows, Godsend remained.

90

Tick, tock. The room remained deafeningly silent. The sound of the clock in the back being the only thing their ears could hear.

It, again, was a Thursday. Pastor Alan had already let the group in. Declan, Milo, Owen, Margot, Hazel, and Calvin quietly shuffled to their seats. They knew that for the past few days, the mysterious masked rebel on the news was someone they knew closely. It was someone who was seemingly absent. Yet, they waited.

Calvin rubbed his hands together, uncomfortable with the silence. Pastor Alan pulled up a chair, sitting in front of the others. A faint knock echoed from the door. All eyes turned. Amara walked in, her eyes fixed on the floor. She took her usual seat, avoiding eye contact with anyone. The air remained thick with unspoken questions. Pastor Alan cleared his throat.

"Welcome, Amara. Glad you could make it." His voice was gentle, but the tension in the room was killer..

The meeting proceeded, though it felt strained. Everyone shared their weekly updates, their voices hushed, their eyes darting towards Amara whenever she wasn't looking. She offered brief, vague responses when it was her turn, her usual energetic demeanor replaced by a quiet reserve. The topic of the news, and what happened earlier that week, loomed over the group. A confrontation seemed inevitable.

"With that being said, let me pray us out," Pastor Alan, following the usual script, started to end the meeting. "Dear Heavenly Father, thank you for our time today. In Your name we pray, Amen."

Pastor Alan looked up once more. The group began to eye each other, unsure of what to do next. One thing was clear: they wanted to know more.

"So Amara—" Declan started, obviously going straight into the topic. The rest of the group internally flinched, hearing this abrupt cut straight to her.

"Hey." Calvin spoke loud and firm, grabbing the group's attention over Declan. "Why did you defend those cops? Didn't you see what they did to that guy?"

The group tensed. Calvin's words were unusual, his demeanor completely changed. They sounded like they came from an entirely different person.

"Guess my 'masked rebel' shenanigans need no intro then," Amara, motionless and looking down, admitted.

"Calvin, what's gotten into you?" Hazel suddenly stepped in.

"Yeah, man. We all want to know too, but that's kinda harsh wording, you know?" Owen chipped in with his own opinion.

"Guys, it's alright," Amara looked up, a stern scowl on her face, "I get it. To everyone, somehow he looked like justice itself. He was defending an innocent civilian, anyway. How do you argue against that?"

"Right, but I'm sure you have a reason!" Milo, sounding concerned, added.

"All of you," Pastor Alan raised his voice for the first time at them. "If you're going to argue like this, please do so outside."

Without a beat, Amara walked out the door with her stuff. The rest of them quickly followed, curiosity taking over their logic. Calvin followed her close behind.

"I'd like to know, too. What's so important that you had to interfere?" Calvin asked.

"What's so important?!" Amara angrily shot back, her usual happy energy completely gone, "*My dad* was there too! Is it truly justice when his coworker's actions nearly get him killed?! Answer that for me!"

The rest of them stopped. The group had re-assembled on the patio outside. Nobody could provide an immediate answer, not thinking from that perspective.

"Did that really mean you had to go out there yourself?" Declan asked.

"YES!" she shot back, "Who *else* is doing anything about it? This unknown vigilante shows up, people call that *thing* 'Godsend,' and people all have some sort of opinion on the matter. Does anybody actually *act* on it? No! They're all talk!"

"Amara..." Margot quietly tried to cut it, "You don't think at all this guy came to fight corruption?"

"I see it! I see that's what he's doing. But you know what? His methods are wrong." Amara began to rant. "What we need is someone with a surgeon's precision to bring these people to justice! We need *reform* not *war!* Godsend is just an angry, unorganized response to the pain of the world. He doesn't *CARE* about the damage he does on the way to 'fix' things!"

Calvin stepped ahead of everyone. Sweat beaded down his face from his forehead. He muttered something, furrowing his eyebrows as he stared into Amara's eyes.

"Huh?" she looked at him, half-angrily, half-confused. "Speak up. I can't hear you."

He bent down, nearly pressing his face into hers. The rest of the group backed off.

"Are you calling **my** method 'sloppy?'" he grinned, still shaking. She couldn't respond. She couldn't accept what he had just said.

93

"You—?" she was cut off. A sudden shove from Calvin ended their confrontation. She fell to the ground. Calvin stormed off the other way.

"WAIT!" Declan immediately went after him. Most of the others bent down to help Amara up after realizing what had happened.

"Are you okay?" Milo asked, helping Amara up.

"Did he just say *his* method? As in..." Hazel drifted off whilst helping with Milo.

"He *was* Godsend. Holy shit, the cops were right," Owen blurted aloud. Margot raised an eyebrow.

"What do you mean by, 'the cops were right?'" Hazel looked at Owen with scorn. All of the eyes around Owen shifted toward him. He put his hands up.

"The cops didn't think I could be Godsend, but they thought he might be in this group. I don't know the details, but they just had me report on people's behavior!" Owen had no problem quickly admitting to what he was up to.

"You were *spying* on us?" Amara quickly lashed out at Owen.

"What exactly were you reporting? That we were *alcoholics*? Do you even really need to be in this group, man?!" Hazel angrily questioned him as well.

"Yes! Yes I promise, I'm just one of you guys! They just... it seemed like they were going to do something to me if I let it out that the cops were looking for Godsend. I'm sorry I kept quiet!" Owen clapped his hands together, begging for forgiveness.

"Interesting," Margot remarked, "I wonder how the cops concluded that Godsend was part of this group."

"Well, looks like they were right. I just can't believe it's *him*..." Amara tightened her fist. She was about to run off, but Hazel grabbed her wrist.

94

"Hold on, masked rebel. I think Declan is on the case. With his identity revealed, Godsend can't stay around much longer. What happens when he exits the suit? What happens when the police find *Calvin*?" Hazel talked some sense into her. She stopped struggling.

"Should we tell them?" Milo suggested, having his phone already out.

"Look up," Owen pointed to a camera that was pointed toward their area, "At this point, I think there's no way they don't know."

"I'm still going to try and stop him, if he isn't arrested immediately," Amara concluded.

"I know why for you, but won't this cause an uproar with the public? Some people are extreme fans of Godsend," Milo brought up.

"I don't know. I'm not sure what's right anymore, but I have to defend what's close to me." Amara started to walk toward where Declan and Calvin ran off too. "I hope you understand."

The others watched her start to speed up, running in the direction of Calvin.

"Let's go too. I want to see what happens," Hazel, sounding curious, started to run. The others looked at each other, then decided to follow Hazel.

As they ran, Declan was about to catch up with Calvin as he ran toward the street.

"WAIT!" Declan shouted. Calvin turned, looking at Declan with a smirk. Declan threw an angry right hook, attempting to hit Calvin in the face. Calvin dodged to the right.

"Wait for what? You to hit me? I didn't know you hated what *Godsend* was doing so much." Calvin put his hands in his pockets, jumping back again as Declan tried to hit him.

"I don't care who you are. You don't end that by shoving someone on the ground," Declan spat, taking a break from throwing jabs. "Plus, you *can't* be Godsend."

"But *I am.*" Calvin stomped down, hitting Declan's foot. But this gave Declan the opportunity to finally make contact, hitting him in the chest. Calvin stumbled backward.

"Your voice is totally wrong. It doesn't match up at all. Even a detective came to me, trying to force me into believing that it was Amara. I didn't fold for a second! I know you two. I've been at this *dumbass* group for too long for you to fool me!" Declan shouted one of the most genuine things he had ever told Calvin.

"I can't believe my brother would go that far just to try and save his own ass. He just doesn't want to be related to trouble. He doesn't want any bad marks on his life anywhere, and just thinks that I'm a nuisance. Good! Let Godsend be the greatest nuisance assholes ever had to deal with!" Calvin shouted back, still backing away from Declan.

"You still don't talk like him. I don't know what's going on in your head, but you're faking this for some reason. Maybe you still get too angry at the news," Declan remarked, hoping to get under Calvin's skin.

It worked. Calvin's face contorted with anger, trying to hit Declan back. But Declan was bigger and stronger, taking the hit, and throwing Calvin to the ground.

"Not so strong anymore, 'Godsend.' If you were really the person in that suit, you could have evaded *that*," Declan panted, out of breath. But without warning, a car came to a screeching halt near the sidewalk where they fought.

"Took long enough." Calvin grinned as the blacked-out car threw open its rear passenger door. He leapt up getting inside. The door slammed before Declan could open it.

"CALVIN! WE CAN TALK ABOUT THIS!" Declan pounded on the door. But the car floored it, speeding out of the area.

The others ran up as Declan just had watched Calvin speed away in the blacked-out vehicle.

"What happened? Where's Calvin?" Amara asked, realizing that Declan was alone there.

Declan still panted. "He... got in some car. I don't know why he's doing this. Calvin *can't* be Godsend. They might seem similar, but—"

"ENOUGH." Margot cut him off. The others all turned to her, not knowing her as someone to speak up like that. "He just told us *plainly* to our faces who he is. He admitted to keeping secrets, and being two-faced. Maybe it's time we stop defending him."

"She's right," Amara backed up Margot, "We just need to accept the facts."

"But now what? We're just going to let him go? We pretend he was never part of the group? We let the cops get him?" Declan started to spiral.

"Since when did you care about Calvin?" Hazel asked. Declan stopped. He dropped his hands.

"You're right." He turned around. "Maybe I'm just overreacting."

"I would just wait to see what the police do, Declan. His declaration was caught on camera so... it's a little out of our control now," Milo explained. The group remained

97

still. Declan remained focused on the roar where Calvin had left.

"I guess we'll just have to wait and see, then." Declan sighed a long sigh.

Their options to interfere had run out. One by one, they all went home.

Inside the detective's workspace, Miller was at work going through the footage submitted to their office. Multiple programs had been set up by the Commoner's Safety Act, and now they had the whole country essentially under their surveillance.

But one individual had constantly managed to escape. *Godsend.* The whole program, created to find individuals like that, couldn't do its job this one time. No matter what, Godsend managed to thwart any connection to their identity.

But then some security camera footage came across Miller's desk. It changed everything. "Silver Prophet," he whispered to himself, watching as Calvin revealed himself to be Godsend. He exclaimed "SILVER PROPHET!"

More detectives ran into the room. Together they watched the entire confrontation. As Calvin continually referred to himself as *Godsend,* the entire group began to look toward Hadley, one of the detectives in the group. The one who had repeatedly defended Calvin.

"Declan is *RIGHT!* It makes no sense," Hadley shouted, his entire group of coworkers staring him down. Suddenly, he was cuffed without warning. Miller stood to his side.

"We're going to have a nice, long talk about why *exactly* you wanted to frame Amara Taylor. 'Kay?" Miller told him, holding his handcuffs.

"I was *not* trying to FRAME her, I thought it WAS her! Come on!" he protested as the whole group of detectives took him out of the room. "Shit," he spat.

They didn't let the news go public, but news was spread around government sectors pretty quickly. The police continued to search, trying to find the now wanted criminal: Calvin Becker.

Another problem arose, however, when they looked at his online history. It didn't make sense, but it appears that the car that picked him up seemingly vanished. The only thing for certain is that it used to be a civilian's vehicle. It disappeared without a trace, was marked as stolen, and then showed back up to pick up Calvin. Footage indicated it went out into the country on some back roads. But where it went remained a mystery.

In an interrogation room, Hadley was found innocent of knowing about Godsend. He genuinely thought there was no possible way it was his brother, and the other detectives concluded he was just in denial about it. However...

"The fact still remains, Hadley Becker," a fellow detective began to tell him, "You tried to implicate Amara Taylor just because you found some weak evidence. You made it out to be very obvious, when most of the evidence was coincidental. For that, we're going to have to revoke your position."

"You're serious? You have to be kidding— do you *know* how much work I put in?!" Hadley fought as much as he could, but his reputation was tarnished. Exactly what Calvin was aiming for.

Calvin now had been gone for five days. Still no trace of him, but many were still looking. The streets of Philadelphia were littered as usual. Many of the "lower class" remained on one side of the gate. Those more "affluent" on the other side of the gate. Above, however, was a different story.

An airplane began its descent. The pilot announced, "We are now descending into Philadelphia International Airport. Please place large device—"

BOOM! The entire plane shook. The people inside screamed as the lights flickered. The oxygen masks dropped.

"Everyone remain calm," the pilot ordered to no avail. Screaming and chaos ensued. Some people began to use the masks as the plane started to lose altitude. From the outside, people on the ground could see that one of the engines had caught fire.

"What's going on? Where are the flight attendants?!" one woman got up, looking around. Despite the lights flashing for their attention, there was a distinct lack of flight attendants. The woman ran up to the front.

"What are you doing?!" a man shouted at her.

"TO SEE THE PILOT!" the woman shouted back, running to the front. She tried desperately to open the door, but it was locked.

"Please remain in your seats," the pilot's voice announced again. This just made her angrier, and she managed to pull the door open.

Inside, there was a cockpit with no pilot. The woman's eyes widened. The descent grew faster.

"Please remain in your seats," the voice played again. Pre-recorded.

"I should have known they would try and pull this," a man grumbled. Aboard the flight, this man was seated in first class. He was the leader to a human rights society, devoted to curing cancer. With him, he held a possible solution to the disease altogether. He was known as "Charles Edwin."

On the ground, people from his association looked to the sky.

"Isn't that the plane Charles is on?!" one of his colleagues pointed to the plane with the fire on the side.

"Yeah... that doesn't happen by coincidence," another of his colleagues clenched their fists.

The plane continued to fall, on target to crash into a large unoccupied piece of abandoned farmland. Their fates were all inevitable. That was until they heard something else.

BUMP— The plane had suddenly stabilized. The people on the ground watched in awe as the plane flew straight.

"LOOK UP THERE! IT'S GODSEND!" a passerby shouted, bringing attention to one of Charles's colleagues. They adjusted their glasses, looking back up at the plane. Indeed, beneath the plane was Godsend.

"So he returns," another passerby commented as Godsend continued to lift the plane up.

"SILVER PROPHET! I REPEAT, WE HAVE A CODE SILVER PROPHET!" the air traffic control spoke over the intercom back to the airport.

The plane seemed to smoothly start gliding down, as Godsend held it up from underneath.

"**YOUR VENTURE WAS SUPPOSED TO END HERE. I CANNOT ALLOW THE HALLOWED TO GO SO EASILY**," the people on the plane heard Godsend's computer-static voice announce to them all. They started to cry of happiness. The feeling of being saved overwhelmed the passengers.

Godsend, outside of the plane, noticed another object flying directly toward them. It was a remotely operated drone, carrying missiles.

Three missiles suddenly shot out of the drone. They weren't going for the plane, but toward Godsend himself. Godsend put forth a hand, sending out an electric wave that caused a small pulse. The missiles stopped in the air, falling directly toward the found. They exploded in mid-air a few hundred feet below the plane.

"Why are there more explosions? What's going on?" one man shouted aloud, looking out the plane window.

"**IT APPEARS THE SYSTEM WANTS TO DESTROY ME. EVEN IF IT MEANS TAKING YOU DOWN AS WELL**."

"YOU GOT THIS GODSEND! FIGHT BACK!" a woman cried out. The plane began to rally. The one in the fluid metal suit smiled.

"**UNDERSTOOD.**"

Godsend shot a bullet through one of its fingers. It penetrated the drone, causing it to explode.

More drones appeared, all in pursuit of Godsend. It detached its hand from its body. Godsend, holding the entire plane with their left hand. Pointed their right hand like a gun. As dozens of missiles were launched toward them, he destroyed them far before they could get anywhere near them.

But this was just a distraction. On the ground, government forces readied a laser cannon. With the power of nearly a gigawatt, this was supposed to be a weapon to take down Godsend.

"FIRE!" a man overseeing the cannon shouted. A nearby robot manned the scope, shooting directly up at Godsend.

The drones had been cleared, and the cabin of the falling craft was at ease once more as Godsend began their descent. But another *THUNK* hit the craft.

"Now what?!" a civilian tried to look down under the craft, to no avail. The beam had blasted straight up, so powerful it looked like a beacon of light. Godsend was hit directly, crashing the metal monster directly into the bottom of the craft.

"KEEP HOLDING! WE'LL FRY THAT SUIT AND DIG THE YOUNGER BACKER OUT OF IT!" the government employee ordered.

Godsend, feeling the pressure, was attempting to move. They were pinned to the bottom of the craft, being pushed upward as the cannon continued its assault. But Godsend couldn't take it anymore. There was no longer an option.

Being crushed under the weight of the laser, Godsend once again charged up. The green energy around Godsend became monstrously huge, charged up by the laser. The entire plane saw a flash of green as Godsend's limbs snapped up. The laser was deflected to the side, straight past the horizon and into space.

Godsend peered down, pointing with their thumb out toward their assailant. A surge of green energy shot out of their hand, zooming down at the speed of light. On the ground, the cannon was blown to pieces, hit by Godsend's wrath.

"IT MAY GET A BIT ROUGH, BUT IN ORDER TO SAVE YOU, I'M GOING TO BRING US DOWN QUICKLY. THERE, THEY WILL DE-PRESSURIZE THE CABIN!" Godsend shouted, sounding more panicked than they ever had been before. The cabin suddenly felt tense again.

"Everyone, grab hold of something!" a man ordered everyone in the cabin. Most buckled up again, holding onto the seat arms.

Godsend grabbed the bottom of the plane, and pushed forward. They essentially went back to crash-landing speed, only Godsend held up the plane this time. Thew flew through the atmosphere, going toward an empty patch of grass.

"AAAHHHH!!" the passengers in the cabin shouted as they flew directly toward the ground. As they were about to hit the ground, Godsend flew to the back of the plane, pulling as hard as the suit would allow, but not so fast that it would kill the passengers from whiplash.

All the passengers went face-first into the seat in front of them as Godsend pulled the plane to a near-stop. Then, on the grass, the plane bounced off the ground, touching down once more and rolling into a tree. The front was damaged, and the people were rattled up. But there was not a single casualty from the incident.

"**SORRY ABOUT THE LANDING**," Godsend apologized. The cabin was mostly okay, offering applause and crying of relief.

News vans following the incident pulled up as fast as they could. Suddenly, Godsend stood on the field with the plan behind him and was surrounded. Paramedics, police, and the media were all on the scene.

"FREEZE!" a cop tried to shoot at Godsend, but the bullet bounced off. They began to hover in the air again to avoid confrontation.

"MR. GODSEND! WHAT DO YOU SAY HAPPENED HERE TODAY?" a newscaster shouted out from below Godsend. Godsend looked down, their green light bar on their face swirled down to form a mouth once more.

"**THE ONLY COMMENT I WILL MAKE IS THIS**," Godsend began, "**I SERVE THE HALLOWED. THE HUMANITY LEFT UNTOUCHED AND UNCORRUPTED**

BY GREED. THOSE WHO HATE ME SHOULD FEAR ME. THOSE WHO LOVE ME SHOULD LIVE BY ME. TOGETHER, WE WILL REBIRTH THE HALLOWED."

With that comment, Godsend charged up once more, launching themselves so fast it looked like they were teleporting.

Then, as the paramedics started to release people from the plane, the newscasters recognized Charles Edwin. One came up to him, hoping for a comment.

"Mr. Edwin, that must have been one hell of a ride. How do you feel now that Godsend has saved your life personally?" the newscaster asked.

"I believe that the government just tried to take me out, to be frank with you," Charles said on a live broadcast, "It seemed to me that due to the lack of a pilot, they planned to bring down my plane. All because here, I have a possible huge step toward curing cancer."

"Is that so, Mr. Edwin?"

"Yes, certainly. After seeing it with my own eyes, I don't think this man, or woman, or being we call Godsend, is a threat to the people. I think he's a threat to those like President Hulls. Nasty fellas. And that scares them powerful folk." Charles Edwin's powerful opinion resonated with those around him.

"Thank you for your time," the newscaster quickly ended it, knowing that the executives that were his bosses weren't gonna like this.

A few people still exiting the plane gossiped. "Was it just me, or when Godsend got flustered, did it sound like he spoke with a Russian accent?"

"Yeah, totally!" another passenger agreed. They continued to talk until they were cleared to go home.

Hours later, Godsend had evaded all the cameras. Going back to their hiding spot, they now had a chance to breathe. Underground, a set of double-doors opened up.

They walked in through the doors, quickly taking off the metallic suit. It compacted itself back into a disk that they held in their hands. Holding it, they went over to the nearby computer, turning it on.

Online, it was clear as day. Godsend was more popular than ever with the people. After what Charles Edwin had said on live television, people identified more and more as "with the hallowed."

The government on the other hand, seemed more irritated than ever. They were wondering why they couldn't find their culprit, who they believed to be Calvin Becker.

"Speaking of Calvin..."

"I'm right here!" Calvin opened a door behind them, walking into the same room, "I got to see everything. Man, I underestimated how amazing you could be! Saving people in that aircraft, gaining all this popularity."

"I do my best, hah. It wasn't easy, but somehow it all worked out. Weird to find out that the government does all this stuff, isn't it?"

Calvin, with giant eyebags, nodded. Calvin appeared like he was in a trance, or had not slept in a long while. "It's hideous. To believe that they were getting away with this for so long. You sure you don't mind me taking the credit for their undoing?"

"Go for it. I don't really want to be known, anyway." They faced Calvin directly, putting the disc of the Godsend suit into their pocket.

"Also," Calvin began to ask, "When am I going to get to go outside again? I get that this is totally for my good but, it's been a while."

"Soon. You'll make an appearance as Godsend soon."

"Ah, okay," Calvin responded, sounding a little disappointed. Calvin began to walk back into the other room. He then remembered something. "Oh! Also, what is your 'next step' as Godsend?"

"Not sure. I've been going as I figure this all out. Don't think, like the public, I'm some sort of mastermind. I'm still just... who I am."

Calvin paused for a moment. It was strange to meet someone who had been so vehemently on his side about everything he felt. It was a change of pace, and it felt strangely good. But it also felt weird in a way. He was so used to being told what to stop doing, that it was odd to have that missing.

"You sure that I can still be a part of all this? That I'm not over-obsessing?" Calvin asked again.

"You're fine just being you. You were right to want to get back at Hadley. Look at you now! You're better than ever!" They held Calvin's shoulders up, trying to cheer Calvin up. "Now you'll live in history as the one who saved the common man. The one who took down corrupt billionaires. Hadley'll just just be remembered as a sham."

"Right." Calvin took a deep breath, sighing in relief. He looked up at who he now knew as Godsend once again. He held so much admiration in his heart for the one who was taking care of all the corruption he hated so much. He was scared that if he met the person, maybe it would ruin things. But no, it stayed. It even grew as she decided she would help him get back at his brother and be remembered for what he wanted to do.

She smiled at him, walking back into the other room. Calvin took another look, seeing again the only person he had been talking to in the last five days while he hid out in a secret bunker she had been taking care of.

Despite all of the battle damage Godsend took, her glasses underneath the suit were undamaged. It was truly a marvel of technology. And it was both of their ways toward fixing the greed that humanity had created.

"Hey Margot," Calvin got her attention. Margot Davis turned back toward him. "Thanks for helping me out."

"Likewise." She grinned, taking the metal disc with her into the other room.

Another week had gone by. Time had dragged all the way onto Thursday. Many of the group members wondered how this session was going to go. With everything that had occurred, it seemed like nothing but trouble could be brought about by the group reassembling.

Pastor Alan, unsure of what to say after the last group, gulped as he opened up the double doors to room 109. Surprisingly, all of the normal participants of the alcoholics anonymous group sat before him. All but one. They didn't make a noise as he entered the building.

"It's lovely to see you all already gathered! I was wondering where—"

"We've all decided not to talk about it," Declan interrupted Pastor Alan, "We knew it would be hard for you and we'd just end up arguing about it, so we're gonna move on for your sake."

"Thanks for considering me. I already knew coming into this week that Calvin may be the first thing on everyone's minds. But we don't need to talk about that. Instead, how about we get back to the root of why we're here?" Pastor Alan asked, leaving the answer open from the room. The only response he got was subtle nods from the group.

"I broke it," Owen said, raising his hand after a prolonged silence. He exhaled loudly, and reiterated, "I broke my sobriety. There. Phew. I just... wanted to get it out there."

The room remained quiet, the silence now heavier than before. Milo nervously shifted in his seat, avoiding eye contact. Hazel looked at Owen with concern, while Declan just sighed, running a hand through his hair. Margot, however, leaned forward, her expression unreadable.

"Owen," Margot said, her voice surprisingly soft. "Do you want to talk about it?"

"Stole the words right out of my mouth Margot. However, I do want to interject and say it's totally okay if you do not wish to touch anymore on it," Pastor Alan rushed in.

Owen flinched, his gaze still fixed on the floor. "I don't even know what to say. It's a dumb story," he took a shaky breath.

"Nope," Hazel jumped in, "I thought it was dumb of me to come here but, I think it was right. So I'm not about to let you tell me that the story was 'dumb.' If you want to tell us, tell us."

He leaned back, eyes fixated on the blank ceiling above. He thought that he wouldn't feel nervous, but somehow his nerves were on fire. "Well, to me this sounds dumb. But... I don't know. After the whole thing with Calvin, I just wasn't sure how to feel anymore. I used to feel safe-ish in my own home. Didn't read into things too much. But if Calvin was this... 'Godsend' guy. I wanted to look more into what 'Godsend' was talking about." He took a pause.

"And?" Margot asked, egging on the obvious question.

"I went down a trail of how rotten and corrupt everything is now. The friggen— surveillance act or whatever it's called. All the way back to the early twenties. This place, this country, it's been turned into exactly what we used to fear." Owen went on scrolling through things he found on his phone, "I couldn't sleep at night knowing there were cases of citizens just being thrown out under wrong assumptions or... the fact that the tax dollars I fund are responsible for murdering innocent people. I don't know why it all hit me so much now. I knew it was always a possibility from rumors and stuff like that but— it's just so plain to see now."

"I'm guessing you took the most effective sleeping pill you know of," Declan added, seeing where the story was going. Owen leaned back, pointing to him and nodding.

"You know it. Straight from the bottle," Owen put a hand over his embarrassed face.

"It's okay, Owen," Pastor Alan said softly, trying to offer comfort. "We all slip up. The important thing is that you came back here to share it with us. That takes courage."

"But you know what stopped me?" Owen kept talking, almost as if he wasn't listening to anything in earshot, "It doesn't have to be this way! And the one who's gonna fix things is CALVIN of all people! Isn't that friggin awesome?"

"Owen." Pastor Alan interrupted with a tone unlike himself. It was stern and brisk. "I understand that your story has to do with him, but we were not going to talk about all that during this session."

"But don't you see how this could be amazing—"

"Owen." The pastor clearly didn't want him proceeding with the topic.

"Alright, jeez," Owen complained in reaction to the pastor's insistence.

"I think I had a fairly normal week, somehow," Hazel jumped in, trying to avoid any silence, "I'm starting my next semester now. I know, it's early. But hey, somehow getting close to the end with pre-law and political science."

"You do *both* of those? That's a lot of pressure," Milo asked her, sitting nearby.

"Tell me about it," she rolled her eyes, "But I'm getting towards the latter of my degree now. Should just be law after that."

"I, uh, second that it sounds hard, Hazel. I would probably drop out in your shoes," Declan admitted.

"So you can bring lawsuits to every corrupt politician soon, eh?" Owen asked in a smug tone. Amara, who had been sitting quietly, had enough of this.

"Alright, Owen. What is up with you? Last week you're spying on us for the cops, now you suddenly hate the government," Amara pointed out.

"I did *not* want to spy on you for the cops! It just— it sorta just happened. I got roped into it, you know?" Owen jumped right into defense mode.

"Were you taking notes of us? What'd you write down?" Margot asked without skipping a beat.

"I did *not* take notes— none of you guys seemed like Godsend to me!" Owen shouted.

"Alright, I really tried to separate current events from what's going on but none of you can go along with that," Pastor Alan interjected, "I can wrap up now and let you all talk on the patio or we can go through the reading. Your choice." The group exchanged glances, the tension electric. Owen looked pleadingly at Hazel, who avoided his gaze. Declan tapped his foot impatiently. Margot's eyes narrowed. Amara remained silent, her arms crossed.

"The reading, Pastor Alan," Margot finally said, her voice stern. "Let's stick to why we're here."

A collective sigh of relief seemed to sweep through the room, even from Pastor Alan. He picked up his worn Bible. "Very well. Today's reading is from Proverbs."

Anticipation grew as Pastor Alan spoke. Almost nobody in the room could pay attention, knowing the unsaid tension was building up.

As he finished up his reading from Proverbs, another silence fell. But this one felt different, less charged with immediate conflict and more with introspection. Owen was the first to speak.

"I guess... I guess that's why I felt so awful, you know? Like I was fleeing from something, even when no one was chasing me. Just knowing all that stuff, it felt like a weight. And then picking up the bottle... that was definitely fleeing. But coming here, saying it out loud... that feels more like the 'bold as a lion' part. Facing it." He looked to Margot, who gave him a warm nod.

"I can relate to that. When I was drinking, it felt like I was always running from something. From feeling inadequate, from expectations. It wasn't until I stopped running that I started to actually live," Milo explained.

Hazel chimed in, her voice softer than before. "And it's easy to get caught up in things that feel like they're outside of our control. But we can choose how we react to it, rather than letting it consume us." She glanced pointedly at Owen. He nodded, embarrassed.

Somehow, the continued discussion went on without mention of Godsend or politics. They focused more on sobriety and how to get back on track, diffusing the situation of conflict.

As the discussion was wrapping up, Pastor Alan smiled gently. "We are all on this journey together, facing our own fears and striving for our own versions of righteousness." He closed his Bible. "Let's end with a moment of silent reflection, a closing prayer, and then we'll conclude for the day."

A final prayer was said, and the group took a collective deep breath.

"Well, looks like we got through it finally," Amara commented.

"I didn't truly intend to end it early, however I'm glad the rest of it went well. I'm looking forward to getting more back-on-track next week," Pastor Alan explained, shortly dismissing the group.

Declan sighed, rubbing his temples. Despite the sweet words, the air still felt heavy with unspoken implications, with the ghost of Calvin and the presence of Godsend hanging over them all. He wondered if the relative calm would hold, or if the unresolved issues would finally boil over.

The group almost silently started to all leave in unison. Usually, they would be talking about something boring or on-topic at this point. Instead of letting this wait for next week, Hazel began to take action.

"I agree with you, Owen," is all Hazel said, but it got the group to freeze. All eyes turned toward Hazel. "I think we should support Calvin."

"You *WHAT*?" Declan couldn't even believe his ears. This sudden shift seemed out of the blue.

"Are you seriously telling me that you're going to support a known vigilante?" Amara snapped, stepping closer to Hazel, "After all we just talked about in there?"

Hazel met Amara's intense gaze, her arms crossed. "I'm not supporting a vigilante, Amara." She nearly stumbled over her words. "I'm agreeing with Owen that the government has gone too far this time, and something needs to be done about it. Calvin may have... unconventional methods... but he's fighting for something real."

115

"So you're just going to ignore the fact that he shoved me to the ground?" Amara's voice was jagged with disbelief. "You're just going to excuse everything he does because he's 'fighting for something real'?"

"Look, I'm not saying what he did was right," Hazel conceded, glancing at the others in the group who were watching the exchange with anticipation. "But this isn't about personal grudges. It's about what's happening in the world. Owen saw it, and honestly, so do I. The news, the surveillance, the way people are being treated... it's not right. Especially when studying the history of the *law*— it becomes clear there's something wrong."

"And you think *Calvin* is the answer?" Declan interjected, shaking his head. "The same Calvin who obsesses over every little headline and then lashes out? That's your beacon of hope?"

"He's doing *something*," Owen said, stepping forward slightly. "That's more than anyone else in power is doing right now. And if he's taking down corrupt billionaires and stopping planes from crashing... maybe he's exactly what we need, even if he's a bit rough around the edges."

"Rough around the edges?" Amara scoffed. "He's a menace! And he's going to get himself, and probably others, killed. You think the government is just going to let him continue to run around causing 'nuisance'?"

Margot, who had been silent up until this point, spoke up, her voice surprisingly firm. "Maybe it's not about who he is, or how he operates. Maybe it's about what he *represents*. People are looking for hope, for someone to stand up to injustice. And right now, he's that symbol for a lot of them."

Milo, looking uncomfortable, nervously shuffled his feet. "But... he admitted to being Godsend. The police know. Isn't that just going to make things worse? It won't look like justice if he's fighting the cops."

"Worse for *them*," Hazel corrected, a glint in her eye. "Not for everyday people like us... the people Godsend calls 'hallowed.'"

The group fell silent for a moment, Hazel's words settling over them. Amara in particular scowled at Hazel.

"My dad's a cop, you know. Are you saying he's done something wrong?" she asked, truly trying to hide her anger. Margot stepped in front of her.

"I think I understand what Hazel is trying to say. It's nothing against your dad, it's just... when in a dangerous position like that—being under the potential control of someone corrupt, it makes him a target for carrying out their actions," Margot attempted to explain, putting a hand on Amara's shoulder.

Amara brushed Margot's hand off. "Then what do you suggest he does?"

"Ignore any calls related to Godsend, get in and out just for the paycheck," Margot firmly answered.

Amara looked back over at Hazel. "Is that what you were trying to say?" Hazel nodded. Amara clicked her tongue. "Whatever. I can't believe you guys are falling to such extremists. There are better ways to fix politics. Like maybe, voting? Maybe *Calvin* forgot about that one."

"Maybe you're right!" Milo spoke up, "People over time should wake up and smell the roses, right? If it's that bad these people will be voted out, things will change! We don't need to resort to that!"

Margot shot Milo a deadly look. One he had never seen her wear before: A scowl, one as if she was looking at trash.

"After everything that's happened, you really still think that?" Margot angrily questioned. The others quickly turned their attention to her. She cleared her throat, going back to a neutral look. "I'm sorry, that was uncalled for. Let me go think it over. I'll see you guys next week, okay?"

She was already on the move, walking away before any of the others could say anything.

"Odd," Hazel commented simply, "Guess I'll go too, then."

"Same here," Owen added, getting his stuff and heading the other direction.

"Yeah. Guess we'll see what happens. But I think Godsend won't be painted in such a positive light," Amara scoffed, heading her own way. Declan and Milo also went their separate ways, all of them awaiting the next move of Godsend.

A lone reporter rushed into the crowded hall. Dozens of other reporters from different outlets were attempting to get to the front of the crowd.

The reporter looked into the camera as the videographer motioned that they were already rolling. "Right here in this very room, President Hulls is expected to sign a historic bill. This would further roll back environmental regulations, allowing for more oil pipelines to be built domestically. Here he is now."

A somewhat-tall, old white male with ghost-silver hair came out from the curtains on the side of the stage. His dead eyes wandered from the audience to the cameras as he took the podium. This was President Hulls.

"Today marks another day that we cut down the red tape!" Hulls announced to hurrahs and applause.

Meanwhile, Hazel was watching this unfold live. She scoffed at the very idea there were so many cheering for something like this.

She was sitting at a cafe, laptop on a table. She decided to tune in and see what was going on, only to find herself how these people even existed.

"What state is this conference even being held in?" Hazel questioned herself, quickly searching for the answer online. She found it in just a moment, remarking, "Well *that* state isn't a huge Hulls fan. How are there so many cheering in that building?"

The broadcast continued. Hazel noticed multiple lobbyists and company ambassadors were present in this emissions rollback announcement.

"Well *there* are the guys who financed this whole thing." Hazel rolled her eyes, pulling up another website.

She went to make a post, complaining about the whole situation. She typed: *Can't believe this press conference. Just another corporate pandering move by Hulls.*

Aaaaaand... post.

At first, she thought about deleting it. What was it going to do for her, anyway? Then she thought, she would just let it be. It's a good outlet. But fearing the debates it might cause in the comments section, she went back to delete it anyway.

Upon going back, she realized the post she made was already *gone*. As if she had never posted it. She quickly went into recently deleted posts, and the post wasn't there either.

A thought popped into Hazel's head. She tried to post the same post a second time. It *also* disappeared. What was going on here?

"Is there some sorta filter deleting this? What's going on here?" Hazel asked aloud. She decided to search for other posts that criticized the emissions rollback. Nothing.

"President Hulls is looking out for us all!"

"Thank goodness for Hulls cutting the red tape. Nobody wanted it there."

"So glad we can have a common sense president."

Nothing but garbage. She couldn't tell what was real and what wasn't. She went into a profile. There were no posts. Clearly this was a bot. So she went into another post. Another nothing-burger of a profile.

"Has nobody picked up on this? Is criticism being openly censored? When did *that* happen?" Hazel panically thought aloud, trying to figure out what was going on. The internet had no answers. Panic clawed at her throat. This wasn't just a glitch, not some random algorithm error. This was deliberate. This was censorship on a scale she hadn't imagined. If they could control the narrative about the President's policies, what else could they control? What *had* they already controlled?

She scrambled, opening new tabs, searching different news sites, independent blogs, anything that might offer an alternative perspective. But the more she searched, the more she found only praise or eerily bot-written slop.

She remembered Declan's earlier, almost offhand, comment about the news being "bullshit anyway," only showing "what they want you to see." As well as remembering Owen's recent dive into the "rotten and corrupt" nature of everything, especially with the surveillance act. It all clicked into place with a sickening realization. This wasn't new. This was a *long* time coming.

"I still don't like how Calvin has to do things, but it seems like he's got no choice. Especially if the law is something people openly ignore now," Hazel pondered what might happen following the event.

But oddly, it was silent. For a few hours there was nothing. Eventually things started to post again as if nothing had happened. The most she got out of it was that the companies behind social media "admitted" to there being a glitch around the time where their filter was "overly sensitive."

Hazel wasn't the only one who noticed these falsities online. People online began to post about the connection between the act being signed and the people attending the President's event. One of which was the head executive officer of the same social platform "accidentally" censoring dissent to the decision.

The name of said executive officer was Aidan Samson, and he was currently leaving the building the press conference was held in. He had curly hair and a tailored suit for the conference, despite recently wearing more casual clothing to relate to the youth. He walked up to a bodyguard.

"Don't worry sir, we're having the car drive itself over now." Aidan was told. He nodded, despite being a little ticked off that it wasn't all timed perfectly.

Suddenly, the bodyguard felt something off. A strange whirring noise suddenly descended upon them. They looked to the sky. A familiar green streak across a metallic fluid suit floated to the ground. Godsend took care to stay far enough away to not incite an immediate reaction.

"**STAND DOWN. I JUST WISH TO TALK,**" Godsend's voice boomed, amplified and distorted. However their movements were calmer than usual.

Aidan, despite a flicker of surprise in his eyes, maintained his composure. He raised a hand, stopping his bodyguard from pulling a firearm. "And what would you possibly want to talk about, *vigilante*?" he asked, a thin, patronizing smile on his lips.

Others began to take notice. Civilians in the area became their own newscasters as they took out recording devices and started to stream the altercation to the internet.

Godsend tilted their head, the green light bar on their face forming a frown. "**THE CENSORSHIP. THE MANIPULATION OF INFORMATION.**"

Aidan chuckled dismissively. "Ah, yes, the 'glitch.' Already addressed it online, so... no need to go right at each other's throats."

"**A HICCUP THAT SERVES YOUR AGENDA, AND THAT OF YOUR 'COMMON SENSE' PRESIDENT.**" Godsend stepped closer, their presence continuing to hum a subtle, low presence of energy.

Aidan's smile wavered. "Look, I can apologize again, but it's back now. You can complain all you want online. But I'm surprised people aren't all up in arms about *you*. You disrupt order. You attack civil servants!"

"**I ATTACK CORRUPTION, SAMSON.**" Godsend's voice sharpened, the air around them crackling.

"Are you getting this?" a nearby girl whispered as she watched her friend pointing her camera at the confrontation. Aidan's eyes darted there and back. Anything he said or did would be broadcasted. But the same went for Godsend.

"So... you said you wanted to come talk about some sort of manipulation. However, on the platforms I'm responsible for, we have clear community guidelines that outline what can and cannot be said. By coincidence, an artificial intelligence whose sole purpose is to moderate posts, flagged a lot of stuff coming in at the same time that could have been bullying or spam. The issue has been fixed. If anything was manipulated, it isn't *us* at fault," Aidan clearly stated aloud, as if acting for the camera.

"**THE PEOPLE ARE TIRED. I TOO, GROW TIRED OF HEARING THIS WRETCHED, CORPORATE DRIVEL.**" Godsend turned, backing away from Samson. "**I WILL NOT CHOOSE OF MY OWN ACCORD, SAMSON. THE PEOPLE, THE HALLOWED MANY YOU SURPRESS, WILL DECIDE YOUR FATE. SO QUIT WHILE YOU'RE AHEAD.**"

Like that, Godsend shot up back into the sky, taking a right angle and flying off into the horizon.

"What was his name again?" Aidan Samson asked his bodyguard, looking up into the sky as his car finally pulled itself up.

"Sir, that's not publicly available information," his guard deflected, motioning to the girl recording. She quickly stopped, running from the area to not be involved.

"We'll talk in the car. Pretty sure that guy's named Calvin. Find him," Aidan told the guard, as both of them shuffled into the car seats.

"The government has been trying since they found out—"

"WELL LET'S MAKE IT GO FASTER! DOES HE HAVE AN ACCOUNT ON ANY OF OUR PLATFORMS?!" Aidan shouted back.

"Uh, yeah, I think so," the guard got real quiet, getting increasingly afraid of scolding.

At the same moment, back in Philadelphia, the confrontation had already gone viral. Hazel was back in her room in her apartment now. She watched the whole thing playing out only moments later.

"Holy shit," Hazel mouthed, looking down at her phone, "I wish I could have done that."

Many online shared the same sentiment. Godsend was right. The people were fed up.

"Did you see Godsend actually stand up to AIDAN SAMSON???"

"I feel like that one confrontation made years of anger with this platform a little alleviated."

"Who the hell is Godsend? Why didn't I know about this guy?"

"Can Godsend ACTUALLY bring change in this anti-consumer economy? I would LOVE that! Godsend, my landlord next! THEN my boss!!"

124

These were just a few posts online following the events. Posts that echoed the frustrations of the many, for Godsend was right. For years now, the people have learned to look at the news and expect something bad. To expect something that looked like a comedically fake headline happening in real time. To see a billionaire like Aidan Samson get talked down to... well... It was a miracle.

Before much longer, many more livestreams started to pop up. This time, from people in downtown Philadelphia.

"What's going on now?" Hazel whispered to herself before opening the livestream with the most concurrent viewers at the time.

Now downtown, Godsend stood atop a tall building, looking down at a crowd of people. Many of which were recording live broadcasts with their cameras.

"We just heard a woosh noise above and suddenly, look who's here! I don't know what he's up to though. Seems to just be standing there right now," the man behind the camera commented. They zoomed in to Godsend. Suddenly, a voice boomed.

"**SAMSON. YOU WISH TO KNOW WHO I AM.**" The Godsend mask slowly came off of Calvin Becker's face. "**I'LL DO YOU A FAVOR. HERE I AM. BUT YOU AREN'T GOING TO FIND ME. I WILL DISAPPEAR AT THE SAME TIME THE LIES, LOBBYING, AND CORRUPTION DO.**"

"*That's* Godsend?! He's just a guy! Well, a guy with a pretty awesome suit," the spectator admitted.

"**I SHALL NOT USE THEIR MEANS OF COMMUNICATING. I WILL NOT HAVE AN ONLINE PRESENCE. YOU WILL KNOW IT'S ME WHEN I APPEAR. SO LET THIS BE MY MESSAGE TO THE WORLD: BE GOOD TO EACH OTHER. ANY GREED THAT PERSISTS, I WILL**

125

EXPOSE. IT DOES NOT MATTER HOW IMPORTANT OR WEALTHY YOU ARE."

With that, suddenly Calvin disappeared without a trace. Nothing but a *woosh* left behind, and people watching as he supposedly flew faster than they could see.

"Man, that guy is insane. I kinda get it though," the commentator stated right as Hazel closed the livestream. She felt exhausted from watching it, as if she were there. Mainly, it was strange seeing Calvin's face like that.

"I knew it was gonna get out sooner or later, but *what* is Calvin thinking?!" Hazel scolded the dark screen, unsure of how to feel.

"Yo Hazel, you alright?" Becca, in the room next to her, opened her door, "I just heard a lot of talking-to-yourself."

"Have you not seen all the 'Godsend' stuff, dude?" Hazel asked in response, seeing that Becca was busy doing something else.

"I kinda heard of it, why?" Becca asked.

"Godsend is someone I know. Or... someone I knew at least," Hazel admitted.

"Whaaaat? The crazy metallic guy, right?" Becca asked. Hazel nodded, "Well who then?"

"A guy who went to the same AA group as me for a few weeks. His name is Calvin. No clue how he got that metal suit and stuff though. He was pretty politically involved and... well I can't help but wanna support him somehow."

Becca whipped around, a double-take being necessary. "You wanna support the crazy metal guy?"

"He's saved people from natural disasters, robberies, and other disasters. He's constantly talking about 'the hallowed,'" Hazel said in her best 'Godsend' impression, "...which is just his fancy way of saying, like, us everyday people who aren't making companies to price people out of single-family homes. He wants to help us, you know?"

"If Godsend can make real change and make it so these wack-jobs aren't in charge, maybe I'd start liking him too," Becca semi-sarcastically responded.

"Maybe you will then," Hazel suggested. Becca grinned and then left the room, closing the door behind her.

Inside the double doors, hiding underground once more, Godsend descended. But just the *idea* of Godsend. It was really both Margot and Calvin, walking down the steps after Margot closed the doors behind them.

"Well, that was quite the performance, wasn't it?" Margot said, her voice light, though her expression was serious as she stripped off the outer layers of the suit. "You really sold it."

Calvin grinned, a manic glint in his eyes. "Did I? I was a little worried but... You did better. Aidan Samson looked like he was about to piss himself! And that whole 'Hallowed' speech? Pure *gold*." He paced a small circle in the bunker, still buzzing with adrenaline. "But why me, Margot? Why did you want *me* to take the credit for it? I just... I just did the voice, and you know, the whole 'disappearing' act you rigged up."

Margot paused, placing the compacted suit disc into a secured bag. She turned to face him, leaning against the cool metal of a workbench. "Because, Calvin, you're particularly useful. A born American. That way, they can't spin the whole Godsend narrative about something... racially motivated. No 'foreign agitator' nonsense. It grounds the message, makes it undeniably about those we're trying to help."

Calvin's maniacal glint disappeared, responding with, "Oh, yeah..." There was a little disappointment there.

She watched him, a bit of concern crossing her face. She wanted to change the subject. "You know, this is a lot for anyone to take on. I'm glad you wanted to do this but... do you ever miss your family? Or your old life, even just a little?"

Calvin's grin faded slightly. He shrugged, avoiding her gaze. "Miss them? No. Not really. What's there to miss? Endless arguments with Hadley, pretending I cared about my parents' whole obsession with how they socially appeared, listening to the same old stories at the AA meeting... This is better. This is real. This is *purpose*." His eyes, still tired from lack of sleep, were now deeply shot with an outlined intensity. "We're actually doing something, Margot. We're changing things. I want to help however I can. Whatever you need. Just tell me."

Margot studied him, a knot tightening in her stomach. His eagerness was almost unnerving. It was one thing to be passionate, another to be consumed. His obsession was growing, bordering on creepy. A sudden pain hit her right hand, taking her out of the moment.

"Ah jeez..." she looked down. Her hand still had a portion of the 'Godsend' suit on it. She took her other hand, and quickly peeled off the piece.

Calvin peeked over, intrigued at what was happening. "Margot... is that part of the suit?"

"Yeah, sometimes this happens," Margot admitted, putting the piece near the unzipped bag, letting it re-combine with the compacted suit. "That's why I had you in that fake suit. So you could just do the talking, and then I'd pick you up myself."

Calvin's grin sparkled again. "It sucks that I couldn't blast off like you did, but having people pay attention was cool. Even if the suit didn't really do much. I wouldn't even be able to figure out the Godsend suit." Calvin paid close attention as Margot zipped the bag shut. "I haven't really been able to ask you much. You've been mostly out so... just wanted to know if *that* was normal."

"Well I didn't really make the suit, Calvin. I think it is, but I don't know," Margot got a little snappy all of the sudden.

"You didn't make it? How do you know how to use—"

Margot's hair whipped back as she shot a scowl at Calvin, cutting off his question. "Look. You and I are doing good together right now. Let's leave the personal aspect out of it. The longer I use that suit, the more it gets a firm hold on me. It gets harder to take off, is all. But let's move on."

Calvin, a little hurt by Margot's words, ignored her warning. "But that would still be good for me to know, wouldn't it? You can't be in the suit for too long, so I shouldn't expect you to. Would it ever come off if you were in that suit for days?"

"Calvin, did you *not hear me*?" Margot's eyebrows furrowed. Taking a moment, she exhaled, calming herself down. "I don't know. I don;t want to know what happens. There's nothing I can't take care of in under a few hours with that suit, so it shouldn't be a problem."

Calvin, testing his luck, pressed further, "How did you even get that suit?"

"Are you going to refuse to listen to me? Is that what this game is?" Margot angrily shot back at Calvin. Calvin immediately recoiled, putting his hands up in a placating gesture.

"No, no, I just... I just want to better assist, you know? But uh... well to do that, I wanna at least know *your* motivation." He hoped to steer the conversation back to their shared purpose, away from the increasingly tense personal questions.

Margot's rigid posture softened slightly, though her expression remained sharp. "I've seen both sides of this coin, Calvin. I've seen the sheer desperation of people struggling just to stay afloat, working themselves to the bone. Others, higher up, casually make decisions that crush those that struggle further. And I've seen the affluent lives of those in power, who genuinely don't care about the impact of their actions. They take advantage, exploit, manipulate... sometimes without even realizing the full extent of the damage they cause, sometimes with malicious intent veiled by 'business decisions' or 'political necessities.'"

She paused, her eyes looking unfocused out into the distance. "This idea of the 'hallowed' people, the ones who strive for good, who help each other, who are untouched by that insatiable greed... that's always been something I felt compelled to protect, compelled to be a part of. But I thought it was ending. I thought greed had become the only way to survive in this world. I didn't think it would be possible to stop it. Not until I found this." She gestured vaguely to the bag containing the compacted suit. "To me, it was like a divine sign that I had to do something."

"You think... pretty deeply about this stuff, Margot," Calvin admitted, his voice also less aggressive, "I really just wanted to be something. Surrounded by those high-class people that do nothing but manipulate, like you said... I just wanted to tear it all down. I wanted to help people like me, I guess."

Margot grinned for a moment, forgetting all about the gravity of the outside world. "Yeah. I've had a lot of time. But enough about me. Sorry, I can't really get into the past right now. I want to focus on what's in front of us."

Calvin nodded in agreement. "Yeah. What *is* the next thing we do?"

"We wait," Margot replied on the heels of his question, "We're going to see what happens. Monitoring everyone through the systems they've set up to protect themselves, we'll assess. I figure they won't change, even if they are scared. But maybe a little intimidating is all they need to quit being openly corrupt."

"Not really sure how you've hacked into the Commoner's Safety Act program either, but I guess now isn't the time for questions." Calvin laughed to himself as Margot went to another desk, pulling up thousands of video feeds.

"Just assume most of this isn't my fault, I just figured out how to use it all," Margot assured Calvin, pushing her glasses up.

Calvin laughed a little. "That's... an odd way to put it." He watched as Margot went through a few of the camera feeds. Calvin saw Aidan Samson, his face contorted in a mixture of fury and disbelief, berating his subordinates.

"Find him! Find Calvin Becker!" Aidan's voice, though tinny through the speakers, still carried his tone. "He just publicly unmasked himself as that... that Godsend character! You have access to every account, every online interaction! Get him!"

One of the employees, a younger woman with tired eyes, bravely spoke up. "Sir, the government has been trying for weeks. Their best detectives, their most advanced surveillance... there's nothing more we can do than what they've already attempted. He vanished without a trace!"

Aidan slammed his fist on a desk, having zero composure. "Then find a new way! I don't care how! This is a direct challenge to my— our authority! We cannot let him bully us!" His voice was thick with a rage that bordered on desperation.

Margot muted the feed, turning to Calvin with a big grin. "Looks like we rattled him pretty good, didn't we?"

Calvin chuckled, satisfied. "Good. He deserves it. All of them do."

Margot nodded, then switched to another feed. The scene shifted to a familiar office, bathed in the glow of overhead lights. It was Hadley's old team. Miller, ever the wanna-be-leader, was holding a meeting.

"Look, Hadley's out. That's done," Miller stated, his voice flat. "But the mission hasn't changed. Godsend is still a threat, and now we know who he is. Calvin Becker. He's shown the whole *world* now. We need to locate him."

A younger detective spoke up, "But sir, his brother, Hadley... he was so convinced it wasn't him. He even tried to pin it on someone else. What if there's more to this? What if it's not as simple as it looks?"

Miller scoffed. "It's never simple with these types. Hadley was in denial, pure and simple. Or maybe he knew more than he let on and was trying to protect his brother. Either way, he's out of the country now. Our focus is Calvin. Double down on surveillance, track every known associate, every old address. We bring him in, no matter what."

The same younger detective spoke up, "Sir—"

"What is it Brad? You *in favor* of Calvin or something?" Miller immediately spat back.

"No, I just got a message from a video analyst. They've used upscaling tech to make out some more from a few pixels and... well... we should talk in the other room," the younger one, Brad, concluded.

Miller looked around, seeing other guards and cameras in the room. It was a fair concern. "Alright, Brad. In my office."

Quickly, the two moved areas to Miller's office with an absence of personnel or cameras to spy on them. Miller motioned for Brad to put his work computer on his desk. The two watched the footage.

It was of Calvin, making his declaration from atop the building in Philadelphia. He was wrapping up the speech and then he seemingly disappeared, only a few frames of him launching in the other direction.

"So what? We know this suit has to have some unknown technology. This isn't new," Miller dismissed the video almost immediately.

Brad moved his cursor, advancing the video. "There's a slowed down and upscaled portion next."

Miller's attention was regained, and the two looked closely at the other version. Now, they could clearly see what looked like to be a different object flying in and picking Calvin up. This object happened to be in the shape of the Godsend suit as well. Still, it was only a few frames, but the implications were serious.

Miller exhaled. "This doesn't leave my room. Only so many people can know about this."

"Does this mean Godsend *isn't* one person? Are there more?" Brad couldn't hold his questions in.

"I don't know what this means. All I know is Hadley might have been a little more right than we thought he was," Miller concluded.

Later in the week, Amara sat inside of a diner at mid-day. A few small groups were there for the lunch special. Orders taken on screens, fulfilled by robots. Somehow they still asked for a tip. At least it was cheaper.

A familiar voice rang at the same time as the door opened, "Hey." Declan entered, waving to Amara. She gave him a warm smile.

"Hey yourself," Amara replied in a friendly manner, motioning to the seat across from her. "Grab a coffee and sit. This is going to be a long one."

Declan walked up to one of the ordering screens, tapping quickly before returning with a steaming mug. "So, about our old pal Calvin... still can't believe it, can you?" He took a sip, making a gross face at the robot-made brew.

Amara shook her head. "No, not really. It's... a lot to process. Especially after everything he said. And the way he just vanished. It just makes you wonder how long he's been planning this, or how he even got that suit."

"Exactly! It doesn't make any damn sense!" Declan agreed. "I mean, I knew he was intense, but *Godsend*? I've seen the video, but I still don't really believe it. Unless Calvin is also somehow secretly Russian. But speaking of the group, I haven't seen Margot or Owen around much lately either. Have you?"

Amara sighed, stirring her own lukewarm tea. "Nope. Margot was pretty quick to leave last week, and Owen's been... Well, Owen's been Owen— aloof recently. Hazel couldn't join us, either. I guess everyone's trying to figure out where they stand after all this."

Just then, the diner door chimed again, and Milo walked in, looking a bit flustered. "Sorry, sorry, I'm late! I

135

lost track of the time!" He hurried over, pulling up a chair and flashing a nervous smile. "So, what'd I miss?"

"Nothing much," Amara said, offering a small smile. "Just catching up. We were just about to dive into the latest... *developments*." She raised an eyebrow, clearly referring to Calvin.

"Yeah... this, uh, whole Godsend thing is wild," Milo agreed, picking up a coffee mug of his own. "Calvin being that guy? I still can't wrap my head around it. He didn't seem put together well enough to be someone secret."

Declan leaned back, laughing at Milo's comment. He then exhaled, crossing his arms. "Honestly, he's insufferable, but he hasn't actually done anything deplorable yet. Just a lot of grandstanding and some verbose theatrics."

Amara's expression tightened. "I don't care. His 'theatrics,' as you call them, are dangerous! He's lumping everyone who doesn't fit his narrow definition of 'hallowed' into this 'greed' category. It's a slippery slope." She clearly felt strongly about this.

"I agree. Knowing Calvin, he can get a little crazy about things," Declan added, "I mean, he shoved *you*. All you've done is be nice, for the most part. When he didn't hear you out at all, that's where I knew I couldn't be rooting for *him* to do this."

Milo furiously nodded. "It's easy to get lost in his message. Godsend... The hallowed... it just all seems like something honored. Er, or like, holy? I dunno. It's like he's an angel sent to protect us. But again, that's just theatrics." He fidgeted with his thumbs in his lap.

"Protecting us all is what's on the surface," Amara began, "Under that, I think he has some sort of vendetta. I don't know much about his personal life, other than what he's said in the group. But it seems like he wants revenge."

Declan, deep in thought, turned back to the conversation. "Not that I knew him super well, but I was one of the first in that group. We all had one thing in common: we were unhappy somehow. No alcoholic goes to an anonymous group because their life is just peachy."

Milo laughed, "We're pretty far from an *anonymous* group now. Aren't we?"

"I feel like I know too much about you guys now," Declan groaned, looking the other way while scratching his beard.

"I prefer it this way. Knowing you all— even if it's gone in a different direction than I had imagined— it's helped me move on. Not think about going back," Milo admitted. The two others, unsure of how to respond, just nodded. "Or, uh yeah! You get what I mean?"

They laughed, Amara calming herself. "Regardless, what do you think, Declan? Revenge maybe?"

"For sure," Declan didn't waste a moment, "He had quite a *thing* when it came to his family. He hated high class, high society stuff. Something about it leading him, through peer-pressure, to gamble all this money away. Little did he know the meaning of money, being raised the way he was. Then, he was shunned. Cast out by the same people who supposedly cared— until the money went away."

Amara and Milo stared. Calvin had never been that open to the two of them. They knew him as some sort of self-important prick.

"Was he... different before I got there? I know I came when the group was pretty tight. Then we had

Margot and everyone else the week after," Amara explained.

"Margot came the week before Hazel, Owen and I? That's weird. She seemed more established than that to me," Milo commented.

Declan nodded. "She was just, quiet. But she blended in really well, and said what she needed to when asked. So she wasn't really questioned. She's only ever been passionate when—" The group collectively remembered her harsh words after Milo expressed an alternative method to Godsend.

Amara didn't like the silence. "Yeah. That was the only time. She was probably sleep deprived, though. Didn't seem like her."

"Well, uh," Milo uncomfortably interjected, "You wanted us to come here to talk about that. What do *you* wanna do about the Godsend situation?"

Amara's expression drooped once more, remembering the reality of why they were there. "Right," she scoffed, "I dunno. We *know* Calvin. There's gotta be something we can do to fix this in a better way than him. Show him it *can* be done differently."

Milo and Declan both looked at her like she was mad. "Uh," Declan spoke up, "How the hell are *we* supposed to intervene?"

"You might be on to something," Milo jumped in, "Maybe instead of interfering directly, we can just get Calvin to talk to us. He's kinda loud and proud, right?"

Declan rolled his eyes. "That's the very definition of Calvin."

"We have to make an example of some small positive change. *Really* help people. Then, goad him into doing the same. Use reverse-psychology, tell him he couldn't. This is *Calvin* we're talking about, so he'd take that bait in a heartbeat," Amara explained.

Declan and Milo exchanged a look, both slightly skeptical but intrigued by Amara's audacious suggestion.

"Okay," Declan said slowly, a faint smirk forming. "Well if anyone can get under Calvin's skin, it's you, Amara. But what can we do that he hasn't?"

Milo piped up, snapping his fingers. "We help people in our own way. Something small, something tangible, that shows him there's another path besides blowing stuff up and making grand speeches."

Amara nodded, determination in her eyes. "We identify a local issue, something concrete that needs fixing, and we fix it. As a group. I'll find a way to get 'Godsend's' attention. All we need to do is tell him we're doing something he can't."

An audacious grin spread across Declan's face. "You know, I'm actually starting to like this. It's got a certain... 'screw you Calvin' vibe."

The three laughed after that remark, continuing on to finalize their plan of what they would change. After that, the three separated, heading to their own plans for the rest of the day.

Milo now walked home, the earlier conversation with Amara and Declan replaying in his mind. The idea of actively doing something, however small, felt strangely exhilarating.

He found himself nearing the income checkpoint, the familiar gate that divided the affluent side of the city from his own.

"Ugh," he rolled his eyes. It was more worn down and gross than ever. The guards around it were ever still.

Milo decided to take a detour, going off into a nearby neighborhood just beyond the checkpoint. It was a quieter area, older homes, well-kept and from a different time. They were clearly not in the same league as the mansions on the other side of the divide, though He rounded a corner, lost in thought, when a familiar figure caught his eye.

From afar, he saw Margot. She was standing outside a particular house, her head tilted back, staring up at the second floor. She looked... different. Less serene.

Milo went to wave, but quickly stopped himself as he looked closer. Margot looked furious. Her grip tightened, looking at the house. Specifically, the 'for sale' sign out on the front lawn. There was a logo on the bottom left of the sign. The text read, "Darkstone Funding Group."

Suddenly, a real estate agent walked out from the front door. There happened to be an open house today. As she walked toward Margot, Margot's expression changed back to neutral.

"Are you here to look at the property, miss?" the real estate agent asked Margot, who hadn't moved an inch.

Milo, ever curious, made an impulse decision. He just wanted to know *why*. "Actually *we're* here to see it!" he boasted, running up next to Margot as if they were buddy-buddy.

The real estate agent looked from him to her. Margot didn't move, making a confused expression at Milo. "I guess so," she sighed.

AHHHH WHY DID I DO THAT?! Milo thought to himself, *I JUST WANTED TO KNOW WHY SHE WAS SO MAD AT THAT HOUSE! SHE'S GONNA HATE ME!* He nervously sweated.

"Alright, well, right this way then," the agent let the two of them go ahead of her.

Margot remained mostly silent as the agent led her and Milo through the two-story house, commenting on little things with a practiced cheerfulness. Milo, trying to act natural, nodded along, occasionally glancing at Margot. He noticed her eyes lingered on the small scratches in the paint, the faint dents in the floor, and the stubborn stains in the rug. Each time, she seemed to fall into a brief, almost trancelike state.

When the agent noticed Margot staring a little too long at a depression in the hardwood floor near the front door, she quickly interjected, "Oh, don't worry about that, miss! Any and all repairs would be included in the purchase agreement, naturally. We want to ensure the new owners have a pristine, fresh start!"

Margot didn't react to the agent's words for a moment. Then, in a low voice that Milo barely caught, she muttered, "They're not flaws. They're memories." She quickly cleared her throat, regaining her neutral expression. "Just— well— for the people that *used* to live here," she stuttered quickly, a bit of nervousness in her tone.

"Yeah, they're not a problem!" Milo randomly jumped in, thinking he needed to help her out. It went awkwardly quiet.

The agent looked as if she had no idea what to say. "Alright, then! Good to know..." she trailed off, moving on with the tour regardless. For the rest of the time, Margot remained neutral. She tried to only look forward, and not show any emotion.

As Milo and Margot trailed the agent, Milo whispered to Margot, "Sorry about this. I was just curious." Expecting something back, he was surprised when

Margot's expression didn't change. It was as if she didn't hear him.

"It's fine," she whispered back, seemingly without moving a muscle. Milo breathed a sigh of relief, even if what she said didn't sound totally genuine.

The group continued to one of the upstairs bedrooms. Milo could see Margot's hands start to fidget as they approached. He was curious, what was the connection between her and this house?

The agent led them into the room. The wallpaper still felt as if people inhabited the house. "This is the secondary bedroom up here. It can be used as a guest bedroom, or..." the agent trailed off. She looked at Margot's expression once more. She was clearly beaming at something important.

Turning around, the agent was met with the view of a picture frame propped up on a dresser. Two parents behind a young, blonde girl. The three were all smiles. A caption at the bottom, in cursive, read, "Jetty Beach: Home Away From Home!"

The agent quickly jumped in front of the photo, covering it. "I'm so sorry! I thought the previous belongings had already been taken out of the house!" she grabbed the photo frame. "I'll get this out of here—"

Margot lurched forward, grabbing her arm, stopping her. She looked back, thinking, *well, at least it's just Milo here*.

"I knew the previous owners. I can take that," Margot grabbed it, putting it under her arm. She squeezed it between her arm and chest, covering the majority of the photo.

The agent, taken aback, chuckled a bit. "So *that's* what you meant by memories. What am I showing you around for, then?"

Everyone froze. Milo was waiting on Margot's response. But she didn't say anything. She looked stumped.

"I was really the one wanting to look, she just knew that this place was for sale!" Milo covered for Margot, lying to the agent.

The agent chuckled again, "Oh, *now* I get it." The others still didn't say anything as the tour continued, ending shortly after they returned downstairs.

"So what did you think, *buyer*?" Margot joked, patting Milo on the shoulder.

"It was a nice place, but maybe I'll put in an offer *later*." Milo couldn't look the agent in the eye after that. They left not soon after.

Milo, watching Margot try to leave without a word, asked, "What was the deal, anyway? Who were those people?"

"Milo..." Margot turned around. She didn't open her eyes. Her smile was clearly forced. "Could you not poke into my business, please?"

It was clearly a cold shoulder. He froze, his muscles tensed. "Oh, okay," is all he got out. She quickly walked off, and Milo was left confused. *Why couldn't she meet up with Amara and Declan? She said she was busy, but this is what she was doing?*

"Wonder what she thinks about Calvin..." is the last thing Milo muttered to himself before walking away.

The news, in that decade, had become a cesspool of negativity. To see it suddenly go silent after Godsend's confrontation with Aidan Samson was a miracle in itself. But as time went on, it only felt inevitable that something big was coming.

The members of the Thursday alcoholics anonymous group convened, a little less "weight" on their shoulders this time.

Everyone conversed normally, the whole 'Godsend' situation out of their minds, for now. Everyone besides Calvin, who was still out. Milo eyed Margot, wondering if she was still upset with him. Owen was mostly silent.

Pastor Alan had just finished the reading, wrapping up on a quite tame session. "Before the ending prayer, would anybody like to make any prayer requests?"

Initially, silence. This was something extra, something the group hadn't expected. To Pastor Alan, it was just a habit. A slip of the tongue after a session with no hiccups. Owen cleared his throat.

"Prayers for, uh, well... My family dog died. I know it's a little off-topic but, it was just really sad to see my folks all torn up," Owen requested, his voice coarse.

"Aw, I'm sorry Owen. Mine passed away not too long ago, I know that's heartbreaking. Was it sudden?" Hazel asked.

"I don't think it should have been," Owen replied, his gaze steady on his hands gripped together, "My parents just saw the bill for vet *consulting*. Yeah, just *consulting* and they couldn't afford it. *Forty-five hundred dollars*. There was no way he was going to a surgeon after that."

"Are you serious? Ugh." Declan looked visibly upset. "How can people look you dead in the eye and ask for something so ludicrous?"

Owen 's grip tensed. "If you're curious, Declan, they don't. The employees don't own the place they... They just do what they're told. They have to." He looked up, his eyebrows furrowed. "Darkstone Funding bought 'em. The whole chain of vets. Prices skyrocketed and well... there's nothing else in the area."

Milo, who had been watching Margot, watched her eyes behind the glasses dart over to Owen. That title: Darkstone. It gained her attention like an alarm.

"Darkstone? The private equity group?" Amara asked. She crossed her arms. "They're like real-life supervillains."

"Yeah, there was—" Milo started to speak up, cutting himself off after seeing Margot glare at him. "...I saw single family homes owned by them in the masses." he lied, not wanting to get on worse terms with Margot.

Owen rolled his eyes. "Yeah, well. Not much we could do, but prayers for that." The others all nodded, moving on to other prayer requests. But none of them piqued Margot's interest, just like that one had. She zoned out for the rest of the night, going back to her lone apartment with nothing but questions.

"Darkstone this, Darkstone that. They seem to be everywhere recently." She angrily opened a laptop that had been cleaned of any backdoors, making it invulnerable to the surveillance of the Commoner's Safety Act.

She looked it up. A trillion dollar company. Stakes in nearly everything. Private schools, healthcare groups, real estate management, social media, fast food, car companies— and yes, *vets*. Even the social media

145

platforms Aidan Samson owned were *really* owned by Darkstone.

Nearly everything they purchased became publicly traded, following with cut staff and exponentially rising prices. This company didn't care about the destruction left in their path, they only cared about a quick buck. A decision made by the *greed* of those who participated in their overly-inflated shares.

She continued to scroll, watching their story. She had *known* about them, but not to this extent. They had actively had a hand in creating recessions, only to receive billions of taxpayer dollars as a bailout to keep them afloat in the aftermath. They had dozens of their own "charities" to avoid paying taxes in the first place.

The government didn't just turn a blind eye to them, they actively *helped* them. Committee members at Darkstone were all buddy-buddy with the members of congress. President Hulls was among one of the worst offenders, openly holding a large share in their stock.

"You'd swear this is insider trading," Margot grit her teeth. She fidgeted with her hand. Many reading this would feel helpless. Margot, however, only felt enraged.

She pushed her rolling chair back, looking up at the ceiling. "They think they can kill *her* and then sell her family home?" she coughed out, her chest feeling light. She coughed out a laugh, feeling hysterical. Her fist came crashing down on the desk with a *bang*. Her jaw tightened, her gaze beaming back at the computer. That bang seemed to accidentally open up an old folder.

"What's this doing on dad's old laptop?" she questioned, opening up the first sub-folder. There was a video. She opened it up.

There was a video of her mother dropping her off at a school for one of the first times. Margot watched, mouth gaping from shock. She watched as her father video-taped her mother letting go of her hand. The camera zoomed in as little Margot ran toward the school gates.

"I didn't know he had these... why would he?" Margot whispered under her breath. Her voice was shaky from a mixed feeling. She couldn't tell if she felt lied to or guilty.

Another video. This time it was little Margot's first doctor's appointment. She looked closely at the video, watching her younger self get into a chair. "I barely remember that place... is that a repurposed house?" she asked, questioning her own memories.

Indeed, her doctor's place was a repurposed house. From other documents she gathered, she found it was simply the house on the corner of her neighborhood. The man lived there, doing personal visits to the people he knew. No public trading, no agents setting up the appointment, just someone honestly helping his community.

Margot was wrapped up in all the documents, looking through pictures from the past. She lingered on another, a house with a beach in the background. It was a little her with another blonde girl. The photo's title: "*Margot_and_Lily.png.*"

Her eyes were taken away from it before she could reminisce longer. In the top right of her screen, a passive news notification. It read "*What a Third Hulls Term Could Mean for The Economy.*"

It ripped her away from the comfort and nostalgia in the past. No private equity, no income checkpoints, no robot replacements... it was different. She yearned for that again. For the longest time, it seemed impossible. How was one going to fight the world?

"Maybe I'll owe Samson an apology," Margot remarked, holding up the disc containing the 'Godsend' suit. "Seems he just has to bend over to *his* superiors too. Not like he's really a good person, either."

Moments later, many reported to see a shooting star fly through the sky. But with that green tint present, it was clear to some that it was truly Godsend on the move. Flying faster than most cameras could even keep up with, Margot flew in the suit straight to the nearest Darkstone building.

"If you don't stop after this, there'll be a *lot* more," she muttered under the suit. She then held out the suit's hand, pointing it at the empty building. She charged up as much energy as she could in a few seconds, and let go.

Headlines were out early the next morning. Despite it being an empty building overnight, they all claimed: "GODSEND ATTACKS DARKSTONE!"

Pictures of the event showed that the building had not been blown away, but a whole half of the building with all the glass windows had been mostly destroyed from the impact. Video from the building revealed Godsend as the culprit. The word "retire" was burned into the building, visible from a helicopter above the scene.

Somehow, the people were mostly in unison— behind **Godsend**. And yet, they tried the same playbook: censoring the posts.

"WE WILL NOT BE SILENCED." The message echoed across the internet, accompanying countless videos of people holding up signs with the same phrase, or chanting it in unison. It was a defiant roar against the digital filter, a response to the broken windows of the

Darkstone building. The public, spurred by Godsend's brazen act, was now actively fighting any censorship. They found loopholes, created new platforms, and overwhelmed existing ones with their support for Godsend, sharing stories of their own experiences with Darkstone's pervasive influence.

President Hulls, visibly agitated, held a press conference. He stood before a backdrop of the damaged Darkstone building, images of the "retire" message starkly visible. "This act of domestic terrorism will not stand," he declared, his voice strained with feigned outrage. "This so-called 'Godsend' is a menace, a destructive force targeting American enterprise and the very fabric of our society. We are working closely with our partners at Darkstone Funding to bring this individual to justice and protect our economic stability." He emphasized the collaboration between government and corporations, a narrative designed to reassure the wealthy and instill fear in the masses.

But the people weren't buying it. The social media feeds, though still attempting to filter, were alight with comments and posts mocking Hulls.

"Economic stability? My rent went up 30% because of Darkstone last month!"

"Protection for who? The billionaires buying up everything?"

"Hulls holding a press conference with Darkstone? Coincidence? Yeah, don't think so."

The narrative was slipping from the control of the powerful. The lines between hero and villain, between government and corporation, were blurring in the public eye. Darkstone's reputation, already shaky in some circles, was plummeting with astonishing speed. Their stock plunged, albeit slightly, for the first time in years.

Aidan Samson, watching the chaos unfold from his personal penthouse, slammed his fist on his desk. He was on a call with other Darkstone executives. "This is a disaster! We have to regain control of this shitshow. Just deleting posts isn't working anymore! And *I'M* the one who's gonna have to take the flack for it!"

"What about that Calvin Becker kid?" one executive's tinny voice asked over the speakerphone, ignoring Samson's plea. "He unmasked himself. Can't we just target him?"

"We've tried! The goddamn government even tried, you know this! Who knows where the *hell* he usually stays!" Aidan roared, pacing his expansive office. "This isn't just about public opinion anymore. This is about physical damage and economic disruption! So quit asking ME about it! Go to your... legal team or something!"

Another executive cleared their throat, still ignoring him. "Perhaps a different approach is necessary, Aidan. The public is enraged. A direct confrontation, or continued censorship, only seems to fuel their defiance. Maybe a... public relations campaign? Something to show our 'benevolent' side?"

Aidan scoffed. "Benevolent? And WE?! It's a little late to change *your* image now!"

"Don't forget who owns you, Samson," another angry voice came through. That shut him up for the time being.

Meanwhile, also that day, there was an emergency meeting. Amara, Milo, and Declan all met up on a whim after seeing the news about Godsend.

"So what in the world happened there? Does anyone else find it odd that Calvin attacked Darkstone the *day* we were talking about it?" Amara questioned aloud.

"I found that odd too," Declan followed up, "I mean, I know that Calvin would be against Darkstone regardless. He's just like that. It's just a little weird that it was the same day."

Milo was wondering how he should respond in this situation. He thought, while Owen was clearly sad that Darkstone played a role in his dog's death, that *Margot* was already angry with them too. But he knew that he haphazardly interjected in her day, and wasn't supposed to snoop on her.

"I guess, yeah, it's weird," Milo shrugged, not adding anything concrete by choice.

Declan looked up, a serious expression on his face. "You know, I'm thinking that *maybe* Owen got into contact with Calvin."

The two looked back at him, surprised. Amara immediately connected the dots, and Milo didn't *really* think that was the case. Although, the small possibility of that being the case kept Milo from mentioning anything about Margot.

"He did just have his dog die. He kept *praising* Calvin weirdly a few sessions ago too. It might line up," Amara said her thought process aloud. Milo just awkwardly smiled.

"Should we try and convince him to take us to Calvin?" Declan asked.

Amara shook her head. "No. We'll finish getting my dad's local laws passed. Then we'll find a way to Calvin, and show that off."

What they didn't account for was the fact they could be listened to. With security in overdrive after Margot's stunt, all of their phones had been tapped. While Margot's was equipped to send back garbage data about scrolling cat memes, theirs were just regular phones.

On the other side, Miller's team listened carefully. All that went through their heads was "Owen knows Godsend."

Detective Miller looked down at the live footage, smirking. "Guess Pastor Alan wasn't wrong about making Owen look out for Godsend. He may have just found him."

The team immediately packed their things to go search.

Owen jolted awake, unsure of where he was. The last thing he remembered, he was alone in his room. Suddenly he was surrounded by a drab gray room and strapped into a chair.

Detective Miller walked in, standing above Owen. "Awake? Good. We're just gonna ask you a few questions about your friend *Calvin.*" Owen tried to struggle against the restraints, but they were too tight.

"Who? Calvin? What Calvin? What are you talking about?" His voice was hoarse, his throat dry.

Miller leaned closer, his expression unreadable. "Don't play dumb, Owen. We know about your little group and your conversations. We know about Godsend." He picked up a tablet, turning it to show Owen a still image from the surveillance footage of the AA meeting. It was a clear shot of Owen talking to Declan and Amara. "We heard you praising him. We heard you talking about his methods. We heard you glorifying his actions."

Owen's eyes widened as he saw the image. *They were listening the whole time?* A cold dread settled in his stomach. "That's... that's just talk! We're an AA group. We talk about our feelings, our struggles. Sometimes those struggles involve current events!"

"And sometimes those current events involve domestic terrorists," Miller countered, his voice losing its pleasant facade. "So, where is he, Owen? Where is Calvin Becker?"

Owen clenched his jaw. He genuinely didn't know. He hadn't seen or heard from Calvin since that chaotic day on the patio. "I don't know! He just... vanished! Like he always does!"

Miller scoffed, leaning back. "Don't insult my intelligence. The 'vanishing' act? We know about that now. It's a second suit. Someone else is operating it. Someone who picks up Calvin Becker after his little performance."

Owen's mind reeled. *A second suit? Someone else?* He genuinely had no clue what any of that meant. He hadn't even come into contact with Calvin since he revealed himself as Godsend.

"You're telling me Calvin isn't Godsend?" Owen asked, his voice trembling. Miller listened, looking at a monitor near Owen's chair. It was a polygraph, indicating that Owen was being truthful with that question.

"We... don't know. Calvin seems to be Godsend, but if he is, he must be using a drone or have a partner," Miller admitted, getting the tablet yet again. He showed Owen the slowed footage where Calvin was picked up by another object.

Owen didn't even know what to make of this. He honestly thought that Calvin was coming clean when he admitted to being Godsend. "What am I supposed to do about it? I don't know where he went!"

"Do you know anybody that could have been Calvin's accomplice? Anybody close to him?" Miller pressed further, watching the polygraph rather than Owen.

"NO! I thought that Calvin was telling us the truth!" Owen shouted in frustration. The machine indicated this was also true. "If you know so much, you should have been able to tell if I was talking to Calvin, you spies."

Miller was taken aback by this. Based on his search history of the same things that Calvin was fighting, they had assumed some sort of connection. They had also assumed there was some way that Owen was bypassing security measures somehow.

"Huh. You barely knew Calvin. You just became a fan of Godsend— not him," Miller commented. This struck a chord with Owen.

"NO!" he shouted back. The polygraph indicated it was a lie. Owen's expression saddened.

"What do I do with you?" Miller wondered aloud, thinking about how he had revealed the "two suits" theory he had concocted to Owen. He wasn't sure if it was irrelevant enough to just send him back. "It's right about now that I wish memory erasure existed."

Owen, continually angered by the situation, spoke out. "Oh, is the government worried about little ol' me? That maybe I'll reveal to Godsend the theories they have? Well you guys decided to trust me *first*. I was supposed to find out who it was. But you already know, I've already completed your favors. I don't owe you anymore."

Miller turned, walking out of the room, closing the door behind him before Owen could say any more. Ahead of Miller was Brad, the other guy in their department.

"Do we let him go and track him? Or do we use him as a hostage?" Miller asked Brad.

"I just started here and you're asking *me?*" Brad paled at the situation. He looked from the door back to Miller, thinking. "Well... we could just use Calvin's old group as hostages if we really needed to." Quite an idea. Miller took a moment to digest it. "But should we really be doing that? The president's already unpopular as ever—"

"Godsend is going to ignite a civil war unless we can get him and his followers under control!" Miller sternly yelled back at Brad. Brad had no response.

"Sir?" another lady was standing by the door, awaiting the decision Miller had to make.

"Drug him up and send him back out. We don't need him here, he can't answer any of our questions," Miller ordered, "As long as he goes back to his group, we can use them to draw Godsend out."

"Are you really going to use people as hostages? Why not try and confront Godsend?" Brad brought up what he thought was a good point.

Miller furrowed his eyebrows, looking back at him. "Do you know how dangerous this man is? He's a terrorist at the least and a global threat at the most. Based on the capabilities he's shown, he might be able to win a war singlehandedly. We cannot risk sending people to *fight* him!"

Brad stood back as Miller stomped into the next room. Despite any warnings, Miller decided to carry on regardless. The people on standby sedated Owen once more, putting him back into his room without a trace.

Meanwhile, Calvin and Margot had already discovered that Owen was captured. The CIA had done their best to hide it, but they were still able to see them stealthily remove Owen from his room, after a dose of a knock-out dart.

"Damn it!" Calvin, rings still around his eyes, pounded the desk, "Do they not let any devices into that room where Owen is?"

Margot sat further back, expression more neutral. "The only device I know of in there is Miller's tablet. It's been firewalled and gutted of microphones and cameras."

Calvin grit his teeth. "Why are they going after Owen, anyway?"

"Not quite sure. I looked through the surveillance on him and came up with nothing," Margot mentioned casually.

"Are you making sure to keep tabs on everyone? I've been focused on the government and Darkstone," Calvin asked Margot.

Margot already felt irked. Calvin started to sound like he owned the operation, and she wasn't a fan of it. "I'm not spying on everyday people, no. I looked into Amara, but just found out her grandparents used to work on exo-suits for the SWAT team and military. That's why *she* had one but— nothing more than that."

"But we have to be vigilant!" Calvin argued, standing to face her. Margot sat cross legged, tapping her knee with her index finger. Looking up at Calvin, she wore a more frustrated expression.

"We have to focus on protecting people. I'm not spying on people who aren't threats," Margot protested.

"You say that," Calvin spat back, "But look at yourself. You flew out in the middle of the night and practically blew up the Darkstone building here."

"I'm doing my job, Calvin. I had an outburst, I'm sorry. But it was against the real enemy, while nobody was there. Clearly, just a protest. I'm not using people we're supposed to be protecting. This isn't a game, so *focus*." Margot's voice was firm, an edge of frustration in her tone.

Calvin paced, running a hand through his already disheveled hair. "I *am* focused, Margot! That's exactly why we need to be more vigilant. I've been using the system, checking all their little backchannels. And I found something big. People are planning a huge protest outside Philadelphia City Hall against Darkstone and Hulls. And guess what? The military is planning to be there in full force to put them down. It would be the perfect place for Godsend to show up— To show them our supremacy!" His eyes shone with a certain intensity.

Margot pushed herself off the desk, her expression tightening. "And that's exactly why we *can't* risk it right now, Calvin! We need to be more careful, not less. The military is on full alert. They're looking for any excuse to paint us as the enemy, to turn public opinion against us. A direct confrontation with armed forces, especially when people are protesting, could be a disaster. It could jeopardize everything we've built, all the popularity we've gained. We need to be smart about this!"

Calvin, already fuming, looked her dead in the eyes. Her dark stare looked back into his soul. He continued, "Godsend *would* show up. He would be there for the hallowed, don't you think?"

"*Calvin.*" Margot attempted to reel him back in, "I *will* save people from this greedy world. But I am not whatever people want me to be. Okay? I'm not just some... political tool!"

Calvin finally backed up after Margot got in his face. "I... I'm sorry. I just..." His fist tightened.

"Trust me. I want to protect those people too." Margot felt a pang of guilt. "I'm not sure how I can use you to safely make another announcement, but I can go."

"Are you sure?" Calvin now took on a more concerned expression.

Margot chuckled, "You just said why it was a good idea and *now* you're having second thoughts?"

"HEY!" Calvin retorted, "I was trying to be more agreeable rather than arguing with you! But of course you had to put down my awesome idea before going along with it anyway."

Margot began to walk the other way. "Yeah, whatever. But seriously— try not to spy on people."

"Where are you going?" Calvin asked, watching her near the door to exit.

"Looks like you're running out of food. If you're gonna stay holed up here, you might as well have some stuff to snack on," Margot told him, closing the door slowly behind her.

Calvin grinned. "Heh, yeah. Thanks." She left right after that.

While that was going on, there was simultaneously a city council meeting they weren't paying attention to. The air in the council chambers was thick with anticipation. Amara, Declan, and Milo sat in the gallery, their eyes fixed on the dais. Amara's father, Andre Taylor, stood before the assembly, a nervous but determined look on his face. This was it. The vote for the Human Jobs and Basic Rights Act.

"All those in favor of Bill 734, the Human Jobs and Basic Rights Act, please signify by saying 'aye'," the Council President's voice boomed.

A chorus of "ayes" filled the room. Amara held her breath.

"All those opposed, please signify by saying 'nay.'" the Council President added.

A few scattered "nays" followed, quickly swallowed by the louder affirmative votes.

"The ayes have it. Bill 734 is passed!."

A wave of relief, quickly followed by exhilaration, washed over Amara. She looked at Declan and Milo, a wide smile breaking across her face. They grinned back, a shared sense of accomplishment binding them.

"Well *there* is some real change!" Amara whispered, her voice a little choked with emotion.

"We barely made it," Declan chuckled, but his eyes were shining with pride. "Surprised it actually happened,

159

honestly. Maybe people in real life are better than the internet makes 'em out to be."

Milo, ever the optimist, beamed. "But it *did* pass! This is huge! This is exactly the kind of change we were talking about, Amara!"

As the council meeting adjourned, Amara's father approached them. Instead of a police officer's uniform, he wore a suit. His expression shouted tired but triumphant. "Well, that was certainly a fight. But worth it, wouldn't you say?"

"Absolutely, Dad," Amara said, hugging him tightly. "This is amazing. This *actually* makes a difference."

"A lot of angry corporate types are going to be making phone calls tonight, though," a passing Councilman remarked, a smile playing on his lips. "But we stood our ground. This law will ensure that businesses can't just replace humans the way they have."

"And that, my friends," Amara announced to Declan and Milo, "is our message to Calvin." The two of them looked back at her. Both of them were a little confused.

Milo spoke up first, "But— uh, how do we get it to him?"

"Where do you think 'Godsend' will show up next?" Amara asked, as if she already knew the answer.

"Even if this is Calvin, I'm not sure we can *guarantee* he'll show up somewhere specifically..." Declan trailed off as Amara held up her phone. It was an advertisement for the protest planned for that weekend.

"I think I have an idea of where," Amara smirked, showing the two the advertisement.

Storm clouds ahead threatened to pour down at a moment's notice. Regardless, it was the set day. Many were getting ready, making signs and planning on how everyone was going to show up at city hall.

The rain began to fall, light at first, then intensifying, mirroring the rising fervor of the crowd. Chants of "No more Hulls! No more Darkstone!" and "Our city, our laws!" echoed off the historic stone facade of City Hall. Thousands had gathered, a sea of umbrellas and homemade signs, fueled by the viral videos and the raw indignation of feeling unheard.

Inside, Governor Thompson of Pennsylvania and Mayor Reynolds of Philadelphia huddled in a gilded office overlooking the square. The shouts of the protest penetrated the thick windows, a constant, irritating reminder of their predicament.

"They're not backing down," Mayor Reynolds said, running a hand over his thinning hair. "Hulls wants us to crack down, but the public isn't having it. Especially now that they think they have some sort of super-terrorist on their side."

Governor Thompson, a stern-faced man with a reputation for being unflappable, looked out at the angry crowd. "We have our orders, Mr. Mayor. Darkstone's propping up the economy right now. We can't afford to let this go under. Not unless you want to live with *them*," he motioned to the people outside.

Aides bustled in and out, relaying increasingly frantic reports from the police chief stationed at the gates. The crowd was growing more agitated, pushing against the barricades.

"Sir, they're attempting to breach the perimeter!" a young aide reported, his voice cracking. "The police lines are holding, but for how long?"

Governor Thompson gripped the edge of his wooden desk. "We're going to have to go with the president's wishes."

"Don't use more force than we need here! We can't *legitimize* the terrorist!" Reynolds argued back.

"We don't have a *choice*!" Thompson spat in his face. The two continued to quarrel as the protesting outside raged on.

"RESIGN NOW! RESIGN NOW! RESIGN NOW!" people were chanting outside the gates of the building, braving the rain outside. The police had riot-controlling robots push them back with shields.

"YOU ONLY WON THE ELECTION BY GERRYMANDERING!" another shouted. People nearby were documenting this for the world to see.

"GODSEND SHOWED US HOW MUCH YOU'RE OWNED BY THE GREEDY! HOW MUCH YOU'VE TAKEN FROM US!" a protester with a camera expelled, pushing themselves up against the fence around the building.

Inside the building, both the mayor and governor stopped fighting. Thompson put his foot down. "Just let the president call in the troops like planned, okay?"

He pressed a button under his desk. The military was on their way.

"I hope they're good at not using force, like you're saying," Mayor Reynolds hoped for the best, knowing full well there would be casualties because of this.

Just then, a loud *woosh* sounded off in the distance outside. People expected Godsend, turning around to see. But it was not what they expected.

Amara, wearing her getup at the *Masked Rebel* was again in her exo-suit. She jumped off of her father's patrol car, who had just shown up.

"GODSEND IS NOT THE ANSWER TO YOUR PROBLEMS!" she screamed at the top of her lungs, landing in front of the crowd in a recognizable outfit.

"DIDN'T YOU TRY TO FIGHT GODSEND?! HOW ARE YOU HELPING?" a crowd-pleaser shouted, trying to get people's attention off of her.

"I DID!" she shouted back, "I did. And I still will because... I believe there's a better way." Amara unmasked herself, not facing a single person in the whole crowd. They all just watched her face as she walked to the front of the crowd. The police even stopped to watch for a moment.

"You tell 'em!" her dad supported her from afar, watching the world watch in his cruiser.

Amara cleared her throat. "Just this week, this council passed Bill 734. Anybody know what that is?" She was met with silence. "Yeah it's not a pretty name or anything. But in this state, with a little work from my family, friends, and I, we passed a law to keep human workers at *all* companies. *ALL OF THEM*. That and some basic rights for every human employee that works!"

The crowd around her didn't know how to react. In the rain, suddenly everyone questioned their mob mentality.

"Don't you see?! Instead of fighting like this, hoping for Godsend to fix everything, *we* can fix things! We can go to our local officials, tell them our concerns, and get things passed!" Amara continued to preach to the crowd, "The internet recently has made us all divided, split up and stuck in our homes. But if we work together just a little bit, we can make change happen *ourselves*! So that's why—"

"CLEAR THE AREA!" a general shouted, launching a gas grenade into the crowd.

"What the...?!" people in the crowd started choking. They had been so engrossed in Amara's speech that nobody had noticed the military forces in active camo moving in.

"Are you serious?!" Amara coughed out, using the suit to boost out of the smoke cloud.

"STAND DOWN!" one of the military guards shouted, pointing a gun into the crowd, "YOU'RE THREATENING AN ELECTED OFFICIAL!"

"This is insane!" Amara shouted, boosting with the exo-suit again. She felt a few bullets bounce off of the back of the suit. Looking at the ground, she saw them fall in a rain puddle. She realized now what danger she was in.

"THE MILITARY IS SHOOTING AT US!" someone shouted, still streaming the whole thing.

"RUBBER BULLETS! WE STOLE YOUR FAVORITE TERRORIST'S IDEA!" another soldier shouted. People were now running and screaming. It quickly became chaos.

While people were trying to get the real version of the story on the internet, those in power were a step ahead.

President Hulls, simultaneously hosting a broadcasted emergency meeting, sat in front of a camera reacting to what was happening in Philadelphia.

"It's truly horrible, the trouble going down in Pennsylvania. You know, they asked me to send the *best* troops down there. They begged. I told them, I gave them my *oath*, I would put the area under my control. I'm going to help these people in ways you couldn't imagine," the President spat falsities on his own broadcast, leading people into deception.

Back on the ground, the people were crying out for help.

"MASKED REBEL! WHY? WHY DID YOU DISTRACT US?!" someone shouted, running the other way before being tased to the ground.

"I DIDN'T!" Amara dodged another round of rubber bullets, "I THOUGHT THESE GUYS WOULD HELP ME!"

Chaos continued, police became useless as the military completely overtook the situation, leaving people bleeding on the ground or quickly in handcuffs.

"WHY DIDN'T YOU JUST LET US DREAM?" a person screamed out from the floor, reaching their arm out to Amara. She froze. This wasn't what she planned. People's trust of her, of everything the system could achieve, was being eroded in real time. This event was creating a defining line, separating people into the cooperators and the vigilantes. Nothing could stop it, and Amara panicked knowing that.

Breathe. Breathe. Breathe please just... Amara was losing consciousness. She couldn't regulate her breathing. A sudden whirring pulled her out of it.

"**IT'S NOT JUST A DREAM.**"

In slow motion, Amara turned, facing to her right. The rain seemingly froze as people all around the whirring sound all followed the familiar voice that accompanied it. In unison, the hallowed many shouted—

"**GODSEND!!!**"

Godsend hovered there, taking in the scenery. The pain of the people being battered by the military for trying to make a statement. The atrocities committed by those in charge. The quick, abrasive actions that would affect people forever. Margot, under the suit, couldn't keep her calm. People began to see Godsend visibly vibrate in the space the suit occupied.

"FIRE!" a military general ordered. Thousands of bullets were shot at Godsend. Not a single one made a scratch. Godsend was unbothered as they all bounced off like little pellets.

"**HOW COULD YOU...?**" Godsend's voice quivered more than usual. "**HOW COULD YOU DO THIS TO YOUR OWN PEOPLE?**"

There was no answer. Just increased firepower by the military. Margot couldn't hold it in anymore. A dark green glow started to surround the suit as it vibrated, pinned in three dimensional space.

"HOLD ON!" one of the military generals shouted. Just then, the green energy shot out of the Godsend suit, blasting in every direction. It went over most of the people, toppling all of the military vehicles and taking out any technology like an electromagnetic pulse.

Godsend looked straightforward in the aftermath. Margot put forth the suit's hand, sending bits and pieces of the millions of nano-bots that caused the suit to go out and trap the military personnel. Soon, there were a bunch of military men and women, trapped floating like bubbles.

"WHAT'S GOING ON?!" one of them shouted, unable to move from the pressure. All of them floated a few more feet up.

"**DO YOU WANT TO FEEL A FRACTION OF THE PAIN YOU CAUSED?**" Godsend asked. The games were over. The gloves were coming off. This would be the first time Godsend was going to hurt a human being.

"CAAAAALVIN!" Amara suddenly shouted, boosting into the scene. She used the suit and sucker-punched Godsend across the face, causing them to lose focus.

"**AMARA—**?" Godsend was pushed back for the first time. Margot caught herself in midair, forgetting that she was supposed to be acting as Calvin.

The nanobots constricting the military personnel shimmered, their grip momentarily loosened as Godsend recoiled from Amara's unexpected blow. Most of them freed themselves.

Amara didn't respond with words, only another swift punch, aimed at Godsend's chest. The metallic suit absorbed the impact, but the force behind it was undeniable.

"You're going too far, Calvin! This isn't what we talked about!" she yelled, her own voice strained through her suit's comms, echoing with desperation. She used her suit to leap back, creating distance.

The military, still partially held by the shimmering nanobots, watched in stunned silence. Their general, released from them, quickly barked orders. "Hold your fire! We can't use the rounds meant for Godsend on a civilian!"

Amara landed gracefully, her exo-suit making pneumatic noise as the joints moved. "They're just following orders, Calvin! I changed the law! The right way, the way we've done it for years! We can still change things that way "

Godsend floated closer, the green glow around them intensifying. "**THEY ARE SHOOTING CIVILIANS. THEY HAVE CHOSEN TO ALIGN AGAINST THE PEOPLE.**" The nanobots still around some of the military tightened slightly.

Amara charged again, a powerful kick aimed at Godsend's midsection. This time, Godsend met her, blocking with a forearm. A metallic clang resonated through the square. "But you're just doing the same thing! You're just putting them down! If not for this crazy suit— the military wouldn't even be here!"

"**THIS IS NOT INNOCENT ON THEIR PART. THIS IS DESTROYING PEOPLE!**" Godsend retorted, finally pushing Amara away with a surge of energy that sent her tumbling. She landed hard, her suit sparking faintly. "**THE HALLOWED NEED JUSTICE.**"

Amara scrambled to her feet, her breathing heavy. "THEY DO!" she agreed, "But this isn't the way to do it. Taking power, forcing things to be one way, how are you any different than the president, Calvin?!" She saw the military holding back, their attention fixed on the fight between the two masked figures.

Godsend hovered silently for a moment, the green light on their face flickering. The energy around them pulsed, almost like a heartbeat. The nanobots around the military personnel shimmered, then slowly, agonizingly slowly, they began to retract, releasing the soldiers back to the ground.

"**I WILL NOT HARM YOU, AS LONG AS YOU LEAVE. I WILL HANDLE THE PROTEST,**" Godsend commanded the military. They started to back away, leaving because they didn't have much of a choice. "**AMARA. YOU WISH TO KNOW THE DIFFERENCE BETWEEN THE PRESIDENT AND I?**"

Passively, nanobots began to leave Godsend's suit again. Instead of trapping the military. They lifted people to their feet. They helped move cloth over wounds. The people, dusty and bruised, looked to Godsend.

"**I DON'T USE MY POWER FOR MYSELF.**" is simply the explanation Margot left Amara with, still acting as Calvin.

"Godsend! Godsend! Godsend!" the people began chanting. People began to recover as the military backed up. The president intentionally cut the cord on his feed, citing technical difficulties. The truth was, he couldn't let the world see Godsend win.

"But— but we were just going to be on another path! We could have fixed things another way!" Amara still staunchly argued. Godsend slowly ascended into the air as the people cheered him on.

"**THE MORE TIME IT TAKES, THE MORE LIVES THEY TAKE. I'M SORRY, BUT THIS IS THE WAY I'LL BE DOING THINGS.**" Godsend shot out into the horizon, leaving that as their parting message.

"Calvin... that doesn't sound at all like you." Amara was stumped, watching as the trail Godsend left behind parted the clouds. The rain was gone, and the people rejoiced.

The mayor and governor were escorted out safely, and the people didn't interfere. But terror was instilled into the political upper class, knowing that there would be someone to oppose them. President Hulls was furious.

"That's it," he said behind closed doors, "Let the CIA know I'm devoting the whole power of the office to them. We have to get rid of this vigilante. No matter *what*."

Amara, after the fight, returned to her father. She was a little worried. "I don't want you to take everything that Godsend said. I... still want you to be a police officer. I think you can still do good things as a cop," Amara told her father.

"Heh, I wasn't planning on changing, but..." Andre, her father trailed off for a moment, "Hearing it from you really confirms it for me. Regardless of what super-person says."

The two of them shared a hug in the aftermath of the protest, the one sunny spot on an otherwise rainy day.

Calvin awaited Margot's return, later on the day that the city hall protests occurred. He knew that Margot indeed showed up as Godsend, but he thought the whole thing was a mess. While Margot came up on top at the end, her presence as Godsend was not the same, not as commanding.

Margot eventually walked into the bunker, peeling off the last of the suit pieces. She looked tired, the usual spark in her eyes replaced by a dull weariness. She tossed the compacted suit onto her workbench with more force than necessary.

"That was... something else," she muttered, not looking at Calvin as she was seemingly out of breath.

Calvin nodded, observing her. "You seemed... different. Less prepared. And you almost hurt those soldiers, even though you said you wouldn't."

Margot finally met his gaze with a scowl. "They were shooting at unarmed civilians, Calvin. What did you *expect* me to do? And what was Amara doing there? I can't believe she tried playing hero *again*."

"She thinks she can win by playing the game. Unfortunately, house always wins," Calvin responded, a flicker of concern on his face. "But that's not the point. The point is, you almost lost control. The suit... it seemed to be affecting you more."

Margot scoffed, turning away to wipe sweat from her brow. "It's fine. Just a lot of adrenaline. And the nanobots... they were acting up a bit. Probably the electromagnetic pulse." She didn't even know if she was telling the truth. The suit had been a part of her for so long now, she couldn't tell when it's will affected her temperament.

"The way you spoke... it wasn't the usual Godsend. It was like... it was just *you*. An angry you," Calvin pressed, concern in his voice.

Margot shot a disgruntled look back. "Calvin you *know* this is all *my* plan right? Are you trying to say I'm not good at playing *myself*?"

Calvin took a step back, surprised by her intensity. "No, no, of course not. I just... I just thought that you were trying to give the public a certain perception of what 'Godsend' is like."

She placed her hand on a nearby rail, her fingers tracing the smooth, cool steel. "People are in danger, Calvin. The government is serious. Hulls is serious. They're going to come after us with everything they have."

"Good," Calvin said, his usual chipper tone returning, "Let them. Let them see what happens when the hallowed fight back, when *we* fight back."

Margot finally exhaled, feeling she had regained control of the situation. Just as she was lifting her hand from the railing, she heard a strange noise as the back of her hand made contact. It sounded like metal-on-metal contact.

Both her and Calvin's eyes shot to where the sound came from. A larger piece of the Godsend suit was stuck to her. A little metallic line from the mid-section of the pinky down the side of her forearm, like a vein.

Calvin's expression paled as she lifted her arm toward her vision. "Margot... is that—?"

"This is why I didn't want *you* wearing the thing," Margot partially lied. *That, and I don't want to train you how to use it,* she thought simultaneously.

"Are you seriously not worried about it? What if it gets worse?" Calvin asked, concerned with the sight.

"Well first off, everyone would know something is up with me. I'd have the same metal as Godsend in my arm," Margot replied, picking up a metal scraping tool, "Second off, I don't know if I'd be me anymore if too much stuck. So yeah, it isn't ideal. But it's what I have, and in this situation I'm damn sure using it. Better than needing to hire a robo-taxi at the last minute just to help me with a getaway. *Especially* if it's from a church." She started to chip off the pieces of the armor slowly, taking a jab at Calvin while doing it.

"Just for reference, in case you start to change," Calvin carefully worded his request, "Who *exactly* are you?"

Margot paused, first not understanding the question. As she processed, she understood what he meant. She hadn't really told him much about herself, just what he could see and know in the here and now.

"Well, what do you want to know?" she cautiously answered, unsure if she would regret it.

Calvin took a moment. This was a rare opportunity. Margot would only ever talk about the present, or future. Most of the time, it was related to the mission of saving the hallowed. He took a moment to think what she might be comfortable with sharing, and what might drive her to rescind her offer.

"How about, where are you really living now, and how?" Calvin thought up a casual question.

Margot's face lit up, she seemed relieved. "Well I *do* live in an apartment. It faces route 13, pretty high up. I get a good view. And no, I'm not actually a waitress. I figured you'd know *that* by now. I did a bit of part-time work a while back. I lie and say I still work there. I think that's also what my bank info says."

"You're lucky you're still not entangled in family drama. Boy am I glad I'm out of that," Calvin sighed, thinking about his own issues elsewhere.

Margot's expression froze. *Family* was a word she was uncomfortable with. She held her arm with the other hand. "Yeah, hah. Well, they're not alive so they can't complain."

Calvin realized he may have just stepped on an emotional landmine. "Oh jeez, I'm sorry I didn't mena—"

"No, no! It's okay. I'm glad," Margot cut him off, realizing what she said sounded even weirder. "Well, not *glad* all the way . But, I'm certainly glad *one* of them's gone." Her face muscles clenched, looking away from Calvin.

Calvin felt even more lost, but was happy getting information regardless. "I... won't ask any further. I might get the picture? Were you an only child?"

Margot nodded. "I didn't have any siblings, no. But I don't have *real* emotional baggage from my parents, I don't think. One of them was just not a good person. I wasn't very involved."

"I wonder how I'd feel if Hadley died," Calvin blurted out, "I don't know if I'd really care." A wash of childhood memories fell over him. A pang of guilt hit his conscience, knowing he wasn't telling the truth.

Margot looked away from his line of sight. "Your brother. I was watching over him for a while. He's a detective, and was probably the first one trying to find me."

"Yeah, and he's a total douchebag. So what? He can be our enemy," Calvin responded.

"I don't really know where he went though. I don't think he's dead, but he may have been thrown out of the country. Last I saw he was boarding a plane," Margot explained, reminiscing on the name.

Calvin whipped back to face her. "Hadley is out of the country?"

"I'm not worried about him. He probably knows about everything, even from another country. Based on media feeds from around the globe, the whole world is watching us tear apart this autocracy." Margot veered the conversation back on track.

Calvin kept his feelings to himself, going back to talk about future plans with Margot. 'Right," he said. But he couldn't help thinking about where Hadley could have gone.

When Hadley was discharged, he became consumed with the idea that he had to come back. He *had* to prove to everyone that he could be the one to unmask Godsend. Despite Calvin revealing that it was him, he refused to believe it. The one key piece of evidence was something he overheard when listening in on one of Calvin's alcoholics anonymous meetings.

It was a quote from Declan: *"But the way [Godsend] said 'them' on the news once was a giveaway to me. Even through the voice filter I could hear the Russian-accented 'zem' instead of 'them.'"*

So his next stop was Russia, only a bag of clothes and tech on his back. Having to use his phone as a translator, he was very thankful that technology had come such a long way.

He came across strangers in Moscow, asking about Godsend. Apparently, their media had been censored as well. Nobody there really knew about Godsend, just that the United States had recently been in chaos.

Every cafe, every market stall, every quiet corner he approached, he repeated the same question in his broken, phone-translated Russian: "Godsend? Do you know of Godsend?" He showed them images, snippets from the viral videos, anything he could. Nobody knew anything about the images or videos.

He was beginning to despair, the cold air getting to him. But then, he saw the flicker of a screen through a window. It came from a small, dimly lit library, tucked away down a narrow alley. It was a blurred image, but he knew it. It was a still from the Philadelphia protest, Godsend hovering amidst the chaos.

Hadley ran inside, manic. The air inside was thick with book dust and the hum of an old computer. A thick-bearded burly man sat alone in a corner, looking at his laptop screen.

Hadley hovered by the man, catching his attention. "Godsend?" Hadley asked, holding up his phone with the image. "This. Do you know?"

The man looked at the phone, then at Hadley, a slow, appraising look. His eyes narrowed. "American?" he grunted in heavily accented English.

Hadley nodded, a surge of hope rising within him. "Yes. I... I thought he might come from here."

The man leaned closer, lowering his voice. "That one... troubles. Much trouble." He gestured vaguely to the screen. "Not for ordinary people to speak about."

Before Hadley could react, before he could even process what was going on, a heavy hand clamped down on his shoulder. He looked up, startled. Standing over him was a tall, imposing man in a dark, unmarked uniform, his face grim. Behind him, two more uniformed figures stood by the door, their expressions equally stern.

"You are coming with us, American," the man said in thick, accented English, his voice devoid of emotion.

"WHAT?" Hadley reacted. But it was too late. Before Hadley could fight back, a bag was placed on his head and he was abducted.

Meanwhile, while Hadley was being taken away by the Russian authorities, Owen stared at himself in the bathroom mirror. He had gone unshaved for a few days now. To him, reality felt like it was crumbling. He had no proof that he was kidnapped, and didn't want to sound crazy, but he had nobody to talk to.

He looked into his own bloodshot eyes. "Do I tell them they're going to be used as hostages? Are they going to kill me if I do?" he muttered, feeling frozen.

The faces of Amara, Declan, Milo, and Hazel flashed before his eyes. Hostages. The word echoed in his ears. He had to tell them, but how? And what if Miller was still watching him, still listening? He ran a hand over his unshaven jaw, the stubble scratching against his skin. The paranoia was suffocating.

He paced out of the restroom, now staring at the muted television screen. News anchors gestured wildly at images of the damaged Darkstone building, their voices unheard but their alarm evident. "Godsend." The name resonated with a strange mix of fear and admiration. He had genuinely believed in Godsend, in Calvin's theatrical promises. Now, he wasn't so sure. He knew that it might not be the way it appeared.

He grabbed his phone, his thumb hovering over Amara's contact. He stopped himself, it was too risky. He needed to be discreet, to act as if nothing was wrong. He threw on a jacket, pulling the hood low over his head. The air outside was damp and cold, matching the chill in his gut. He had to warn at least one of them.

As he walked through the streets, he had a thought that might work. *What if Declan is working?* He had overheard the story of Milo running into Declan. He remembered where it happened too. That way, it'd look like he was just going out for a late snack.

He made his way to the diner he had heard about. It was almost midnight, but the place was still open, its neon sign casting a faint glow on the wet pavement. He pushed open the door, the chime announcing his arrival.

The diner was mostly empty, save for a lone figure wiping down the counter. It was Declan. Owen felt a wave of relief, quickly followed by renewed anxiety.

Owen found his way over, going to the counter. "Declan?" Owen's voice was barely a whisper.

Declan looked up, startled, his eyes widening when he saw Owen. "Owen? What are you doing here? It's late."

Owen glanced around nervously, then pulled up a stool at the counter, leaning in close. "Do you have any devices on you?"

Declan's expression shifted, a flicker of concern replacing his surprise. He shook his head, pointing to his phone on the counter. He then motioned for Owen to follow him to a booth in the back, away from the robot servers and the few lingering patrons.

"Alright, what's going on?" Declan asked, his voice low. "Make it quick, boss isn't here right now."

Owen took a deep breath, trying to steady his shaking hands. "We're being watched. The government has access to every public device we own."

Declan scoffed, playing it off like it didn't affect him. "Owen, what the hell are you talking about? Listening to what? Our AA meetings?"

"Everything! They... they took me. They interrogated me about Calvin. About Godsend. They probably knew I would open up because I helped Hadley." Owen's voice cracked, the memory terrified him. "They think there's two of them. That Calvin isn't really Godsend, he just puts on a show in a second suit."

Declan leaned forward, his eyes fixed on Owen's. "I'd say you got into something that gave you hallucinations, but you're an alcoholic not an acid-head."

"I'm serious, Declan! After I refused to tell them anything, they drugged me. I woke up back in my house. But before that, I heard something. Something important. They said... they're going to use the group. As hostages. To draw Calvin out."

A cold silence fell between them. Declan's face was grim. "Hostages? You're serious? For *Calvin*?"

Owen nodded, unable to focus. "I don't know what to do. I just... I *had* to warn someone. But I think they're still watching me closely. We should probably go back to the bar. Just... serve me food or something. I'll pay you back." He turned around, facing back to the front.

Declan ran a hand through his hair, his mind racing. "I can't believe you're serious, Owen. But I can't for the life of me figure out why the hell you'd lie about this either."

"I'm *serious*, Declan! We have to find a way to tell them," Owen shouted back, frustration bubbling to the surface.

As the two walked toward the dining area once more, Owen opened the swinging door to see multiple armored agents in the restaurant.

The two parties froze, staring at each other. Declan knew now that it was definitely for real. Owen just slowly closed the door, leaving the barrier between them.

"I think we should go..." Owen trailed off, about to take off into a sprint.

Another armored agent came out from the darkened part of the back of the restaurant, grabbing Declan's arms. "Going somewhere?" he asked.

"Get *off* me!" Declan tried to free his hands, but they were already handcuffed.

More agents burst in through the front. "You didn't think we'd just let this slide, did you, Owen Park?" another agent boasted.

Before they could even struggle, both of them were pushed outside and taken away into an unmarked military vehicle.

While all this happened, Calvin watched from back at Margot's bunker. He watched the screen in horror as Margot moved around boxes of various old computers.

"Are you seeing this? They're taking away Owen and Declan!" Calvin shouted, trying to get Margot's attention. She looked over from where she was.

"This is pretty usual activity for a government concentrating power at the top. They make a bunch of outrageous humanitarian claims, cover tracks, and rid themselves of any threats. They'll claim it's for safety, or for rebuilding the country," Margot explained, bringing out more boxes.

Calvin's expression changed. He seemed disheartened. "I'm assuming you didn't just go to our group as a cover-up too. But it sounds to me like you don't care about them."

Margot froze as she put another box down, shadows covered her eyes. "No Calvin, that problem is real. Imagine having that suit, the things you could do with it. You'd need to numb the nerves a little to actually do anything with it."

"Then you should care about those in our group. Are they not people that are 'hallowed' too?" Calvin accused her.

"I DO CARE!" she shouted back, her arms tensed up. Calvin took a step back, not realizing she was hurt. "I care, Calvin, but what am I supposed to do? Go rescue them specifically when the government is doing that to everyone they don't like? They'll be free, but after we fix things for *everyone*. They won't kill those two."

Calvin, still emotional that they were taken, didn't take that for an answer. "How do you know all this, Margot? You act like you've been through this before, like it's all part of the plan. How about you tell me how?"

Margot turned quickly, walking toward Calvin. "*Calvin*. There are some things—" She accidentally brushed her arm by one of the boxes. An old cassette player with a speaker fell out. Both of their eyes darted to it. A cassette tape fell out of the player, marked by a piece of tape. Written in handwriting, the piece of painter's tape on the cassette read "On Beaches."

But that was the less interesting part. Calvin was more focused on the player itself. It was not of United States origin. It was primarily red, and had Korean writing on it. There, however, was one line of English. It read, "D.P.R. of Korea."

Margot rushed to pick it up, unsure whether or not Calvin saw it. But looking up after grabbing it, she knew that he certainly did.

"Were you... not born here?" Calvin asked, taking a shot in the dark.

Margot put away the cassette player and tape. She didn't face Calvin after that. "I'm going to fix things. You're just going to have to trust me on this."

She quickly left, going into another room. Calvin realized then that she wasn't being uncaring about the situation. She was just overwhelmed with everything that had to be done, and was thinking of it as more of a problem to solve.

"I might have pressed a bit too far..." Calvin muttered to himself, regretting his shouting.

Across the world in Russia, Hadley was taken into a secret facility for questioning. The ceilings were tall, and the building itself was so full of color compared to United States facilities.

One of the guards approached Hadley at a table he was chained to. "Tell us, American," Major Anya Petrova, a gruff woman with sharp eyes, began in heavily accented English. "Why are you here? You do know we're keeping news about this 'Godsend' man out of the public. Yet you shove it in people's faces."

Hadley swallowed, his heart hammering against his ribs. He had to be convincing. "I had to get officials attention somehow... I came to warn you," he said, his voice raspy. "Godsend... he's not just an American problem. He's a threat to anyone in power. He attacks corporations, he undermines governments. He'll come for you too, eventually."

The officers exchanged glances. Another, a younger man with a cynical smirk, scoffed. "And we're supposed to believe you... why?"

"I know whoever decided to censor Godsend labeled them as a threat. Obviously the government here cares," Hadley pointed out, "He is dangerous. He has technology... like nothing you've ever seen. He's seemingly invulnerable."

The younger man spat in his direction. "Still doesn't mean we have anything to do with it."

"If you wait, if you let America fall into chaos, he'll just move on to the next target. Better to deal with him now, when he's focused on us." Hadley hoped this convinced them.

Major Petrova narrowed her eyes. "And what do you propose we do, American? We have no jurisdiction."

"You have resources," Hadley pressed, leaning forward. "Intelligence. You can observe. You can prepare. If you want to avoid civil wars across the globe, you need to be ready. And I can help you understand him. I know his methods, his motivations." He hoped his desperation sounded like conviction.

The officers murmured amongst themselves for a moment, then Major Petrova turned back to Hadley. "You will tell us everything you know, American. Spill that, and we'll collaborate with what we know." Hadley nodded, a small, weary triumph settling over him. It was a long shot, but it was a start. "What was your name?"

"Hadley." He extended a free hand. He shook hands with the gruff woman.

"Petrova." She had mimicked his introduction. She then released him from the chains.

After getting clearance, a military vehicle came and picked up Hadley and Petrova. As they rode in the back, Hadley looked around at the place he had been taken to. It was a cloudy, gray day over the Russian military base. Different squadrons walked along the streets of the base. Hadley knew he was in deep now, no turning back

They pulled off the road, going into an empty aircraft hangar. From inside, there was a downward driveway that went underground. The vehicle took Hadley and the others down, parking inside. They were now in what looked like a command center. They had camera feeds and people monitoring all important intelligence coming into the center.

Petrova got off the vehicle, motioning for Hadley to follow her. The two walked over to the other side of the intelligence center, where a tall man with a nearly shaved head stood. He had gray hair and a mustache, wearing a military uniform that was higher prestige than his colleagues.

"General Makovsky. This is the foreigner," Petrova introduced Hadley. Hadley bowed, not sure how to act in this situation.

"Get your eyes off the ground, little man," Makovsky grumbled at Hadley.

Hadley shot up, standing with his hands behind his back. "Yes sir. I am the American they speak of, sir. I was assigned to find out who the 'Godsend' character was, but they grew tired of me and threw me out."

General Makovsky laughed, a hearty sound coming from his lungs. "We know who you are, Becker. You had to use your passport to get here, after all. So you'll tell us all about your 'Godsend' problem, huh?"

Hadley was taken off guard. Makovsky's demeanor switched from terrifying to friendly so quickly. "Uh, yes sir. Should I start from where I got involved?"

"Just tell us everything you know. That's a perfect starting point," General Makovsky ushered him on. Very quickly, Hadley spilled what he had. He started from when he was assigned to be a detective on the Godsend case to when his brother suddenly was accused. Then, he moved on to being kicked out.

"...So with that one quote I saw on camera about the accent, I thought maybe I'd find Godsend's origin here— AND warn you all. Since Russia's, like, another giant country," Hadley wrapped up, adding that last part to make sure his story was consistent.

"Mmhmm." The general had just been nodding the whole time. Acknowledging, but not commenting. Now, there was an awkward silence. Hadley had finished up.

"And... yeah. That's it, here I am," Hadley added, feeling awkward that he didn't have anything to add.

Makovsky smirked. "You're certainly right about one thing, Becker. It's impossible that 'Godsend' is your brother. Nobody could use that suit without training. But I am not telling you to ignore your eyes and ears, either. Your brother is being used as a front by the real person in the suit."

Hadley perked up. That was the first person to say to his face, without a doubt, that he was correct. "But how do you know? He could be using an AI to pilot that thing. Maybe it isn't a person in it most of the time, after all—"

"We know *exactly* what that thing is. That suit. We just thought it was never completed." Makovsky moved over to a computer, pulling up an image. It was dated twenty years back, and looked like an in-progress version of the Godsend suit.

Hadley stumbled backward. He had no clue how, in Russia, they had evidence of Godsend's origin. Maybe he was spot-on with the accent.

"So... so there's a Russian soldier in that suit?" Hadley panted out, in complete disarray.

"No, there is not," Petrova interrupted, "When 'Godsend,' as you call him, was leaked online, we were just as confused as your current administration."

"Then what the hell is this?!" Hadley pointed at the image of the suit-in-progress.

General Makovsky grabbed the mouse and went to the file name. "This is not Godsend. It is what eventually *became* Godsend." The file name was *Proyekt_Stal'noy_D'yavol-23.jpg*.

Major Petrova scoffed. "Project Steel Devil. There was no actual steel involved, but there were plans to build a sort of 'super soldier.' However, we could not complete it. There was an element we believed was housed in the United States that could make it work. In theory, this one soldier could become a bigger threat than any nuclear bomb."

"Again, how do you guys not know what happened to it? This looks *pretty* important," Hadley asked, ignoring the fact that Russia was trying to create a world-dominating weapon at one point and he had no clue.

Makovsky banged his hand on the desk in front of him. "The element we were after didn't exist. At least, we thought it didn't. The man in charge of it, Aleksandr Davis, was killed when the project was supposed to reach a conclusion. The nuclear battery was never complete, making it impossible to run that thing for more than a minute or so."

Hadley thought for a moment. *Nuclear battery... Aleksandr... Davis?*

"Hold on a moment, Aleksandr... Davis?" Hadley asked, thinking back to the people in the alcoholics anonymous group.

"We assumed people from your government found him, and took his assets into hiding, no?" Petrova asked.

"No, no, no. I have security clearance. Or... had. We never knew about Aleksandr. We never took his things either. But that name, that name is the same as one of the people suspected to be Godsend," Hadley explained. "Her name was Margot Davis. Aleksandr... was her dad. He just had a sail boat business."

General Makovsky laughed heartily again. "That was no sail boat business. That was a cover for shipping in

187

foreign goods, little man. Aleksandr changed his last name to blend in there, looks like it worked well."

"Aleksandr never had a daughter, did he?" Petrova asked aloud, looking down at the console of the computer.

"He married a Korean woman from the north. I don't recall them having any children. However, our American friend here says otherwise," Makovsky motioned to Hadley.

It was all coming together now. It all started to piece together in Hadley's brain.

"What was his wife's name?" he asked, piecing together everything he had just heard.

"Hmmmm. Something like, Nah-ray?" Petrova mis-pronounced the name.

"Yeah, yeah. It was Narae Davis. I forgot both of their last names before that," Makovsky added.

That was it. Hadley knew one thing for sure now. Between the alcoholics anonymous group, the origin of the Godsend suit, and Calvin's last friend he made before disappearing, he had found the identity of Godsend.

"Then our friend *Godsend* is indeed the daughter of the two of them. Her name is Margot Davis, and she's living in Philadelphia, Virginia right now," Hadley declared. The others all looked at him.

The Russian general sounded surprised. "You're certain?" Makovsky asked. Hadley nodded.

"Narae and Alec Davis were listed in the United States registry as the parents of Margot Davis, and I've seen her in the flesh. I just assumed she was Korean-American," Hadley told them both, boldly declaring what he believed.

Suddenly, it was quiet. Hadley was wondering if he had said something outlandish, or maybe something just plain unbelievable.

"They had a child...?" Petrova asked aloud, seeming distraught. "That must have been rough." She put her fingers to the bridge of her nose.

Even the general seemed a little let down by this statement. Hadley was confused.

"I just told you the most likely candidate for Godsend, there's probably nobody else it *could* be. Why are we sad now?" Hadley asked aloud, his pride hurt from their lack of response.

Makovsky coughed, looking up at Hadley. "Well, Narae wasn't... the most fond of him. So we thought the Americans paid her to kill him. If you say the Americans didn't even know... then she just murdered her husband after having a child."

The room went silent. *There was nothing like that on the United States Registry,* Hadley thought. But he knew it had been tricked before.

Petrova gave Hadley a whack on the back. "Luckily we had someone crazy enough to come here with just one clue leading back to speaking Russian, eh?" she asked, laughing and joking around. Nobody else joined her laughter.

She clearly didn't read the room.

Decades back, Aleksandr stood in the very same room where Makovsky and Hadley would converse in the present. The general structure of the Godsend suit was laid out, called the "Steel Devil" back then.

"Дэвис, ты готов к поездке?" [Davis, are you ready to go?] a commanding officer in the Russian military asked from behind him.

"Да, наверное. Какая она, Америка?" [Yes, probably. What is America like?] Aleksandr asked in return.

"[Between you and I, I believe starting a family would be the best way for you to blend in.]" This advice the commander gave left Aleksandr confused. He then remembered how he told the commander in passing about a woman he had been seeing.

"[The Korean woman from the military? Her and I? No, sir. That's a transactional relationship.]" Aleksandr Davis laughed at the suggestion.

"[Seriously, Davis. If you're married, and a child is on the way, the United States turns a blind eye. They call those types 'Nuclear families.' Become one and you'll blend in perfectly.]" The commander swung his hands wildly as he spoke. Aleksandr started to notice the insistence in his tone.

"[This sounds like a command for taking the 'Steel Devil' with me,]" Aleksandr pointed out. The commander nodded. With a big sigh, Aleksandr agreed to making relations with this woman he frequently visited.

Later that same day, he boarded a military plane headed for the North Korean border. Once at the base on the other side of the border, he got clearance, with his friends in the North Korean military, to come through. They then drove from Kraskino to Sonbong, through the border. He had previously been involved in joint operations, and was largely welcome there.

At the small, unknown military base was a woman who Aleksandr only knew as "Narae." He walked through the gates to the main field. There, another commander escorted Narae to him. He bowed as he left her in Aleksandr's company.

"안녕하세요. 이번에는 얼마를 제시하시는 건가요?" [Hello again. How much are you offering this time?] she asked at the sight of him in Russian-accented Korean. Narae was a beautiful woman in Aleksandr's eyes. She was just the right height with fair, soft skin. But she was also cold enough to stand her ground. He liked that about her, along with her beautiful eyes and black ponytail she wore out the back of her military cap.

Aleksandr took a deep breath. "English now, Narae. I don't come for... 'Services' this time." he switched languages. She looked around, confused.

"English... why?" she asked, bringing the language to the surface of her mind again.

"I have to go to America. The military... They want me to find the secret to what they call a 'Nuclear Battery.' They would like it if I had wife, maybe child too," Aleksandr explained.

Narae felt a pit in her stomach when he explained that. "You can't. You aren't speaking in English properly. 그들은 당신을 쉽게 알아낼 것입니다 [They will easily figure you out!]"

Aleksandr looked around, fearing someone heard her shout in Korean. "Narae, English. I can not be talking about this here! Let's stick to English. I *really* need you here."

191

"You want me to go to America, *with you*? You think what I have shown you resembles love, do you?" Narae asked, accusing him.

Aleksandr stayed quiet as other soldiers passed by, not wanting to cause a commotion. He then spoke up, "Yes, I know this is crazy. But you are the only one I could think of. Your military is willing to send you off with me. Would you not rather be a housewife than this torture you endure everyday?"

"I would rather be myself," Narae spat back in his face, turning to face the other way. He put his hands on her shoulders.

"Narae, I have no choice. For the sake of our countries, for *your* country. I need you. I have the permission already. I will have you returned here in only a matter of years, and you will be released! You will have the riches to do as you please!" Aleksandr begged, making it seem like her duty to complete.

She furrowed her eyebrows in anger. Gritting her teeth, and watching the other commanders observe from afar, she caved. "Fine. If that is how I can serve."

In the following months, Narae went with Aleksandr to the other side of Russia. There, the two were prepped and trained on their new identities. They were the Davis family, the owners of a sailboat company that operated out of Philadelphia with the majority of its workers on Jetty Beach or just "The Jetty" in Atlantic City, New Jersey.

The workers at their sailboat company were all in on the operation. All of them had ties with the Russian government and were secretly importing goods and sending them to Aleksandr.

Meanwhile, Aleksandr and Narae were settling into American life. There were so many wacky characters out there that they never really stood out. Aleksandr just acted like himself and was constantly driving between Virginia and New Jersey to manage the "business."

Narae started out as very reserved. She mostly stayed inside of their house, a two story blue and white home outside on the outskirts of Philadelphia. They had a generous porch and a small backyard. It appeared to the people around them that they led a peaceful life. This wasn't exactly the truth.

Aleksandr, now going by Alec in the United States, came home from work at fairly irregular times. His relationship with Narae was truly distant. They were uncoordinated.

Alec came home later one night. "I'm home," Aleksandr said aloud. Narae didn't respond, but he saw her watching television in the other room. "Not that you care," he muttered to himself, looking the other way.

Narae, without warning, got up and turned to face him. "This country is different than I thought it was, Aleksandr."

"A little more, freeing? I get that a little. We live like kings and queens of old," Aleksandr motioned to the house and the furniture.

Narae shook her head. "There is that sense of freedom, at least from where we came from. But neither of these places are perfect. The way things are heading... they'll be a surveillance state too. Their authoritarianism is a little less out in the open."

Aleksandr nodded. "They are somehow not at all, and *exactly* like what we've been told."

Narae, ever cold, actually returned a laugh for once. Her usually frozen demeanor warming for a moment. "You don't really want to go back to how it was, do you?"

Aleksandr paused. He didn't know how to respond. Both because he didn't know what he thought in the first place, and he didn't know how to verbalize it. "I... I wish to change things."

"How so?" Narae pressed, immediately interested in what he meant.

Aleksandr thought for a moment. "We bring this suit back. We fix our home. We don't let them use it, and we live like this back home."

Narae smiled. Perhaps it was Stockholm syndrome, or maybe it was just the fact that they were close together now, but she liked this idea. "I hope we can do that... for her."

Narae put her hand to her abdomen. Aleksandr nodded. She had been pregnant for a while now, and was hopeful for the future for once.

Years passed. Their daughter, Margot, was born. They adored her at birth, but very quickly Aleksandr had been sidetracked by work. This project was taking longer than anticipated, and the Russian government was not happy. Margot largely grew up without a father around. Even on her first day of school.

"Mom," little Margot began to ask, still having a slight Russian accent, "Is dad... not coming?"

Narae sighed. "Your father will join you later. You know he's a very busy man. But he cares about you very much and told me to wish you luck."

Little Margot nodded, heading in without much help. She tended to keep to herself.

As she grew up, her father, and the Russian government, got closer and closer to making a nuclear battery. The United States, after all, didn't have a completed version. They were close though, and Aleksandr

194

had made the correct connections to monitor the battery's progress in real time. This gave him a little more time, after years of constant work.

Narae confronted him one night. "You're home more now. Why don't you do something with your daughter?"

"Narae. You remember why we're here, don't you?" he shot back, drinking a glass of bourbon.

She clenched her jaw. "She's more than just a political chess piece, Aleksandr. She's a living, breathing person. Can't you find some way to—"

He put his drink down aggressively, cutting her off. His tense eyes looked back, clearly tired from the government barking orders at him. "Fine, fine. Whatever you say, honey."

Despite sounding like he was brushing her off, he meant it. But the way he found time to spend with Margot was a little odd.

After middle school, Aleksandr picked her up. She was happy, but he didn't say much until they got home. "Margot," he began, "Do you wanna learn how to be a badass?" He grinned.

Her face lit up. For once, she felt like he was actually acknowledged. "Hell yeah!" she responded, despite not knowing what he meant.

"How about... rock climbing?" he asked her. She was confused at first, but it soon became her favorite pastime.

Every day after school, she was strength training or challenging herself to climb another portion of the wall at the local climbing gym. She became obsessed, trying to earn more of her dad's attention as she continued to train.

But he only added on to the tasks, also suggesting that she do martial arts. Despite the ever growing demands, she pushed herself to do it all, somehow further isolating herself.

Margot still kept one person close. One good friend that her dad wasn't keen on. "Dad, can I go to Jetty with Lily again for the weekend?" Margot asked. Lily was the daughter of a neighbor to the sailboat business. But they were considered "lower class" by society. Yet, they still owned a family beach house. Likely from generations back.

Aleksandr grunted, "Yeah, sure. At least it's by my place. But don't go to too many public places, Margot."

"Why?! You say she's not supposed to go to the private school with me, but she's there every day!" Margot argued.

Aleksandr explained to her. "We worked hard to get you into a respectable private school, Margot. Their reputation isn't exactly our 'class,' I hope you know."

"I don't care!" she shouted, slamming the door. This was really her only point of contention with her parents for the longest time. It was until one day, she stopped seeing her. Neither of the parents asked.

Now almost going into high school, she had incredible grades, was a proven martial artist, and had done every course in the gym by her house. Despite all that, she had less of her dad's time than ever.

On the other side of the family, Narae watched this all happen. She liked that Margot was motivated, but saw as her father continued to pull away. He didn't speak to her much anymore. He always seemed tired. She felt more distant than ever from him.

One night, she went to talk to him. "Aleksandr... is our plan still to fix things back home?"

He didn't respond, slumped over in a chair. His eyebags were worse than ever. He propped himself up a little more, meeting Narae's gaze. "Narae. I did intend for all that. But... I don't know. I thought of training Margot to use the suit in case I was ever killed by the military. I'm glad she's achieved so much. But we don't have to drag ourselves through that. We could simply complete our mission, and return when she's an adult."

It was everything Narae had feared. She could tell he wasn't feeling like he used to, but to believe it had come to this? Betrayal washed over her.

"Is that *really* how you feel?" she angrily asked, her arms trembling.

He sighed, unmoving. "I'm tired. They'll guarantee us safety and a good life there."

"They'll destroy this place! You *know* that! They believe every inch of the Earth is theirs to conquer! And your *daughter* lives here." Narae shouted back.

"Does this country, and every other, not think exactly the same?" Aleksandr looked away, relaxing his muscles.

"No! Most people *don't* want to pillage other people's worlds!" Narae shouted at him, stomping away and up the stairs. "I thought you cared about your daughter at least, even if you didn't care about me." He was left alone, sleeping on the couch.

The family was all skewered. Margot came home, day after day, going straight to her room. It felt impossible to talk to anybody. Regardless, Narae knocked on her door.

"Margot? Do you have my cassette player again?" she asked, giving herself an in. Margot sighed, opening the door to her room.

Margot lifted the cassette player with Korean writing on it to her. "Yeah, sorry mom. It just sounds better on the cassette."

Narae took it from her. The two stood there, awkwardly. "So, how's rock climbing going?" she asked.

"Fine," Margot responded, not sure what to tell her. She already had glasses, and they started to fall off her face. She caught them, putting them back on.

"Margot. I'm sorry if this is coming out of nowhere. How much do you... *know*?" Narae asked. This caught Margot off guard.

She still knew what her mother was referencing. "You do know I was briefed on it, once. Where I really come from. Russia. The DPRK. It's also literally on your cassette player. Why else would you have bootleg American songs on cassettes? Smuggling them in, you guys didn't have streaming so this was the option. I haven't told anybody. But what am I supposed to do? Tattling would ruin my life."

Her mother never knew that she knew. "Somehow, I knew your father told you at some point. Sometimes I swear he talked to you more than me."

"Not like he really talked to me, either," Margot chuckled. The two sat on her bed.

"Has he shown you his... bunker?" Narae asked. Margot nodded.

"That and the Steel Devil, facing completion. And then you two want to move back, right?" Margot asked. Narae shook her head.

"I don't want any of that. I wish we could fix some of the issues in this world, but I want to stay here," Narae

198

admitted. She felt a tinge of awkwardness. "I shouldn't put this on you. This is for adults to figure out. Maybe... I can talk to him."

Margot nodded, letting her go. She gave her back the cassette with the one song she loved in it. After the conversation, Narae had the courage to face her husband.

Narae found her way to the bunker, the entrance imposing like a chasm. At the bottom, the space opened up into a surprisingly large, well-lit chamber. Wires snaked across the floor, connecting an array of blinking monitors and humming machinery. And in the center of it all, bathed in the cool glow of overhead lights, stood the Steel Devil, in completion.

Aleksandr stood beside it, a smirk on his face. He turned as he heard her footsteps. "Narae. Perfect timing. It's done. Our ticket home." He gestured grandly at the suit. "Stole the schematics to the nuclear battery. Every fragment of this has one now. As for the Americans, I destroyed any trace of success. We'll be the only ones with this technology.

Narae's gaze hardened. "Home? Is that what you call it? A golden cage for the two of us?"

Aleksandr scoffed, walking towards her. "Don't be dramatic. We'll be heroes, Narae. Royalty. The world will bow before us, thanks to this. We can finally return, live the life we always dreamed of, without this... charade." He swept his hand around the bunker.

"The charade was blending in, Aleksandr. Not destroying everything we built here," she countered, her voice low. "This bunker wasn't for hiding from *the Americans*. It was for hiding from *both* of them. From all governments. We could have a life here. We could use this suit as a threat to never mess with us."

199

He stopped, his eyes narrowing. "Free? You think we're free here? We're still pawns, Narae. Always have been. Always will be. We can just do it more comfortably back home. Free from these babbling idiots..."

"And what about Margot!?" Narae asked, her voice trembling slightly with suppressed rage. "What about the life she has here? The one you helped build, even if you didn't mean to?"

Aleksandr laughed, a harsh, dismissive sound. "She's a part of the plan, a means to an end. She was always meant to be. Just like you."

The words hit Narae like a physical blow. The last shred of hope she held for him, for their future together, shattered. He truly saw them as expendable, as tools for his ambition.

"Of course. That's always been you, Aleksandr," she whispered, tears running hot down her cheeks. She grabbed a pistol, laying out on one of the tables with ammo nearby.

He turned back to the suit, his hand reaching out for the sleek, cold metal. "You're really going to turn against me? I'll return home alone, if I have to!"

He began to lift his arm, preparing to step into the Steel Devil. Narae aimed without a second thought. She raised it and fired. The bullet went through his skull, killing him instantly. The liquid metal released, causing his body to fall to the ground below.

Outside of the bunker, still years before Godsend, Narae ran for her life. It was only a matter of time before the other operators of the "sailboat business" found out that Aleksandr wasn't responding anymore.

She burst into the house, her mind racing. Margot heard the door swing open downstairs.

"Mom? What's going on?" Margot asked, walking down the stairs, rubbing her eyes. She'd been fast asleep.

Narae didn't respond. She just stared at her daughter, her chest heaving, tears streaming down her face.

"Mom, you're scaring me. What happened?" Margot pressed, a knot forming in her stomach.

Narae stumbled forward, pulling Margot into a fierce, desperate hug. Her hands were shaking as she clutched Margot's shoulders. "We have to go. Now. Get everything you need, quickly."

"Go? Where? Why?" Margot was bewildered. Her mother was never like this.

"There's no time to explain," Narae whispered, her voice hoarse. She released Margot, pushing her gently towards the stairs. "Just trust me. Your father... he's gone. And if we don't leave, we'll be next."

Margot froze, her mind struggling to comprehend. *Gone?* Her father? A wave of fear washed over her. "What do you mean, gone?"

Narae shook her head, tears still falling. "Just... pack everything important. That's our only option."

Margot, seeing the raw terror in her mother's eyes, didn't argue further. She raced upstairs, her heart pounding. She grabbed a small backpack, stuffing it with a

201

few changes of clothes, her cassette player, and the photo of her and Lily at Jetty Beach. She hesitated for a moment, looking at the familiar objects in her room, the life she was leaving behind. It felt unreal.

When she came back downstairs, Narae was already by the front door, a small duffel bag clutched in her hand. She looked even more frantic. "Is that all you have?"

Margot nodded, confused by her mother's sparse belongings. She noticed a compacted metallic disc, not something she had ever seen before. "Where's your stuff, Mom?"

"No time for that," Narae said, already pulling open the door. "We have to go before they realize. Before they find us. We'll take a way that they can't track."

"Who?" Margot demanded, but Narae was already half out the door, pulling Margot along.

They ran. Breezing through the quiet suburban streets, the night air pressing up against Margot's face. Narae didn't look back, her focus solely on moving forward. They didn't speak, leaving only the sounds of desperate breaths and footsteps.

They finally stopped at a bus station on the edge of town, a dimly lit, deserted place. Narae pulled out a wad of cash, buying two tickets to a city Margot had never heard of, a small town hundreds of miles away.

As they sat on the bus, Margot finally found her voice again. "Mom, please. Tell me what happened."

Narae looked out the window, her expression unreadable in the passing streetlights. "He… he wasn't honest about who he was, honey." Her voice was devoid of emotion, a chilling contrast to her earlier panic.

"What do you mean!?" Margot whispered, her stomach churning.

Narae turned to her, her eyes hollow. "He was going to go back to the Russian government. I don't even know if he really *ever* meant he wanted to change things. Maybe he was just stinging me along. But... I had to stop him from taking the suit there— and stop him from betraying us."

Margot was completely lost. *Betray? What was she talking about?* "What did he do?" Margot asked, a desperate tone in her voice.

Narae sighed, a long, weary sound. "He said he didn't mind returning home alone. Back to Russia. I had to... stop him."

Before she had time to explain further, two gruff men burst into the small building where they had purchased tickets.

"FREEZE!" one of the men shouted, his voice echoing in the small, empty bus station. He held up a device, a small black box with a blinking red light. "We know you're here, Narae Davis!"

Narae's eyes widened in terror. She shoved Margot forward. "Run, Margot! They won't come after *you*. Get on the bus!"

Margot, still reeling from her mother's confession, hesitated for only a second. The men were moving fast, already closing the distance with their firearms in hand. The bus driver, oblivious to the drama unfolding behind him, was about to close the doors.

"Now!" Narae screamed, pushing her daughter with surprising force, sending her onto the bus.

Margot fell to the bus floor, looking back just as the first man reached her mother. A struggle ensued, brief but brutal. As the bus started to move, the driver seeing the dangerous situation, Margot noticed the compacted metal disc had been shoved on with her.

"**MOM**!" Margot cried out, reaching out for her as the bus accelerated. Through the grimy window, Margot saw a flash of movement, a blur of fists and dark uniforms. Then, a sharp, sickening sound. Her mother collapsed, and was now out of sight.

Margot, tears streaming down her face, slumped herself forward onto the glass between her and the outside, clutching the metallic disc to her chest. The small town, her home, the only life she had ever known, was rapidly disappearing in the rearview mirror. Her father was gone, her mother was dead, and she was alone. The only thing left with her now was the metallic disc. The disc that she would soon find out was the project that could bring down countries on its own.

But Margot would do nothing with this disc. Horrified of where it came from, Margot buried it for years. She attempted to move on, using the luxurious funds left over by the Russian government to get by. She was never in financial peril, thanks to her father giving her ample amounts of funding to support her. But she got an apartment, and she tried to move on.

Living now seemed impossible. How could she ignore the things she had been through? Every day, more corrupt men were cast under the spotlight. More men and women that remind her of her father. The man she hated most.

Aleksandr was going to give everything away for riches and the profits of the men greedily going after domination of the world. Margot realized after living alone, being with the common folk, that he wasn't alone. Nearly every powerful person around her was in the same boat. She couldn't fathom the amounts of corruption she witnessed. It was comedic.

Despite trying to be her own person, despite trying to move on, the past kept luring her in. She figured there was no way for her to change things. Every time she thought about doing something about it, the memory of her mother would curl up like a pit in her gut. It terrified her. So she just worked as a waitress, trying to get by.

One night, she lost her mind. "I'm... home," she blabbered, coming back into her apartment after a late shift. She already swiped a few margaritas from the bar. The dark loneliness of her apartment drove her into further despair.

On the floor was a slip. She was genuinely confused at what it was initially. But then, it came into clear view. *An eviction notice?*

"I'VE NEVER HAD A LATE PAYMENT!" she shouted, tearing up the pink slip. Her arms were shaking, her nerves getting to her. She poured another shot to calm her nerves. At this point, she was a functioning alcoholic.

After passing out, and waking up when her apartment's office hours were, she stormed to the property manager.

"WHAT THE HELL IS THIS?" she shoved the taped-up pink slip in the property manager's face.

"Sorry, Margot. We have to make space for another tenant. Your... coming home late has become a nuisance to the other tenants," the property manager explained to her.

"This has to be illegal. There's no way you're just... making me leave! That's when I work 'til, it's not my fault!" she desperately pleaded.

The property manager shook his head. "The new bill passed under President Hulls states that we can evict any tenant who is being a nuisance to others."

"WHAT?!" she continued to argue. But it was too late. She had to pack up and leave in the next week.

That night, she went out drinking. She couldn't figure out what the point was anymore. She just wanted to feel okay.

The chill of the autumn night caused Margot's breath to be visible. The city lights, once a comforting glow, now mocked her with their indifference. Each passing car seemed to carry people with lives, with homes, with futures. She had none of it. Her family, gone. Her home, stolen. Her very existence, deemed a nuisance.

She lifted the nearly empty bottle to her lips, the last drops of the cheap liquor doing little to dull the sharp edges of her despair. Tears, hot and bitter, mingled with the rain that had begun to fall down her cheeks. Time and memory constantly forcing her into the pits of her own mind.

"What's left?" she slurred to the indifferent pavement, her voice cracking. "Ain't shit left."

She closed her eyes, wishing for an end, for the oasis that the alcohol promised but never delivered. She fell to the cold ground, her jacket barely padding behind her. Laying there for a while, she thought maybe she could drift away.

But that wasn't what was in store for her. A burning memory surfaced. Her mother wanted to make things right. She wanted to believe in fixing things, regardless of where they were. *Could I do that?*

Margot's eyes fluttered open. The streetlights blurred, but the image of her mother's face materialized in her mind's eye. Her mother, who had fought, who had risked everything, for a better world. Her mother, who had refused to let a weapon of control fall into the wrong hands.

A fire ignited within her, small and fragile at first, but stubbornly persistent. What had all those close to her died for, if not for this? To fix this brokenness, to defy the greed of the world. She had the means, the very tool her father had created and her mother had sacrificed for. The metallic disc, buried deep and long forgotten in her apartment, suddenly felt like a beacon, a dangerous, terrifying, yet undeniable path forward. With that, she could finally complete a certain promise she made. One for the Hallowed.

She had a place outside of the reach of governments, her father's abandoned bunker. A place she could go to hide the suit and store it safely.

She pushed herself up, her limbs heavy and uncooperative. The cold concrete floor had served its purpose. It was here, in the depths of her despair, that a new resolve hardened. She would use it. She would use everything she had, every ounce of her training, every piece of her shattered past, to fix what was broken.

"My mother and Lily both loved many people in this world." Margot, now smiling with her tears drying, got up. "What did she call what she loved... 'Hallowed' to her?"

With a twisted, burning desire, Margot sprinted forward. She no longer cared if she got it right. She no longer cared about the strength of the world pushing her down. She would prevent the end of the 'Hallowed' people. She would follow up on the desires of the past. The first part of that was moving back to Philadelphia, along with joining an Alcoholics Anonymous group. Sobered up, she was sure she could use *that* weapon against greed itself.

When she finally arrived at the bunker, a space she followed her father too long ago, it was empty and musty. Not used for years. The Russians must have abandoned it quickly, seeing that they had left a pile of decayed bones lying on the floor. It was a safe bet to believe they weren't returning. She promptly removed the evidence of anybody ever being there. She looked in disgust, remarking, "It's time for your burial."

Not too long later, she had become the enigmatic 'Godsend.' For years she trained indoors to attain mastery over the suit. When she chose to go to apprehend robbers as the suit's first appearance, the people had a new name for the suit created to be a devil. She was now determined to be a savior, someone to change the corrupt reality that she lived in. She was willing to do *anything* to meet this end. Even if she had to fight, or succumb to the will of the armor itself.

She walked back into the bunker, Calvin sitting on a chair by the computers. "Calvin. I have a new task for you." She handed him a piece of paper.

He soundlessly accepted it, reading it over. It was a speech. One to the people. To Calvin, it seemed like a dangerous rally cry.

"Are you sure you want a call-to-action message *now*?" Calvin asked, seeming apprehensive about the whole situation. Calvin, seeing Margot's face, was terrified. She looked more angry than ever.

Margot beamed down at him. "This is how we rebirth an era of the hallowed people. We bring people like them to justice. I warned them time and time again to change their ways. If they don't want to, that's their choice. But they'll have to accept the consequences."

He nodded, quickly getting off his chair. He saw the time, and the speech would be best told to the people as soon as possible, before the government had time to prepare a statement against what happened between 'Godsend' and Amara.

Hours later, Calvin looked out on the desolate streets of Philadelphia. The income checkpoints, the divide between the have and have-nots. The city was as tired and broken as Margot was the day she lost everything. With Margot behind him, using nano bots from her suit to give the illusion he was levitating with his fake suit, he was ready to go.

Margot nodded to Calvin. He jumped off a ledge, flying out above the many in the city. A giant *whoosh* sound alerted people to his presence.

People began to look up, seeing the prophetic presence that appeared to them as *Godsend*.

"**HALLOWED, BENEVOLENT, PEOPLE OF THE BROKEN. HEAR MY CRY TO YOU,**" Calvin began, the speakers around him boosting his voice to around the entire city. "**THE TENDRILS OF GREED REFUSE TO LOOSEN. THEY PLUNDER YOUR WAGES AND TAKE ADVANTAGE OF YOU. THEY STEAL YOUR TIME AWAY, TAKING HOURS OF YOUR LIFE AWAY FROM YOU. THEY TAKE THE ESSENCE OF YOUR LIFE AND COAT THEIR OWN WITH IT.**"

More and more people gathered. More streams on the internet now showed Calvin's face. Organizations and governments were immediately on it, seeing what their options were.

Calvin continued, letting the thousands hear his plea. "**THEY HAVE BEEN WARNED. YET THEY STILL STEAL. THEY BELIEVE YOU'LL DO NOTHING ABOUT IT,**

REMAINING POWERLESS AS EVER. THEY AREN'T AFRAID OF ME, BUT MY MESSAGE. MY MESSAGE TO YOU HALLOWED, BEAUTIFUL HUMANS. THEY FEAR YOU MAKING THE REALIZATION THAT YOU *CAN* FIGHT BACK!"

The people in the streets erupted into a roar. Calvin raised up his hand, making his face visible to the masses. They all shouted in unison, all in a ferocious battle cry. They too, lifting up their arms.

Suddenly, a bullet flew toward Calvin. A nanobot caught it, bringing it in front of him.

"EVEN NOW, THEY WANT ME GONE. THEY WANT YOU GONE. HOLD THEM ACCOUNTABLE. LET THEM KNOW, WE WON'T JUST STAND HERE AND TAKE IT!"

The crowd erupted again. People stormed off in different ways just as the police arrived.

Calvin made one last announcement. **"LET THEM ATTEMPT TO CONTINUE TAKING FROM YOU. THEY WILL SEE ME REAPPEAR FROM THE SHADOWS."**

He then retreated, Margot bringing him back in, and quickly boosting them out of the area using the suit. The two retreated as the everyday person and her had a reiterated goal: to fix the broken.

"There's really no coming back from this, Margot..." Calvin warned her as the two flew back toward the bunker.

Margot smirked, her face tense. Her face was a mix of angry and twisted emotions. "Not once in my life was there a chance to go back."

The uneasy feeling of chaos filled the days after Calvin's most recent appearance. Most politicians hadn't made a public appearance since. President Hulls had gone mostly radio silent as the news continued to try and sweep Godsend under the rug. It wasn't working.

On one hand, glorious protests were being won. Bosses were caving to workers. Many of the ultra-rich did as the smashed building said and retired. Greed, in the eye of the public, wasn't glorified anymore.

On the other hand, bad actors saw this as an opportunity to pillage stores and create disruption, the exact thing that Margot put an end to during her first appearance as Godsend. But despite the commotion, there had not been another 'Godsend' appearance either.

Seeing what the conditions were, Hazel worried for her colleagues. While the chat for the alcoholics anonymous group had become quiet due to recent events, she didn't care. She texted the group.

"**HAZEL**: *So are we still doing our group later today?*" is what popped up on everyone else's phones that Thursday. After a minute of waiting, a reply came through.

"**PASTOR ALAN**: *I will still be there for those of you coming. The group is still on as far as I am concerned.*"

After that, the chat went silent again. But Hazel, spinning on an office chair in her shared apartment, thought that was enough.

Hazel, later in the day, walked up to the church. The usual chatter outside was notably absent, replaced by the quiet hum of the nearby lights. She walked into the familiar doorway, and into room 109.

"Sorry I'm late!" Hazel, thinking they may have started without her, burst into the room. But there were even less people than she expected. Pastor Alan sat with Margot, Milo, and Amara.

Calvin hadn't been in a while, but Hazel wasn't expecting Owen and Declan to randomly no-show.

"Don't worry about it. I hadn't heard from Declan or Owen, so we were waiting for them as well. Seems they may just be busy, though," Pastor Alan let Hazel know as she pulled up a chair as well.

"I tried calling them, but neither of them picked up," Amara said, her voice a little hoarse. She had a few visible bruises on her face, and a fresh scrape on her arm, evidence of the chaos at City Hall. She seemed to be trying to play it off, but her posture was stiff.

Margot watched Amara, a pang of guilt hitting her. She knew exactly why Amara looked so roughed up. The images of the "Masked Rebel" being tossed around by both the military and her as "Godsend" flashed in her memory. *I really am sorry, Amara. But you were standing in the way.*

"Well, let's go around the room then," Pastor Alan said, seemingly oblivious to the tension, or perhaps choosing to ignore it. "Hazel, why don't you start us off?"

Hazel nodded, straightening up in her chair. "Alright. So, things have been... intense. With Godsend's recent appearance, and all the protests, it's like the world's been turned upside down. It's hard to focus on... well, on sobriety. Especially when everything feels so chaotic. But I'm here. One day at a time, right?"

"That's right, Hazel," Pastor Alan affirmed. "The world will always have its storms, but we find our calm within ourselves." He then turned to Margot. "Margot, how about you?"

Margot shifted, playing her part as a normal person. "It's... been a lot to take in," she said, choosing her words carefully. "Seeing the protests, seeing people react... It's a powerful thing. It makes you think about what really matters. And I've been trying to keep my head straight, to not let the... external chaos, affect my 'internal peace.'" She glanced at Amara again, her gaze lingering on the bruise above her eye. *I just want to fix this world, Amara. Please don't get in my way again.*

Pastor Alan nodded, a gentle smile on his face. "Indeed. And Amara?"

Amara sighed, a small, tired sound. "I... I was at the protest at City Hall," she admitted, her voice low. She figured after news broke out, they all knew about her antics against Godsend. "I saw firsthand how... how easily things can go wrong. How quickly a good cause can turn into a battleground." She flexed her injured arm slightly. "It was... sobering. Sobering in a different way. It made me realize that even when you're trying to do the right thing, there are always unintended consequences." She looked down at her hands, clenching them.

"Thank you for sharing, Amara," Pastor Alan said softly. "It takes great courage to confront such difficult experiences. Milo?"

Milo, who had been unusually quiet, cleared his throat. "Well, after hearing Amara, I guess my week wasn't *that* eventful. But... it was still weird, seeing everything on the news. It's all so... extreme. I'm just trying to keep a low profile, honestly. And stay away from... well, from anything that might lead me back to old habits." He fidgeted with his hands, avoiding eye contact with anyone.

Pastor Alan, ever chipper, nodded at Milo's statements. But before he could respond, or lead them to the next topic, a loud set of footsteps banged down the hallway outside. It wouldn't be unusual to have church guests, but it sounded like a weighty, forceful group of people approaching. It quickly put everyone on guard.

What the hell? Margot thought, her mind racing. *Did they find me? I don't have the suit on me!*

The doors to the room crashed open as a large group of military men in tactical gear held both Declan and Owen captive with mouth guards. They quickly pressed into the room, pointing weapons at the other attendees.

"GO, GO, GO!" one of them shouted. The attendees didn't even have time to think they immediately put their hands up as Owen and Declan were quickly shoved over to where the rest of the group was.

Behind the group, coming through the door last, was Detective Miller with a camera.

"CALVIN BECKER! I COULDN'T REACH YOU, SO HOPEFULLY YOU CATCH THIS STREAM!" Miller shouted, his boots clashing with the floor as he stomped forward. He pointed behind himself, where he now had the majority of the group on his camera feed.

"Bleh, what the hell?!" Hazel coughed as dust around her was whipped up by the commotion.

"YOU WANT TO PLAY THIS GAME, CALVIN? WHERE YOU GET TO DICTATE RIGHT FROM WRONG? YOU GIVE US NO CHOICE BUT TO HOLD THEM HOSTAGE! REALIZE NOW THAT YOU'RE ONLY DECIDING JUSTICE FOR YOURSELF!" Miller continued his theatrics, beaming into the camera.

In the background of the footage, Margot was clearly shaking her head. She grit her teeth, knowing exactly the kind of trap Calvin was going to get himself into.

He doesn't even know where the suit is, but he'll find this stream for sure, Margot thought, *But dammit, don't come here! I'll figure this out!* She attempted to make more signs telling him not to come.

But Calvin was indeed watching from the bunker. He watched the feed immediately get traction. The government was now pointing loaded assault rifles at civilians, just to get *his* attention.

His hands trembled, not with fear, but with a surge of fury that threatened to consume him. *Hostages.* The word echoed in his mind, overlaying Miller's sneering face. *They're using them.* He saw Margot, shaking her head, her lips forming silent pleas. *Don't come.* But he couldn't ignore it. This was his group, the people he once called friends, caught in a trap set for him.

"*Godsend,*" Calvin muttered, his voice barely a whisper. He looked at the compacted suit on Margot's workbench, the very one he had worn, the one that had given him a taste of true power. He knew it wasn't the real thing, not like the one Margot wore, but it was enough to make a statement. It was enough to get him in there, to buy time.

He slammed his fist on the desk. "They want me to show up? Fine. I'll show up." He grabbed the fake suit, his movements swift and determined. He knew it was a desperate gamble, a chaotic response to a calculated move, but he couldn't sit back and watch. He wouldn't. After all, *this is Calvin we were talking about.* A man of war.

He burst out the bunker doors, concealing weapons. He then realized that some of the nanobots from the main suit were still attached to the fake one. It allowed him to do a controlled hover. After pushing off the side of the hill, he hovered at motor-vehicle speeds toward the church.

He thought of a plan of action. *I just have to distract them long enough so they step away from Shepheard Church. Margot will get them out of there after that.* He knew at that point that different cameras were likely already picking up his location.

He flew above the highway, now passing cars with built momentum. As he neared the church, he noticed an armored convoy already forming a perimeter. Miller, always one step ahead, had anticipated his arrival. Calvin cursed under his breath. He had to draw them away, create a diversion. He spotted a large, unoccupied building a few blocks away, a defunct corporate office with gleaming glass facades. *Perfect.*

He turned sharply, aiming for the building, boosting his speed with the borrowed nanobots. He knew the fake suit wouldn't hold up to direct engagement, but he could create enough of a distraction to grab their attention. He ascended, a dark silhouette against the city lights, the faint hum of the nanobots barely audible over the rush of wind.

Miller's voice, amplified by the camera feed, echoed from the church. *"Don't waste a second chasing him. Keep your aim on the targets."*

Damn, saw through me, Calvin thought. Miller was too good, too focused on his objective. The convoy at the church didn't budge. Their weapons remained trained on the doors, on the innocent people inside. His eyes darted to the church, then back to the building he was approaching. He had to try something.

"STAY STILL, THEN," Calvin mimicked the usual Godsend script, holding his hand out as if he was going to shoot a blast of energy. This suit couldn't actually do it, but he hoped Miller would fall for the bluff. Nothing happened.

"*Shoot already.*" Miller was taunting him at this point. His voice sounded unimpressed coming from the speaker at the convoy. "*We're too close to your friends for you to do something that damaging. Plus, murder hasn't been in the cards for you. Killing isn't your thing.*"

"**NOT YET**," Calvin threatened, jumping off the building and quickly hovering down. His eyes scanned the church's exterior, trying to remember any leads. *The courtyard.* There was a sewer access door there, he recalled from one of their earlier AA meetings. One of those manholes hidden by overgrown bushes. He thought he might be able to bypass the main entrance and get closer to the group. But he needed a bigger distraction.

Miller burst out the main entrance. "Take him in," Miller suddenly ordered. The military convoy aimed at him as soon as he took out a pistol. He aimed down the sight, hitting a fire alarm on the outside of the church.

A shrill, piercing wail immediately tore through the air, momentarily stunning the military personnel. A chaotic murmur rose from the streets as people looked around, confused.

"What the hell was that?" Miller's voice, now tinged with irritation, was just another distraction. "Don't check the fire alarm! It's a diversion! Don't let him—" Miller cut himself off, seeing that Calvin was already gone.

Calvin used the momentary disarray, boosting with the nanobots into a nearby manhole. After quickly throwing the cover back, he sprinted through the sewer straight toward the other cover under the church courtyard.

Meanwhile, a soldier noticed an oddity. "Sir... did Godsend just use a firearm?"

Miller, caught up in everything going on, hadn't even noticed. Their actions were indeed very off for the normal Godsend, lending credence to the two-suit theory. But Miller, knowing that the government just wanted Godsend gone, didn't want to confirm anything just yet.

"It's something we've seen him *almost* do before, but we need to *FIND HIM!*" Miller lied through his teeth, trying to get the convoy back on track.

At that moment, Calvin burst through the manhole at the church courtyard. He landed, using the manhole cover as a shield with his weapon in his other hand. Guards positioned on either side of him started firing, the bullets bounced off of the manhole cover. Calvin shot at the sky, diverting their attention. He then knocked them out of the way with the manhole cover as he burst into the building.

"**YOU THREATEN INNOCENTS, YOU'LL GET ME**," Calvin declared, fighting through more military guards, pulling off what seemed like a miracle. Margot still sat with guns drawn on her, unhappy with the situation. No matter what, she didn't see an easy way out of this.

Calvin, fueled by a surge of righteous anger, flew through the halls. Two guards, momentarily stunned by his sudden appearance, raised their rifles. Calvin didn't hesitate. He slammed the manhole cover into the first guard's chest, sending him sprawling, then spun and delivered a powerful kick to the second's knee.

"Get back!" Miller's voice bellowed, as more agents poured in from the main entrance. "Don't let him near them!"

But Calvin was already there. He lunged, his borrowed nanobots giving him just enough burst to reach the room with the group in it. He threw the first two guards out the front door, and tossed the manhole cover across the room like a frisbee to knock the third out a window.

The Godsend mask mechanically moved upward, revealing Calvin's face. "You guys miss me?" he smirked as he broke down the wall.

"Calvin, the church is gonna have to pay for that!" Pastor Alan complained as Calvin undid their restraints. They both heard banging noises as the guards attempted to break into the room.

"As long as we leave alive, we'll figure it out," Calvin assured him, dragging the others who were tied up on chairs into the other room. This other room was mostly tile, used for the Sunday school there. Calvin threw a table into the hole in the wall, blocking it momentarily.

Amara, now untied, suddenly headbutted Calvin as he turned around. "That's for making me look stupid. I'll save the rest for later."

"Glad we can be on the same page— for now," Calvin projected over the sounds of the military breaking down the door in the other room.

Margot, also now untied, looked toward Calvin with a glare. He looked back with a half smile. He was looking for approval— she wasn't giving any.

"Calvin, what was the point of coming here? You didn't need to. They wouldn't have killed us," Margot asked, still trying to seem unassociated.

Calvin's half smile disappeared. "You don't know that. They're getting crazier every day."

"Yeah, well, now we're stuck here!" Declan complained, now free, gesturing around the small, tiled room. The banging on the barricaded door intensified. "You didn't think this through, did you?"

Calvin rolled his eyes, a glint of frustration in them. "Relax, I've got it. Just need a moment." He looked up at the ceiling, assessing the old plaster and wooden beams. "Everyone, get ready. We're going up."

He jumped, boosting with the nanobots still clinging to his fake suit, slamming his shoulder into the ceiling. Dust and plaster rained down. He hit it again and a large hole appeared, revealing the dark, unused attic space above them.

"One by one!" Calvin shouted over the splintering of walls behind them. "Milo, you're closest. So you're first!"

Milo, looking terrified, scrambled up, pulling himself through the makeshift opening. Pastor Alan followed, then Hazel and Amara. Their movements were clumsy but quick.

"This better go well, for all the shit you've pulled," Declan gave Calvin the evil eye.

"You got this bro. Kick their asses," Owen added as he escaped above with Declan.

"Oh, haha. Thanks, bro," Calvin responded, unsure where the sudden admiration came from.

Finally, only Margot and Calvin remained in the chaotic room. The cracking of wood was getting closer behind them.

Margot's muscles tensed. "Calvin, you don't even have the suit, so why?"

Calvin ignored the commotion around them for a moment. "I couldn't leave you to die."

"This was *meant* to trap you. They have weapons out there to take out the real suit! How does this end well for anybody?!" Margot, frustrated, berated Calvin. His hands shook. He had no response. She huffed, continuing anyway, "Seriously, Calvin. I chose you for who you were, not these superhero antics!"

Calvin looked down at himself in the suit. These were not the limbs of Godsend. These were his own, fleshy, mortal limbs. He had been high of the idea of Godsend. Panic began to set it. His breathing got harsher and faster, all accelerating until...

No... Calvin thought, *I can still be Godsend.* He exhaled deeply. He thought back to the days he endured before meeting Margot.

"Margot," he began, his voice now low, "Before you, I had to be a prideful jerk. It was the only way I knew how to exist, because I wasn't anybody before. I was the tool of my family of rich assholes. That was it." He tightened his grip, forcing a smile. "Now I can finally *be* someone. That's all I care. Even if I'm just your partner in war."

Margot shook her head. She was determined to find a way out of this. "Calvin, we might be able to escape—"

"No." he cut her off, "It's me they want. They won't kill you if they think they have *Godsend*." Calvin picked up Margot, throwing her into the attic space.

"DON'T DO THIS!" she shrieked back at him. He forced another grin as the military finally broke into the room. The mask flipped back on to his face.

"**BEGONE, TOOLS OF GREED**!" He threw some of the nanobots off of himself, causing them to collide with the soldiers. But this now meant he had less boost capacity.

He crashed through the windows, flying above the military convoy. "**THESE TRICKS OF MANIPULATION WON'T WORK ON ME, MILLER!**" Calvin boomed, hovering overhead. He started to boost upward.

Miller screamed, a raw, frustrated sound tearing from his throat. "FIRE! ALL OF YOU! DON'T LET HIM ESCAPE!"

A torrent of bullets ripped through the air, converging on Calvin's ascending figure. But with each desperate boost, each minute tilt of his body, he seemed to dance between the deadly projectiles. They whizzed by, harmlessly missing his limbs, a symphony to his waltz into the sky.

"HOW IS HE DOING THAT?!" Miller roared, his face contorted in anger. He watched, furious, as Calvin became a speck against the clouds. He stood at even height with the tallest buildings in downtown. "GET HIM DOWN! GET HIM DOWN, NOW!"

Calvin looked upon the cityscape. It was his own, personal hell. A mob mentality to falsify one's social status. A bunch of wannabe rich folk, all faking it, driving each other to depravity. The income checkpoints, a stark reminder of where people drew the line. Money was this city's god, and likely the world's. He was rising above it.

"**TO ALL THE AUTOCRATS AND OLIGARCHS, I PRAY YOU KNOW THE WORLD WILL NO LONGER STAND IDLY BY. THEY KNOW YOU NOW, AND THEY WON'T FORGET**!" Calvin's filtered voice pierced through the speakers of the nanobots, filling the city. He raised his arms high, looking up at the clouds— now in his hands.

Snipers suddenly positioned themselves among the rooftops around the city. But Calvin peered back down. He had gathered quite the audience, also while saving Margot.

He grinned. "I win," were the words he muttered as a lone bullet broke through his chest. It pierced the suit, causing him to start to free-fall. Before his body could even reach the ground, it was full of bullets.

The suit shattered as Calvin's already lifeless body crashed onto the pavement below. The military quickly surrounded him, unsure of how their bullets suddenly began to work. Miller was speechless as a unit came, taking away Calvin's body in a bag.

Behind him, the others had come out of the church when the military had left the building. They watched in horror as Calvin's body was taken away. The others started to shout, saying something bad to the military people there. Something Margot couldn't hear.

She fell to her knees, seeing Calvin being taken away. *No... no, no, no...* She couldn't believe it. Were those her last words to him? Did the world just take another from her? She went numb. Her ears heard something, her brain didn't process it. Tears welled up. *I didn't care. He was just a tool!*

She couldn't really convince herself of that. Her brain didn't want to, but it still processed the images she saw. Even the people on the street Calvin rallied started to heckle the military people as they took away the body.

Just a partner in war. How could you be satisfied with something as simple as that? Margot's eyes could barely see through the distortions caused by tears.

Miller exhaled, slapping himself on the cheek. "We got him. The infamous *Godsend.*" It was as if he didn't believe it.

Margot could only despair at the sight in front of her as the military fled the scene.

The others from the group stayed sitting on the stairs of the church long after Calvin had been taken away. It was dark and cold out, but they still felt like moving on that soon would be wrong.

Hazel, looking around, noticed Margot's absence. "Wonder if Margot made it home okay." She had left, tears in her eyes, nearly right after the incident.

"I think the whole thing was just... a little much for her," Amara added as the somber group took in the dreadful atmosphere.

Owen was a distraught mess. He hadn't really said anything aloud, but had been whispering things under his breath. Declan, getting annoyed by this, would target him.

"Owen, we were *both* captured. I get it you're pissed. I'm sure as hell pissed, look at this goddamn mess. But you need to talk about it or you're just gonna feel miserable!" Declan blew up at Owen a little. Despite his harsh words, everyone could tell he secretly just wanted to make sure he was okay.

"The hell do you want me to say?" Owen's tone didn't match his usual mood. "We're down the shitter, Declan. We're done for! Godsend was the one man keeping the powerful in check. Checks and balances? Don't make me laugh. All those goddamn guys are getting Sunday brunch behind the curtains— after pissing each other off live. They can't wait to take a bite of this place without Calvin."

Declan looked as if he were ready to argue back, but he stopped himself. He realized whatever he was about to say would have just been targeted at fighting back, not

224

at getting closer to any kind of truth. So he stood there, accepting his words.

"Do you guys really think that the people are just going to forget all of the sudden?" Amara interrupted. Everyone starkly turned, her words desperately grabbing their attention. "Calvin's final words were that the world would no longer stand idly by. They *didn't*. They didn't even let the military get away with his body without heckling them."

Hazel got up, standing by Amara. "She's right, you know. I mean, sheesh, with the help of her dad, they passed bill 743. That's something tangible. You saw it at your work, Declan, didn't you?"

He scratched his head. "I heard about it. Think the manager was talking about getting rid of some of those machines. They were getting old anyway," Declan explained.

"But now more humans are getting jobs. All because of a few people making the right connections and getting things passed," Hazel extrapolated, "Cartoonishly evil groups like Darkstone win when we think there's nothing we can do about it. I guarantee you, with Godsend gone, they're going to try and show the amount of control and power they have. They'll brag, I'm positive. But the last message was not one of defeat."

The group went silent again. Hazel looked to them all, seeking approval. They still seemed distant.

"I don't know, Hazel," Milo spoke up, "I think that sounds right. It's just... I can't feel right just moving on like that. We barely got to see him, or *actually* reunite with him. He just went out on a last stand, suddenly sounding like the old Calvin I knew. It's bitter, seeing a friend who was a star go."

She looked down, her eyes covered by her hair now. The group's silence indicated they felt similar.

Hazel, exhaling, looked back up. "You're right... I just wanted to carry on his last message. One of everyone's power, not just his. Even your power, Milo, to change things."

Pastor Alan, who had been busy assessing the damage in the church, walked back over to hear that part. "He's in a better place now. I'm so sorry you had to experience that. We'll have to install a church security system."

Declan scoffed. "Don't bother. Nothing that crazy will happen again."

"One can only hope," Pastor Alan responded, looking up into the sky where Calvin flew to his final fate. The others followed his gaze, knowing soon that this would just be another memory. One by one, they resigned themselves to accepting that. They all dispersed at their own time.

Margot, having left early, was the most distraught of them all. Earlier, she had roamed the streets. Unsure where to go both physically and emotionally, her vision blurred as she stumbled through what looked like city streets. The darkness grew around her, eventually only showing the city lights through her dizzy vision.

The blurry city lights became streaks of color, then indistinct blurs. The ground beneath her feet swayed, a cruel mockery of stability. She was falling, not physically, but internally, a precipitous drop into an emotionally bottomless chasm.

Her legs, numb and unresponsive, somehow carried her. Her vision, a kaleidoscope of distorted shapes, eventually honed in on a faint glow in the distance. A beacon in her personal storm. Some sort of establishment in front of her.

She stumbled through the doorway, the sudden warmth and the clatter of glasses assaulting her senses. The smell of stale beer and cheap perfume hit her first, then the low murmur of conversations, too loud, too close. It must've been a bar. She bumped into a table, sending a chair scraping across the floor. A few heads turned, but no one cared enough to comment. Just another drunk, another lost soul in the city's endless night. She hadn't even had a sip yet.

She found an empty stool at the far end of the bar, practically falling onto it. The bartender, a burly man with a faded tattoo on his forearm, merely grunted in acknowledgment.

"Give me whatever," Margot slurred, her voice thick and unfamiliar. "A shot. Make it a double. Tequila I guess." The burning liquid slid down her throat, searing a path of brief, blissful numbness. It was a desperate attempt to drown the image of Calvin's shattered body, to silence the inner demon parroting all her loved ones' deaths.

"Another," she mumbled, pushing the empty glass across the wooden counter. The bartender obliged, his face uncaring. Each refill chipped away at the fragile wall she had built around her sobriety, a wall now crumbling under the weight of grief and guilt. She was supposed to be better than this. She was supposed to be the solution, the savior, the unwavering force that fixed the broken. But here she was, succumbing to the very escape she had once sworn off.

With each drink, the world grew hazier, the edges of her pain softening into a dull throb. The faces of her parents, Calvin, Lily, all blurred into the background of her mind. The suit, the power, the mission—it all seemed too much to bear. Too hard to go back to.

What was the point? She thought, *What was left when everyone you cared about, everyone you fought for, was taken away?* The bar became a void, as if the outside world didn't exist. It was too much to go back to. She lifted the glass again, chasing the oblivion.

"Miss," the bartender's voice suddenly cut into her drowning sorrows, "You look like you've already had too much. Are you alright?"

Margot could barely get her head to look straight at the burly bartender. Every muscle and fibre in her being screamed no.

"Dunno," was all Margot managed to muster up. The bartender looked at her with concern.

The television they had above the bar was playing the news. "Going back to today's events, we have the death of the vigilante known as Godsend.' He was known for—"

The bartender, seeing Margot's bad reaction to the news, quickly turned the television off. "You know, I had a lot of regulars who really liked that guy. A little extreme, but he made it seem like anything was possible. Even for someone like me," he commented.

"But he's gone," Margot angrily retorted, looking off into the distance to avoid eye contact.

The bartender realized this was a touchy subject. "Still, our power to change things is around. Now that we've seen real change, things won't go back to the way they were."

Margot essentially ignored him, going down the train of thought in her own head. "You know we could likely cure every disease. We could save every child. But guess what? That's not *profitable*."

228

"Miss... I get that, but I'm failing to see your point here," the bartender replied, confused. "Are you saying the change we need isn't possible?"

"I'm saying they won't let it happen. Even if things don't go back to the way they were. They'll find ways to drain our lives. Whether it's taking away our money, our health, or our time, they'll find a way." Margot slurred her words, clearly just angered with her mind wandering.

The bartender stopped for a moment, considering just leaving her the bill. But he exhaled, her words bringing up a memory. "I had a friend who had muscular dystrophy. He was honestly one of the coolest, nicest people to be around. He was told he wouldn't live past twelve. The guy made it to twenty five like a champ. He might have made it longer too..." the bartender started to trail off, "If funding wasn't severely cut."

The words hit Margot like knives. Just hearing that made her enraged. The memories of another igniting her own. The drinks had made her mind fuzzy, as if everything was a one way tunnel. This was all she was thinking about now.

"I bet they told you that 'everyone dies sometime,' and that it wasn't worth keeping someone alive who was 'going to die anyway.' Those asshole, bastard, shitfaced politicians. Hope they know they're just gonna die anyway," Margot spat out, her words slightly less slurred as she ranted.

The bartender felt the emotion in her voice. She was right about what they said, nearly exactly. He thought that, maybe, she had known someone like that too.

"Right on the money. Did you also have a friend like that?" he asked.

Margot's breath immediately got shakier. He could tell after asking that, there was no going back. Usually, Margot wouldn't say anything and would storm off. But with the tunnel-vision effect of the alcohol in her system, she just began to blurt out what was on her mind.

"When I was younger, that person for me was the girl I was closest with," Margot began, revealing the start of a story that went deep to her core.

Years earlier, at a time when Aleksandr still hadn't completed the suit that would be known as Godsend, Margot knew a girl named Lily. Her family owned a house close to their business on the Jetty in New Jersey.

Despite owning the house, Aleksandr looked down upon their family. They had no real riches or luxury outside of that, and were semi-retired. They were just focused on raising their daughter. To him, it was disgusting to resign oneself from their life's mission for another.

But the friendship began by accident. On one of the days Aleksandr had work, Margot asked to come.

"Where do you go for the whole day, daddy?" little Margot, now eight, asked her father. Her father had been rather uninvolved in her life up to this point.

"I go to the beach. Where the land meets the sea. There, I help people work on sailboats," Aleksandr explained to Margot in his forced cheerful tone.

"Can I come? I've seen the beach in movies before!" Margot asked, all excited. Her mother walked over to quell the commotion.

"Sorry, honey. Your father has a lot of work to do," Narae, Margot's mother, told her. Her expression drooped.

"I don't see the harm, why not?" Aleksandr asked Narae, suddenly bringing back Margot's smile.

"Aleksandr, are you sure?" Narae asked. He nodded, and Margot excitedly ran up the stairs to pack up her stuff for a beach day. The two hopped in Aleksandr's truck.

The drive was less thrilling than Margot thought it would be. Lots of traffic and many cars honking at each other. But eventually they got there, it was the beach at last.

"Can I go touch the sand?!" Margot asked, her eyes completely enthralled by the ocean. Her father sighed.

"Just a moment. I need to meet with the guys first," he told her, making her wait. He pulled up to a parking area. There, he stepped out to the "sailboat business" and asked if one of the guys could watch Margot for the day.

A tall, lanky man named Victor walked up to the car with Aleksandr.

"Margot, this is Victor. He'll be watching you on the beach for today," Aleksandr introduced him.

"I won't be in your way," Victor assured her. Margot was too nervous to say anything, so she just nodded.

"This is basically like a free day off, so make sure she's safe. Okay?" Aleksandr whispered to Victor. He nodded furiously.

But the day went on well. He sat back as Margot went and discovered the ocean, walking with just her feet in. She was captivated by the salty water and the waves alone. Victor watched from a beach chair in the distance. She looked back every now and then, waiting for his thumbs up to approve what she was doing.

Margot suddenly encountered a horseshoe crab, nearly all the way washed up on shore. "What's this thing?" she shouted back to Victor.

An unknown voice beside her responded. "A horseshoe crab!"

Margot whipped around to see another girl standing beside her, not knowing how she was snuck up on.

"What are you by, Margot?" Victor asked as he walked over, seeing the crab and the other girl.

"Don't worry about it, it's fine!" Margot, embarrassed, replied to him. He stopped, scratching his head.

The other girl began to poke the horseshoe crab. It didn't move. "Who's that, your dad?" the girl asked.

"Nuh-uh. Dad's friend though," Margot admitted, looking closer. The girl looked to be about her age. She had short blonde hair and blue eyes that complimented her seafoam green attire. Her skirt whipped in the wind.

"My name is Lily! What's yours?" the blonde girl announced joyfully.

"Margot," Margot simply responded, unsure how to really converse. She hadn't had many friends at school, so this was a first for her.

"Mar-go? You have a funny name," Lily taunted, laughing as the waves washed over the crab.

Margot, flustered, didn't know how to respond. "Yours too. Like a lilypad"

Lily laughed, walking away from the water. "You wanna see something cool, Margot?" she asked. Margot nodded. The two went over to another part of the Jetty, looking at the cove that went inward. They ended up exploring together all day, finding new cool things and warming up to each other. The whole time, Victor was scared Aleksandr was going to kill him if he didn't get her back on time.

"Margot! Time for us to go back to your dad!" Victor shouted, as Margot and Lily were collecting pieces of sea shells.

"Aww man," Lily looked dejected. Just then, her parents also shouted out.

"Lily, the sun's going down! We should return to the house!" her mother shouted from the opposite direction.

233

"Quick, Margot! Run away with me!" Lily challenged her.

"Wha—?" Margot was so taken off-guard. Lily started to run towards her parents, and Margot followed.

"Lily, you can't do that to a new friend," her mom stopped her, meeting her halfway. "I'm so sorry sir. My daughter looks like she wants to steal yours." Lily's mom joked around.

Victor didn't know what to do. "Uhh, I'm not her father. Just a babysitter. Actually I have to take her *back* to her father," he explained.

"How am I gonna see you again?" Margot asked Lily, ignoring the parents. Lily put her hand to her chin, doing a thinking pose.

"How about I give your parents our contact information?" Lily's mom interrupted. Both girls gave their approval. Lily's mom gave Victor a card where Aleksandr could get their contact info.

For the next few weeks, while it was still summer, all Margot would do was beg her dad to take her to work again.

"You're going to see that Lily girl again, aren't you?" Aleksandr asked.

"At least she's got a friend, dear. They seem like decent people. Why not just have her parents watch over both of them?" Narae suggested.

Aleksandr sighed. "Well it gives you something to do over the summer."

Every chance she could, Margot would go down to Jetty Beach. Her and Lily went from awkward friends to inseparable. The two would have adventures on the beach, go inland to the marshes, walk the streets to get ice cream, and more. Margot essentially lived with Lily at a beach house that her parents had come to inherit nearly every time she was over there.

"Wanna have a sleepover?" Lily asked one day, where the two had just gotten back to her beach house after adventuring.

"I dunno... I wonder how my dad will feel about that," Margot responded. But Lily cheered in the background as Margot gathered the courage to call her dad.

Aleksandr sounded like he had been worked to the bone. "I don't have to come in for another day, so it would have to be a two day sleepover. Are her parents okay with that?"

The two looked at each other as if they had just won the lottery. They ran across the old beach wood floors, getting Lily's mom to sign off on it. "Yay!" Lily screamed. "I bet you'll get scared from my... spooky stories."

"Nuh-uh," Margot smirked, thinking that Lily was full of it. "I have a better one."

The two quickly set up a fort in Lily's living room, grabbing every blanket and pillow in sight. They dragged a flashlight in, and several snacks they had managed to get from Lily's mom.

"Okay, okay. My turn first," Margot said, her voice a low whisper, barely audible over the crickets outside. The flashlight beam danced across their faces, illuminating their wide, excited eyes. "Have you ever heard of the legend of the Drowning Man of Jetty Beach?"

Lily, nestled deeper into her sleeping bag, shook her head, a shiver running down her spine. "No. Tell me."

"They say," Margot continued, lowering her voice even further, "that years ago, a fisherman drowned just off the coast here. His boat capsized in a sudden storm, and they never found his body. But every few years, when the

235

tide is low and the moon is full, you can see his ghost. He walks along the shore, dripping wet, looking for his lost fishing net."

A gust of wind rattled the old windows of the beach house, making both girls jump. Lily clutched her pillow tighter. "What happens if he finds you?"

Margot paused for dramatic effect. "He tries to pull you into the water with him, so you can help him find his net. And if you go... you'll never come back!"

"AAH!" Lily shrieked, burying her face in her pillow, then peeking out with one eye. "You thought you got me. I'd just bring a fishing net. My turn!"

They continued like this for hours, giggling and screaming in equal measure, fueled by sugary drinks and the thrill of the dark. The moon climbed higher, casting long, eerie shadows through the windows. Eventually, exhaustion won, and the two girls drifted off to sleep, curled up amidst their blanket fort, the sounds of the ocean like white noise.

The next morning, sunlight streamed through the curtains, bathing the living room in a warm, golden glow. The blanket fort, now looking less menacing and more like a pile of laundry, was a testament to their late-night adventures. The smell of waffles filled the air.

"Girls, breakfast is ready!" Lily's mom called from the kitchen.

Margot and Lily scrambled out of their fort, rubbing the sleep from their eyes. They found Lily's mom bustling around the kitchen, setting plates of fluffy waffles on the table. Beside Lily's plate, a small, white pill organizer sat, with several different colored pills neatly arranged in the compartments labeled for the day.

"Morning, sleepyheads," Lily's mom said with a smile. "Dig in before they get cold."

The girls wasted no time, pouring syrup over their waffles. Lily, still a little sleepy, barely noticed the pills on the table, her attention fixed on her delicious breakfast. She was hyper-focused on maximizing the fun that day.

"Mom, can we go to the grove after this?" Lily asked, her mouth full of waffles. "We want to explore a marsh where we saw a huge fish."

"Of course, honey. Just make sure you stay on the marked trails and don't go too far," her mom replied, sipping her coffee.

Lily nodded, quickly finishing her last bite. "Come on, Margot!" she exclaimed, jumping up from the table, completely forgetting the pills in her excitement. "Let's go!"

Margot, equally energized by the thought of a new adventure, quickly swallowed her last bite of waffle and followed Lily out the door. The pill organizer, with its neatly arranged pills, remained on the table, forgotten in the morning rush.

Lily and Margot ran about their way. Lily laughed as the breeze rushed through their hair. "I can't believe we both live in Virginia! You didn't know this was just our summer house until *yesterday*."

"I live in the same house always. Didn't know people had two. Luckily, your other house is also in Filly-delfia," Margot mispronounced the city name.

Lily stifled another laugh. "Philedplphia?" she asked, letting the laughter burst out.

"Whatever! I'm gonna find a big fish before you do!" Margot announced, running ahead of Lily.

Lily sped up as well. "No fair!" She ran to match Margot's speed, the two of them ready for another day of exploring. They navigated through the winding paths of the marsh, the air thick with the scent of damp earth and blooming wildflowers. Dragonflies, iridescent jewels, zipped past their heads. Margot led the way, eyes peeled for any ripple in the murky water that might have a large fish.

"See anything?" Lily called out, a little out of breath. She was looking in a different area.

Margot shook her head, pushing aside a curtain of reeds. "Not yet! But I feel like we're close." She moved further, her gaze fixed on a particularly wide stretch of water. "Lily, Lily, look! I think I see one!"

She turned, ready to point, but Lily wasn't right behind her. "Lily? Where'd you go?" Margot scanned the dense foliage, a flicker of concern replacing her excitement. "Lily?" Her voice grew a little louder, a touch of worry creeping in.

Finally, she spotted her. Lily was a few yards back, slumped against a tree trunk, her usually bright blue eyes wide and unfocused. Her chest was heaving, her breaths coming in short, desperate gasps.

"Lily!" Margot cried, her heart leaping into her throat. She rushed to her friend's side, kneeling down. "Lily, what's wrong? Are you okay?"

Lily tried to speak, but only a choked sound escaped her lips. Her hand went to her chest, fumbling at the collar of her shirt, as if trying to pull more air into her struggling lungs. Her skin was starting to take on a pale tint.

In complete panic, Margot called Lily's mom who had the ambulance over in no time. Lily was picked up and rushed off. Margot was left with Lily's mom, panicking about her friend.

"Where are they taking her?" Margot demanded to know. Lily's mom looked down at Margot.

"Her dad is already waiting for her at the hospital. She's going to get some treatment, see her father, and get better!" Lily's mom, obviously acting and barely keeping it together herself, told Margot.

Margot, sniffling up tears, asked, "What happened to her? She seemed fine. Suddenly, she wasn't breathing."

Lily's mother took deep breaths, trying to remain calm. "You see, Lily isn't like you or me. She sometimes gets clots in her throat. She makes too much mucus, the slimy stuff in your mouth. So she takes pills in the morning. She might have just forgotten them."

Margot looked out onto the horizon where the ambulance had rushed off to. "So she sometimes stops breathing."

This, to Margot, was already horrifying. Their sleepover had been cut short, and Margot had to go home early. But Lily called back, after a day, and before they knew it, Margot and Lily were back to their usual beach adventures.

Summer ended, and the two found each other in the same middle school. They hung out, saw each other in the mornings, talked crushes, played video games, you name it. The two were an inseparable pair through and through. As the two grew, got pimples and headed into their awkward years, they fought a few times. But just as friends do, they forgot about what they were fighting about weeks after.

After school, outside of the gate, Margot waited. "Hey," she said. Lily had just walked through the gate.

"I thought you said we couldn't hang out anymore," Lily raised an eyebrow. Margot scoffed.

239

"No... I didn't— you know what. Shut up, you owe me a burrito bowl and you know it," Margot pointed her finger at Lily, leaning over and having her newly-bought glasses fall off her face.

Lily jumped over, catching them before they hit the ground. "Man, you look like a nerd with these. They suit you." She gave them back to her.

"Guess you're just a nerd's friend, then," Margot snatched the glasses back. Within no time, they were at a fast-food place having two burrito bowls.

When summer came around, the two always made time to go out to Jetty beach. That place was the foundation of their friendship, the place where their parents had the beach house and where their adventures began.

One day, while hanging around watching television, Margot nudged Lily.

"Would your parents kill us if we had a party here?" Margot asked, raising an eyebrow. Lily spit out the tea she was drinking.

"Margot this house is a party for two. *US*. We're not having our classmates trash it!" Lily staunchly fired back. But it was only a matter of time until Margot convinced her, and they had a small beach party.

But most of the time, it was the two, their bathing suits, and the sea. They would still somehow spend hours out with sunscreen on. Even if it was just tanning in the sun. Margot would usually tan, Lily would burn, they would poke fun at each other, the usual stuff.

It felt, at the time, like it was destined to be for life.

Margot and Lily were now in their high school years. The two somehow, despite the odds, stuck together. Margot noticed Lily spending more time out of class, and in the hospital. The hospital by their beach house had already been bought out and shut down. The same thing now faced the local Philadelphia hospital as well.

Despite that, the two still returned to Lily's beach house for the summer. It was tradition, and they weren't gonna give up that easily.

On the beach one evening, Margot broke through the usual friend stuff. Her words began to turn personal out of concern for Lily. "I see you've been taking more pills now."

"People like me are hospital babies. If I can spend more time outside of one, I'll take whatever pills I gotta," Lily stood firm, watching the waves. The two were still soaked from going in earlier, hoping their suits would dry off quickly.

"Does it not scare you?" Margot asked, looking at Lily as she looked into the horizon.

"It terrifies me."

"Me too."

The two stood silently as the wind blew through their hair. It was a reminder of the good old days they barely remembered.

Lily turned to Margot, her blue eyes reflecting the fading light of the sunset. "Sometimes I just wish I could take one deep, full breath and know it's not going to be interrupted by a coughing fit, or a sudden tightness in my chest."

Margot felt a familiar chill run down her spine. The casualness with which Lily spoke of such a terrifying reality always unsettled her. "There has to be something, Lily. Business assholes can't just buy up *all* the hospitals."

Lily shrugged, wrapping her arms around her chest. "Doctors try. Pills help. But it's always a new problem, a new symptom. They're talking about specialized clinics now, maybe even out of state. More tests, more medications. It's... a lot." Her voice trailed off, a hint of weariness creeping in.

Margot's stomach clenched. "Out of state? Like, you'd have to leave?" The thought was like a mental knife. Their summers at Jetty Beach didn't seem so endless anymore.

Lily picked at a loose thread on her bathing suit. "Maybe. It's not set in stone. But the doctors here are running out of options. They say my case is... complicated." She offered a small, sad smile. "Just like you, Margot. Always complicated."

Margot didn't return the smile. She looked at Lily, at the thinness of her arms, the slight tremor in her hands when she wasn't actively holding something. The fear, ever present but usually pushed to the back of her mind, now surged forward, cold and undeniable.

"I don't want you to go," Margot whispered, barely able to get the words out.

Lily reached out, her hand finding Margot's, a surprisingly firm grip. "I don't want to either. But if it means... if it means more time, then I have to."

Margot nodded. She knew something big had to be done, but it was scary. Scary that time kept relentlessly pressing on.

Lily, living with this her whole life, wanted to ignore it more than anything. "What if this is the last day? What would you do?"

Margot tensed. Her brain faltered, unsure of what she was supposed to answer. "I'd ride off a cliff in a shopping cart with fireworks. Or... something dumb."

"I'd give the guy who bought the hospital and turned it into a data center cystic fibrosis and see how *he* likes it," Lily, usually cheerful, sounded full of hatred.

Margot forced a laugh, not used to this side of Lily. "I didn't know we were allowed to do supernatural things. I'd save all the people you like from the evils of the world!"

Lily paused for a moment, smiling. "All of them, huh? How about all the things hallowed to me?"

"Hallowed?" Margot asked, "You mean like the church word?"

Lily laughed. "It's just a poetic word *I* like. The fisherman we see down at the other side of the Jetty? Hallowed. The ice cream lady that pulls to the curb by the beach house? Totally hallowed. Just people, living in the moment. People being friendly, and caring for each other. That is what's hallowed to me."

Margot paused, stopping to think about what she said. "That could be most of us, huh? Every time I think about wanting to move away because of manipulative politics and big business billionaires, I think about the people I talk to every day. The common folk who are just minding their business but looking out for each other. That's what I think is 'hallowed,' I'd say."

Lily grinned. Margot was getting it. "I'd agree with you, Margot. But you know what's most hallowed of all?" Lily asked. Margot looked at her, waiting for her to continue. "The beach," Lily followed up with, "This hallowed

243

end between land and sea. This place *we* conquered, Margot. Which places *you* above all that other junk."

"Yeah?" Margot couldn't help but feel a little joy. "You're 'hallowed' to me too." The two were wordless as they looked out onto the sunset. The beautiful refraction of the sun against the clouds, turning them all pink. They stood for nearly half an hour before they decided to turn in for the night, the thoughts still heavy in their mind.

Time went on, ever unmerciful. The other hospital shut down. Lily was out, weeks at a time. The prescriptions were adding up. Her parents couldn't afford them anymore. The debt climbed faster than they could imagine.

Margot, still doing her climbing and martial arts, would constantly invite Lily. She couldn't anymore. Or she would just come to watch. It worried Margot.

One day after school, Margot caught Lily's attention. "Hey, you haven't come climbing. Not in months."

"I can't, Margot. I'd run out of breath halfway up the wall," Lily angrily responded. Margot tried to be supportive, but she didn't know what to say. "But... you used to love it. We could try something easier? Maybe just a few feet up?"

Lily shook her head, tears welling in her eyes. "It's not worth it, Margot. It's too hard. Everything is too hard now." She turned away, pulling her backpack tighter around her shoulders. "I just... I can't do it anymore."

Margot watched her walk away, a cold knot forming in her stomach. The helplessness was suffocating. She wanted to fix it, to make Lily better, to make the world fair. But she was just a teenager, and the world seemed too big, too broken.

That night, Margot found herself staring at the ceiling in her room, the words of Lily echoing in her head. She seemed helpless. Margot wanted to change the world,

244

and make it so she could live happily. But Margot was just as helpless as she was.

The next day, Margot went to school. Everything was usual. Everything besides a certain person's absence. Lily wasn't there. Nothing too unusual, though. She often had to be absent for treatment. What was strange, however, was that Lily didn't tell Margot ahead of time.

"Dude. I told you to tell me when you have to go in for treatment," Margot texted Lily. No response.

"Seriously dude. Don't scare me."

"Lily. Don't be like this."

One missed call. No pick up. She tried calling Lily's mom. No response. Margot went into full blown panic mode. She ran outside her classroom calling her mom immediately.

"Mom I think there's something wrong and I need to go to the hospital—" Margot started ranting into the phone, faking that there was something wrong with her. The nearest hospital was now a forty minute drive, and Narae gave Margot hell for it. But Margot ignored her, jumping out of the car as soon as they got there. She saw Lily's mom's car in the parking lot.

Margot burst in, trying to convince them that she was Lily's sister. They weren't buying it. She ran, ignoring them all. She looked through each door of each patient's room, trying to find where Lily might be. She eventually found the room. The door was open, a sliver of light escaping into the dim hallway. She pushed it open slowly, her breath catching in her throat.

Lily lay in the sterile white bed, a tangle of tubes and wires connecting her to beeping machines. Her skin was ashen, almost translucent, and her lips were a faint blue. Her chest barely rose and fell, a shallow, desperate struggle for each breath. Lily's mom sat beside the bed, her face buried in her hands, silent sobs shaking her slender frame.

Margot looked down, distraught. She rushed to the bedside, her hand reaching out for Lily's, but her fingers trembled, afraid to touch.

Lily's mom looked up, her eyes red and swollen, a raw agony etched into every line of her face. "Margot..." she choked out, her voice barely audible. They embraced.

Margot peaked out, looking from the machines to Lily's fragile face, then back to her mother. "What happened? Why isn't she...?" She couldn't finish the sentence.

"They... they just couldn't stop what already started. Her lungs, Margot," Lily's mom barely got out, tears streaming anew. "I couldn't... I couldn't keep affording new pills. They kicked us off insurance after that last hospital... I didn't even know half the time what the doctors wanted... there's nothing more the doctors can do now."

Margot's head went static. It seemed impossible, unreal. *Nothing more they can do.* How much could be taken from her in so little time?

"No," Margot said, her voice rising, a desperate, raw sound. She kicked a chair. "If they hadn't taken over our god damn hospital—"

Lily's mom gently took Margot's hand, her grip surprisingly strong. "I'm sorry." Tears fell. She couldn't keep it together anymore, feeding herself some of the blame.

Margot let go, walking to the side of the bed. "Hey. Lily. Can you hear me?"

She slightly moved her hand. Margot saw she had some life left in her. Tears welled up in her eyes.

246

"I'm going to protect it all. I'll find a way. I'll save everything you found hallowed," Margot proclaimed.

"You... did..." a whisper escaped her breath, being artificially kept alive.

Margot couldn't endure it. The tears came crashing like waterfalls. Lily's heart rate flatlined.

"HONEY!" her dad rushed in, uniting the family. Margot could only stand by as the doctors came rushing in with him. They revived her momentarily, her parents cried over her. Margot didn't want to leave, but she couldn't watch anymore. She could witness the world taking away her best friend. She ran. She ran away from everyone, and everything.

Her mom found her passed out on the concrete in the city, hours later. She got scolded for what could have happened to her. Margot didn't care. She didn't care about anything anymore. She kept living life, but it felt like it had lost all meaning.

Not long after, her father and mother also met their fates. Margot kept enduring it. She kept living with the idea that everyone close to her was going to die eventually. But she couldn't just end it all. She had promised to protect everything that Lily loved, everything that was hallowed to her.

But Margot thought she was a failure at that too. She tried to move on, to run away. She tried to drink her problems out of her life, and sat on the Steel Devil that was the goal of her fathers life. At first, she didn't want to touch it. It was a memory of the corrupt man her father was, like the politicians and mega-corporations of the world. She eventually gave in, knowing that there was one sure-fire way she could change the world, and save the hallowed that Lily loved so dearly.

The months came and went, and she achieved what she wanted. She strived for fixes and won the people's trust. But she lost friends along the way, and found herself in a similar rut. Now in a bar, ranting off Lily's story to a bartender she had never met before.

Margot slurred her words. She smelled of liquor. "And then, and *then!* Guess what I found out? The healthcare group that took over her insurance? Owned by Darkstone. The new building that went where the hospitals were? Owned by Darkstone. And *GUESS* who bought out her parents house after they moved out of Philadelphia?" She looked dead into the bartender's eyes.

He knew the answer, but was afraid to even say it with how passionate Margot was getting. "Uhh... Darkstone?"

"YES!" she slammed on the bar, "These people are comically *evil*. I wish we could just... er! Get rid of them!" Margot's head fell on the bar as well. She quieted down. "I don't know what to do."

The bartender wanted to wrap things up. But he also thought of something that maybe she needed to hear. "I don't think your friend would want you here, drinking away your sorrows."

Margot froze. He was right. She knew he was right. It killed her to think that she might be disappointing her.

The bartender continued. "I think she'd want you back out there, protecting what she treasured, right? And you were part of that something."

Margot took a deep breath, trying to recompose herself. "How could I be—"

"You clearly were. Take care of yourself. Bill is on me tonight, now get out of here," the bartender told her off.

Margot was left there, staring with nothing ahead of her. She was given one command, one to protect the hallowed which she herself was a part of. She quickly got up from the bar, heading back home to her apartment.

"I promised. I *will* fulfill that promise," Margot told herself, wiping tears from her eyes on that fateful September night.

September. The sky, and the people below, were in gloom. The sun was gone, and it felt that the hopes of the many had followed. Godsend, to the public, was dead. While people didn't forget "him," those who were against him now felt free to resume their old ways.

The group had not yet contacted each other since the death of Calvin. Due to reconstruction, the church was closed. The alcoholics anonymous group was cancelled, at least for that upcoming Thursday. Hazel knew that this time, there was no chance of it going back to being the way it was. The group had too much history now.

She sat alone in her room, her roommates out and about. She fidgeted with one of the tokens Pastor Alan gave to her. She smiled, knowing she hadn't touched booze since. But at that moment, as she replayed Calvin's final words in her head, she got a notification on her computer.

She rolled her eyes, scootching her chair over. "What is it this time? Another ad?" She peered at her inbox. Instead, it was an email she had been hoping for. One that she was beginning to think she'd never see. The sender was Charles Edwin.

"WHAA—?" her mouth gaped open. She then shook her head, thinking it had to be a fake.

"*Hello Hazel. I would love to set...*" the preview read before she opened the whole message. She gulped, thinking that this had to be fake, but she opened it up regardless.

Hello Hazel,

I would love to set up a time for us to meet. Your inquiry about my political future is intriguing. I mostly get questions about my career as a pharmaceutical scientist.

I see you must have noticed with the social media team going into gear, that I plan to make a move into politics. I have always been associated with political figures, but now plan to get involved personally. I feel the need more than ever with the recent 'Godsend' controversy.

I'm sure this could make for a good paper, since you're in political science. I can do Philly Coffee on Main St. What times work for you?

Regards,
Charles Edwin

Hazel was ecstatic. "WHAT IN THE WORLD? HE ACTUALLY RESPONDED TO ME?" She spun around in her chair. She stopped, the realization hitting her. "I need to respond. What am I gonna say?! Uhhh..."

She thought for a moment, realizing that her Thursday afternoon was now definitely free, since the group was cancelled that week. She quickly responded.

Before she knew it, she was barely keeping herself standing as she walked toward Philly Coffee. It was a bit chilly that evening, and she wore a jacket, but the nerves are what kept her shivering.

It was bustling inside Philly Coffee, quite the contrast to the quiet streets. The aroma of roasted beans and warm pastries filled the air. Hazel scanned the room, looking for a familiar face, or at least a face that matched the professional headshot she'd seen online.

Then she spotted him. Charles Edwin sat at a small table in the corner, sipping a cup of black coffee. He looked exactly like his pictures. He was impeccably dressed in a tailored suit with a quiet authority about him. He looked up just then, and his eyes met hers. A polite smile formed on his face.

Hazel took a deep breath and walked towards him, extending a hand as she reached the table. "Mr. Edwin? Hazel Schulz. Thanks for meeting with me."

He rose, his handshake firm. "Please, call me Charles. And the pleasure is all mine, Hazel. I'm always happy to speak with bright young minds." He gestured to the empty chair opposite him.

Hazel sat, trying to appear composed despite her racing heart. "I appreciate you making the time. Your work in pharmaceuticals has always been fascinating, and now, with your potential move into politics, it's... even more so."

Charles let out a small laugh. "A smooth transition, I hope. Though, I imagine the political arena will prove to be a far more contentious environment than the lab."

"I can only imagine," Hazel replied, nodding. "Especially with everything that's been happening. The... ongoing political controversies," she watched him carefully, gauging his reaction.

He took a sip of his coffee, catching on to what she was talking about. "Indeed. While I certainly believe in the power of the people to voice their concerns, I also believe in upholding order and established processes. Unsanctioned vigilanteism, however well-intentioned, often leads to more chaos than solutions." His tone was measured, calm, and utterly devoid of any overt emotion. "What are your thoughts on it, if I may ask?"

She reeled herself back. This didn't sound right. "Based on what you've put online, I figured you'd be more pro-Godsend than against. He did save you from a plane crash, didn't he?"

Charles put down his mug, a grin sprawling across his face. "Sorry, Hazel. Usually, that's how I begin things. Most people I talk to are staunchly against the vigilante. I did say it *often* leads to more chaos than solutions. Not that it doesn't."

Hazel glowed. It was like she correctly answered a puzzle. "So what do *you* think?"

Charles looked around the coffee shop, scanning for anybody listening in as he spoke to Hazel. "The political landscape today had no choice but to let someone like Godsend, who I know now was your associate Calvin, to rise up. The people in power continue to abuse it, setting up like minded individuals in every office. There needed to be a disruptive force. But now, it's up to the people he left behind."

"EXACTLY!" Hazel couldn't help but blurt out. People started to look over, and she covered her mouth, knowing her mistake. "That's exactly what I think Calvin was saying before... you know," she whispered.

Charles nodded. "So I think I have to step in. With my long list of cancer treatment contributions, I have the political footing to step into any of the big elections. Almost nobody on either side of politics can argue with low-cost life saving treatments."

Hazel realized the implications of this. He was going to use his likeability to step into politics, likely inspired by Calvin's words. "So what are you going for? Governor of Virginia?" Hazel asked, mostly joking around. She thought that office might be a bit too high up for a first-timer.

Charles looked her dead in the eye, making sure nobody was listening. He covered the microphone and camera on her phone on the table as he leaned over. "President." he mouthed, keeping a finger to his lips.

"Huh?" Hazel reacted. She could barely comprehend what he had just said.

"Yeah, maybe I could be a district board member!" he heartily laughed, winking at her as he fell back in his seat. She knew what this meant. He didn't want wind of anybody knowing. Not the people around, or the people from the government monitoring their activity.

"Yeah," Hazel responded, pretending to not be freaking out. She then thought of something, trying to get the full story here. "Did you want to... maybe take this to go? I know a nice spot nearby. A cool garden."

Charles caught on to what she was saying. It was risky, but he figured it would be fine. "Oh, certainly! If it's as nice as you say."

The two got to-go cups for their coffee, and walked out the front doors. Charles kept a scarf around the bottom of his face and glasses on. With those on, nobody recognized him on the way there.

It was just a short walk down the road over to a garden that was open for the public. With the cold weather, there was essentially nobody there. More importantly, there were no cameras in certain places.

"I'm just going to put this in my bag real quick," Hazel told Charles, burying her phone under a bunch of things in her bag. "How about yours?"

"I already predicted Hulls long ago. This phone doesn't have anything they can spy on," Charles responded, looking around at the mossy vegetation around him.

"So you're going big, huh? Calvin must have inspired you," Hazel asked, trying to sound more buddy-buddy with him.

He laughed. "That, and my hypothesis about Hulls." He left it vague. Hazel wanted to know more.

"What's your hypothesis?" Hazel asked, needing to know more now that he could speak freely.

Charles looked up, his gaze unfocusing. "I've traveled the world. Especially around this country. Wherever I go, there are a few staunch followers of Hulls. People who are superfans, and defend him like he's some sort of divine figure. However, these people are few and far between. I never really meet many of them at once. Nor has Hulls ever filled a stadium, due to 'safety concerns.' What do you think of this?"

Hazel remembered back to Godsend's conflict with Aidan Samson. The censorship, the manipulation of information. "I just thought it was weird. You see so many of his fans online, and especially in those times where he's met with opposition. All those accounts usually don't even have any friends or anything—"

Hazel stopped herself. She made a realization. Charles noticed, nodding at her suspicion. "You mean... they *aren't real*?"

"Hazel," Charles changed his tone, more serious than ever. "If you collaborated with the largest artificial intelligence companies in history, and they wanted you in power, do you think they'd have the power to deceive the government? To put a bunch of 'real' people and 'real' addresses in the system, to get 'real' votes in return? And then, in turn, fool the people?"

Hazel froze. The surveillance, the unpopular president, the people in power extorting their positions, it

255

all made sense. They weren't afraid of any kind of pushback, or any opposition. They had a way to make sure they won regardless of the competition. A loophole so convincing that the entire country bought it.

"I could give myself nearly unlimited overreach, all while making it seem like the people asked for it," Hazel responded in a coarse, desolate voice.

Charles followed her situation. "And if one of your main political opponents accused you of this, it would sound like you are trying to discredit the people. So the political opponent would need an outside party to try and popularize the idea *before* using that against them."

Hazel turned to him. "You don't need to say any more. I think I get it."

Charles continued regardless, "And you could have got a third term if it weren't for those meddling kids." The two laughed, despite not knowing where this situation left them.

Hazel cleared her throat. "Guess what Calvin would have wanted is for the voices of the people to return. So, I guess I should start a rumor."

"Not forcing you to. It would be helpful though. Maybe you'd get hired after your degree, too. Depending on who's in charge, of course," Charles added.

"That's bribery. But I guess sometimes, you do need to fight fire with fire," Hazel joked, walking away from the garden. Charles smiled, waving as she left.

Hazel walked away appearing more confident than ever. But she was internally a mess. *AHH WHAT AM I GONNA BE ABLE TO DO ABOUT IT?* She thought. Then her mind shifted as she continued down the street. She was wondering if anybody she trusted was good with technology. She knew Owen was, but his state was less than optimal the last time she saw him. She decided to look at who else was in the group.

"Declan...? No. Amara doesn't seem like the type. Milo...? Eh..." she read as she went down her contacts list. Her thumb then floated above Margot's name. "Well... if she's feeling better, she could probably give me advice. Maybe she's a techie, too."

She messaged Margot to meet up. Margot, alone in her apartment, planning on what to do with her newfound resolve, saw her phone screen light up.

"**HAZEL**: *You any good with tech? I've got something extremely important that I need help with whenever you're free*," is what the message on her phone read.

She groaned. "This is just going to side-track me." She initially put the phone down, but felt bad. She picked it back up, and they scheduled to meet the next day.

Margot stood on an apartment building's balcony, knocking on the door that was presumably Hazel's. She had followed her directions, and it was the day after Hazel had met with Charles Edwin. The door swung open, and Hazel, looking disheveled but wired, pulled Margot inside.

"Margot! Thank God you're here. Last night was a whirlwind, and I swear I haven't slept a wink." She shut the door quickly, showing urgency.

"What's going on? You look like you've seen a ghost," Margot said, her eyes scanning the living room. It felt strangely empty.

"Worse, maybe. Come on, let's go to my room. I've got something huge to tell you." Hazel practically dragged Margot down the short hallway. Neither of her roommates were at the place, but evidence of them lied around the apartment.

When they entered Hazel's bedroom, Margot immediately noticed it. The desk in the corner was bare, and the areas of dust showed where monitors usually would have stood.

"Where are all your computers?" Margot asked, suspicious of the whole situation.

Hazel ran a hand through her already messy hair. "That's part of the whirlwind. I had to move it all after my meeting. It's... complicated." She sat on her swivel chair.

Margot raised an eyebrow. "This isn't like you. Explain."

"First, phone goes in the closet," Hazel commanded, pointing to her sliding closet. "They could be listening," she mouthed.

258

She knows more than I thought she would, Margot thought, immediately doing what she said.

Hazel got right to the point. "I met with Charles Edwin yesterday. He wants to become a political opponent of the president. But he can't do so if the *current* president is using fraud to stay in office."

Margot stepped back. "Hold on," she reacted. *Fraud? Edwin? What is she talking about?* Margot's mind raced. "You met Charles Edwin? How? And *what?*"

"It was originally for a college interview assignment, but things changed. He believes that Hulls is using his connections to not only give everyone the illusion that he has millions of followers, but also to rig elections," Hazel continued to explain.

Margot put her hand to the bridge of her nose, pushing up her glasses. "Give me a minute. It's... a lot at once."

Hazel continued. "I know it is Margot. But if we are going to do something before they catch on, we have to find evidence and make it public quickly. That's why I asked for your help. Would you be able to find and collect evidence on this? I'm not the biggest tech person," she admitted.

"HAZEL!" Margot finally burst back. Hazel stepped back. "You're telling me that all of the Hulls advocates are works of artificial intelligence? That he was able to... put on a show that he's actually popular. Then used his connections to get elected?" Hazel nodded furiously.

It actually makes sense, Margot though, *with his connections to the private equity firms that essentially make up all of the top companies. Well, they could all be in bed together.*

Margot sighed. "You need help? I can help. Not like I particularly like the guy either. Especially if he's doing that." She masked her anger. She needed to stay calm, and sound like the normal Margot that Hazel knew. The one from the group.

"YES! Thank you. Here, we can go right to work. The computer stuff is all still *here*, it's just in the other room," Hazel told Margot. "And before we go out there... I wanted to let you know that I was going back and forth with him last night. There's an event scheduled for next week. Wednesday. It's just supposed to be a regular town hall, but he's going to announce his candidacy there. Do you think it's possible to have sufficient evidence by then?"

Next week? Margot thought, *That won't be easy. But it's doable.* She grinned. "It'll be possible."

The two wasted no time, going out to where Hazel had moved all her computer stuff.

"This is driving my roommates Becca and Emma insane, but my stuff is out here in the living room," Hazel motioned to the room. She had a monitor and a computer connected to it on the rug.

Margot cringed at the setup. "This is your computer?" She pointed at the monitor, visibly not pleased.

"Yeah? Why? Dude, I'm a college student not a tech guru." Hazel took a *little* offense.

Margot shook her head. "Best we could do is research and some screenshots on this machine. But you want internal documents, I'm assuming. To do that, we'd need a server grade computer."

"Dude, again, I'm a poly-sci major. Not comp-sci," Hazel retorted.

"I'm gonna pretend that I know what that means," Margot responded, "I had quite a lot of time to mess with computers, figuring out how they work. Basically ever since after high school. So let me use my home computer."

Hazel froze. "I can't let you tell others about Edwin's plan."

"Woah, woah, woah! I believe you, okay! Do you really think after Calvin died at the men Hulls hired, I would just help him get away with more?" Margot angrily shot back.

Hazel, seeing the raw anger in Margot's eyes, decided to trust her. "Okay, okay. You're right. It's just... a lot. And this is too important to mess up. If you're gonna go back home, what do you need from me to start?"

Margot took a deep breath, pushing down her frustration. "Give me everything you have. Any names, any dates, any companies Charles mentioned. Anything that might give me a lead."

Hazel scrambled to retrieve a small notebook from her bag. "Right. He mentioned some AI companies, but didn't give names. Just that they were the 'largest in history.' Which means basically anything owned by Darkstone." She handed the notebook to Margot, her fingers trembling slightly. "The town hall is next Wednesday. Can I trust you'll have it done before that?"

"I'm sure I'll even have time to spare," Margot said, taking the notebook. This wasn't about fighting physically, not yet, but it was still a battle against the same faces. "I'll keep you updated."

Hazel nodded, a glimmer of hope in her eyes as she gave her trust to her friend. "Be careful, Margot."

She ran off, hailed a cab, and gave the driver an address far from her apartment. It was a quiet residential street she rarely visited. Once there, she paid him generously and walked for several blocks, making sure no one followed her before finally turning down a secluded path that led to the hidden entrance of her father's bunker. The metal door, disguised by overgrown plants, creaked open with a familiar groan, revealing the bunker down below.

Inside, Margot approached her primary console, a behemoth of custom-built hardware and multiple monitors. Most coming from when her father inhabited the place.

"Alright, Hulls," she muttered, her fingers flying across the keyboard. "You manipulator."

She started with public records, cross-referencing political donations with known Darkstone subsidiaries. She searched for any anomalies in Hulls's past campaigns, looking for sudden spikes in online support or unusual voter turnout in specific districts. The information was vast, a tangled web of shell corporations and political action committees.

Hours bled into each other. Coffee replaced sleep. The hum of the servers became a constant droning noise.. She delved deeper, bypassing firewalls, cracking encrypted data, and tracing digital footprints across the globe. There were fake social media accounts, bot farms, manipulated poll numbers, and more. It was all there, a crafted illusion designed to perpetuate Hulls's power.

The sheer scale of the deception was staggering, a testament to the lengths the powerful would go to maintain their control. Margot felt a cold fury simmering beneath her focus. It was much more than a stolen election. It was a vast deception covering the idea of free will. Manipulation so far, so intense, that the common public was gaslit into thinking that Hulls, and by extension all his cronies, were the only way.

Margot could only chuckle. "I knew Hulls was a corrupt asshole, but it looks like he and his team around him are also criminals. Nobody even lets them be questioned, anyway. His *actual* followers are convinced he's god or something."

A few days had already passed. It was nearly showtime. Hazel was stressed, not having been contacted by Margot. But then, the night before, a message.

"**MARGOT**: *We're about to crack this wide open. We have pages of irrefutable evidence. Where's the town hall? I'll give you this folder beforehand.*"

Hazel was so relieved she was about to pass out. She sent the address and time right over. She was a little worried, since Margot wasn't responding. But back at the bunker, Margot had just fallen asleep.

The next morning, Margot woke up early. She was still in yesterday's clothes, with food left at her desk. She realized that she had fallen asleep by accident.

"Ah jeez," she sat up, putting on her glasses that had fallen off. A faint smile formed on her lips, "We're close now, Lily. A world where you would have lived. Where the things hallowed to you are safe and sound."

She got up, exercised, and was just about ready to go. She collected all of the documents and the pages she used to explain the data points. It was set in motion.

She looked over at the storage area. "I wonder if I should wear something fancy?" But looking where some clothes were left over, she saw the cassette player. The one her mother had when she was younger. That, and her favorite song. She walked over, about to hit play on the cassette player with speakers, having her favorite song from when she was younger in it, "On Beaches."

BANG! A loud crash resonated from outside of the bunker. Margot quickly threw the loaded cassette player into a safe, locking it. Another loud *BANG* shook the entire room.

"How the hell did they find this place? Was I followed?!" Margot questioned. She grabbed the manilla envelope she had printed all of her evidence against Hulls in, running over to the workbench.

There, sitting on top, was the suit. The 'Steel Devil.' The 'Silver Prophet.' The suit the masses knew as *Godsend*. If Godsend came back now, everyone would know it wasn't Calvin. Margot tensed herself, hearing another *BANG* as the doors to the bunker started to break open. It felt as if the suit was calling her name.

"Let's do this, Lily," she angrily declared, reaching out her arm. The door broke open, and bullets whizzed through into the bunker. But the suit had leapt out, meeting Margot halfway and covering her once again. Godsend had returned.

"**THE HALLOWED DESERVE TO KNOW THEY'RE NOT ALONE**."

Margot, wearing the Godsend suit, readied herself. She was ready to fight. However, looking around, the manilla envelope was ripped to shreds by the bullets. *Ah, come on!*

Two suited men dropped in, holding rifles. Their affiliation was unclear. Margot didn't care, zooming past the two faster than they could perceive. She caught herself from going too far, now floating outside of the bunker.

"**IDENTIFY YOURSELVES, OR FACE ERASURE**." Margot boomed from the suit. Below, she recognized someone. It was *Hadley?!* He was wearing business attire, a red exo-suit, and a translucent helmet.

Hadley wildly grinned. "I found you, Margot. Your dad's cronies knew his bunker was around here somehow!" He held some sort of weapon. One of unknown origin to Margot.

"**WHERE DID YOU DISAPPEAR TO**?" she questioned Hadley. He fired the weapon, thinking she would be caught off-guard. But Margot zipped around the blast, only barely. *It was a bright blue, and was much faster than a bullet,* she thought.

"RUSSIA!" Hadley boosted himself into the air, taking aim again. Margot flew to the side, dodging the blue blast once more. "That's where I found all about your 'Steel Devil.' I knew it couldn't have been Calvin. And here I return, just to find him DEAD!"

He continued to fire his weapon, with Margot flying around and barely dodging each time.

"**HIS DEATH WAS HIS OWN CHOICE. I DIDN'T WANT HIM TO DIE.**" Margot vocally shot back.

"It's still *your* fault. I don't care *what* you say!" Hadley, barely coherent, shot again. This time, the burst of energy made contact.

Margot was caught by the blast, being blown back a few meters. She looked down, seeing the damage the suit had taken. The plasma had phase-changed the liquid crystals in the suit. A small portion where she was hit, her left shoulder, became essentially an inoperable chunk of metal.

"**INTERESTING**." Margot remarked, largely unaffected for the time being. But whatever this weapon was, it cancelled out her invulnerability. Hadley fired again, a rapid succession of blue blasts. Margot, now fully aware of the weapon's effect, moved faster than he could see. The suit's damage was essentially nothing, but it proved that damage could be done. She weaved and dodged, a silver blur against the grey sky, each movement a calculated swing around the destructive energy bursts.

"YOU CAN'T KEEP THIS UP, HADLEY." Margot's voice boomed. "YOU'LL EXHAUST YOUR WEAPON'S CHARGE BEFORE YOU EVEN TOUCH ME."

Hadley snarled, his helmeted face contorted in frustration. "I'LL EXHAUST YOU FIRST, YOU DAMN MURDERER!" He increased the intensity of his firing, his arm trembling slightly with the effort.

She suddenly appeared behind him, her voice a low growl. "FOOLISH. YOU'RE OUTMATCHED." She delivered a powerful kick to his back. The exo-suit, though strong, buckled under the force, sending Hadley hurtling forward. He crashed into the side of the hill the bunker was in, leaving a Hadley-shaped dent in the ground.

Before he could recover, Margot was there, pressing further. She seized his weapon arm, twisting it sharply. A sickening crack echoed in the air as the strange device shattered. Hadley roared in pain, his translucent helmet flickering with internal alarms.

"YOU THINK THIS CHANGES ANYTHING?!" he shrieked, lashing out with his other arm, a clumsy punch that Margot easily deflected. "THEY'LL STILL COME FOR YOU!"

"YOU DON'T THINK THERE'S STILL A 'RED SCARE?' YOU'LL HAVE A LOT OF EXPLAINING TO DO." She reached for his helmet, her fingers closing around the base. With a swift, decisive motion, she ripped it free, revealing his bruised and contorted face.

Hadley spat, defiance in his eyes. "I'LL NEVER LE YOU—"

266

Margot tightened her grip, the suit's power now a tangible threat. "**EITHER I'LL TAKE YOUR LITTLE EXO-SUIT APART, PIECE BY PIECE, AND LEAVE YOU FOR THE AUTHORITIES, OR YOU CAN SCREW OFF.**"

The fear in his eyes was palpable. He knew she wasn't bluffing. His defiance crumbled. "Fine," he rasped, defeated. "Just... don't kill me."

Margot moved the Godsend mask up, revealing her face. "I'm not a murderer, Hadley. Unlike those you serve," Margot stated, releasing him. He collapsed to the ground, panting, bruised, and utterly broken. The two Russian men who attacked with him earlier immediately went to check his pulse. "Now, get going. All of you. I've got a speech to prepare."

Hadley, despite his broken weapon, had one last desperate trick. As Margot turned, he lunged, a concealed blade glinting in his hand, aiming for a weak point in the suit he had studied in Russia. Simultaneously, the two Russian men, surprisingly agile, threw themselves at Margot, one going for her legs, the other for her head.

Margot dodged effortlessly, doing a flip in the air above all three of them. "Don't regret that," she scoffed, holding one arm out with the other. She shot rubber bullets through her fingertips, taking them down.

"GAH! HOW COULD YOU?! YOU SAID YOU WEREN'T A MURDERER!" Hadley shouted back, his two cronies also in agony.

She looked down on them like scum. "I gave you the least lethal option I had."

Margot turned back to the ruined entrance of her bunker. The evidence was gone, shredded by bullets. But she had a better plan now. A much more direct approach.

"The town hall is starting soon. I need to get going," she whispered, the suit humming around her. She leaped into the air, the helmet falling back over her face. Again, she gathered the digital green energy around her, making full use of the suit's power. Each little nanobot with its own nuclear battery attached to it, running in parallel.

WOOSH— She burst through the air in a nanosecond. She flew just as fast as she always had in the suit, making it impossible to trace her path. But the destination was clear.

"YOUR TIME IS RUNNING OUT, HULLS."

The wind whipped around in downtown Philadelphia. The clouds passed over quickly, with some sun peaking through the cracks in the gray sky. Hazel looked up, waiting for Margot. She felt betrayed, Margot was late.

"Damnit," Hazel scoffed. She pouted, going the other way, over to where Charles was standing on the other side of the stage.

"Your friend chicken out?" Charles asked while two people got him ready, prepping his suit.

Hazel frowned. "I guess so. We have my version here, but I bet this is nothing compared to what she got. I wonder if Hulls' people caught up with her." She passed him a folder that she had made personally.

"It's alright Hazel. This'll do," Charles told her. Another speaker began to finish up on stage.

"And that's why we must fight. Not only for what we believe in, but against those who want to use their legal power to bully us into submission. That's why today, I've decided to reveal my endorsement for the primary next year," the woman on stage finished up her speech, leaving the stage with audience applause. It was already a big, crowded event.

Charles took a deep breath, smoothing down his suit jacket. He walked confidently onto the stage, the applause for the previous speaker still echoing. A ripple of murmurs went through the crowd as people recognized him. His presence was unexpected, a famous pharmaceutical scientist stepping into a political town hall. He adjusted the microphone, nervous as ever.

"Good afternoon, everyone," Charles began, his voice cutting through the lingering chatter. "My name is Charles Edwin. Many of you know me from my work in medical research, particularly in cancer treatment. But today, I stand before you not as a scientist, but as a concerned citizen."

He paused, letting his words sink in. The murmurs grew louder, turning into confused whispers. This wasn't the usual political endorsement. He wasn't introducing another candidate; he was taking the spotlight himself.

"For too long," he continued, his voice gaining a quiet intensity, "we have witnessed a system that seems increasingly disconnected from the will of the people. A system where power is concentrated, and the voices of everyday citizens are diluted or ignored entirely." He glanced towards the side of the stage where Hazel stood, a subtle acknowledgment. "I believe it is time for a change. A fundamental shift in how we govern ourselves, and how we empower those who truly represent us."

He looked out at the surprised faces in the audience, then directly into the cameras broadcasting the event. "That is why, today, I am announcing my candidacy for the presidency of the United States."

A collective gasp swept through the crowd, followed by a sudden burst of excited shouts and a scattering of applause. Reporters in the front rows scrambled, pulling out notebooks and adjusting cameras.

Hazel watched, a mixture of pride and utter disbelief washing over her. "Here we go," she muttered.

Charles continued the speech. "I feel as if the current administration has left me no choice but to take up this political mantle." Another pause, the words lingering. "The corruption I see from the other side of the aisle has only been sneakily expanding since the death of Calvin Becker. To you and I, he was known as a vigilante..." Charles looked into the sky. It caught the people's attention, seeing his face look up higher.

"What's he doing?" Hazel heard him slowing down, trying to figure out where Charles was looking.

Charles, looking up in disbelief, finished his sentence, "...A vigilante many would come to know as Godsend."

The humming increased in volume. The people all started to hear it, looking into the sky. Godsend had arrived. Margot, still with the whole suit covering her, descended to directly above the stage.

"Holy shit..."

"No way!"

"Is that him? Did he not die?!"

"**THE CURRENT ADMINISTRATION WISHES I HAD DIED. UNFORTUNATELY FOR THEM, I STAND BEFORE YOU NOW**." Margot's filtered voice boomed. A chilling presence. People didn't know how to react. Journalists looked like they had encountered a gold mine.

"You're flying so, you must be the 'Godsend' we all spoke of. Are you not Calvin Becker?" Charles posed a question, looking up.

Margot decided to be vague. "**I AM THE PROTECTOR OF THE INNOCENT. THAT'S WHO I AM. AND TODAY, I EXPOSE THE CURRENT ADMINISTRATION FOR ELECTION FRAUD**."

The crowd exploded. None of them knew what it meant. All they knew is that seemingly, the dead had risen.

Charles smirked. "Well it seems you beat me to it. I was about to stand up here, telling them all how the Hulls

271

administration used artificial intelligence to fool people into thinking he had a huge following."

"**PRECISELY. BUT IT GOES FURTHER THAN THAT**," Margot picked up after him, "**THEY HAVE THOUSANDS OF SHELL COMPANIES, AND SYPHON MONEY FROM ALL CORNERS OF THE ECONOMY**."

"You mean like the equity firms that transfer money from people's everyday necessary purchases to defense contractors building a system to herd them in like cattle?" Charles played off of Godsend. Margot grinned under the suit.

"**LIFE, LIBERTY, AND HAPPINESS, ALL USURPED FOR PROFIT. CORRECTING THIS CAN NO LONGER WAIT.**"

"The only person who would have been working on that... The only person that would have come here..." Hazel looked up, having a hard time believing the situation.

Charles, originally liking what he was hearing, now was apprehensive. "That sounds like a threat. I would be careful there."

"**HULLS IS NOT OUR LEADER. JUST A SAD MAN THE GREEDY USE AS A PUPPET. HUMAN GREED HAS CONTROLLED YOUR LIVES FOR FAR TOO LONG. WE HAVE TO FIGHT BACK**!" Margot pressed further, not giving in this time.

Charles immediately retorted. "That's going a little far—" he was cut off by the crowd roaring in response.

"HE'S JUST A DICTATOR!"

"A CRIMINAL IN OFFICE!"

Margot as Godsend raised her hand in the air. The people began to shout, raising their hands to imitate her. It was a war cry.

Just then, bullets whizzed past Margot. Police snipers on the roof nearby had just obtained permission to shoot.

"**I WANT TO SAVE YOU. THEY WANT TO BE RID OF ME**." Margot's filtered voice boomed. She leaned slightly back pointing her right hand forward. She held the suit's thumb up and index finger out. She charged up energy in her fingertip, about to shoot back.

"HEY! STAND DOWN!" a cop shouted, getting Margot's attention. But their complaint was toward a civilian, holding a textbook as a shield.

"We get *one* person who stands for us. The government desperately wants them gone. I am *not* letting Godsend die again!" the man with the textbook shouted.

People began scaling the buildings, crowding where the police were. There were so many people eventually, they couldn't fire.

At this point they were all over the news. Hulls watched in horror, from the Oval Office. "I thought we had the body of that kid?! How the hell are they there?!"

"Sir, I'm getting intel that Calvin was just a stand in. That, there, is the *real* Godsend," his secretary told him. He started to pull on his hair.

"DECLARE MARTIAL LAW! WE ARE GETTING RID OF GODSEND ONCE AND FOR ALL! GET THE NATIONAL GUARD IN THERE, NOW!" Hulls shouted at the top of his lungs.

Meanwhile, they had already pulled up to the scene. Troops were starting to unload off of military trucks all around where the town hall meeting was taking place. Margot, seeing the incoming forces, moved with blinding speed. The first volley of bullets from the National Guard clanged against her, flattened and harmlessly falling to the

273

ground. She spun, deflecting a rocket with a roundhouse kick, sending it upward like a firework.

"**YOUR WEAPONS ARE FUTILE**," Margot announced, her voice resonating with a dismissive tone. "**THEY ARE BUT TOYS AGAINST THE WILL OF THE HALLOWED**."

"PRESS ONWARD!" a general on the battlefield commanded.

She didn't engage them directly. Instead, she became a silver whirlwind, moving amongst the troops, disarming them with precise, non-lethal strikes. Rifles were twisted into knots, riot shields were bent into pretzels, and stun grenades were tossed like trash. Her movements were fluid, and too quick to predict. One by one, the soldiers found themselves without a means to attack, their faces a mixture of confusion and awe.

Charles Edwin watched from the stage, a rare look of astonishment on his face. Hazel, beside him, was openly beaming, a mixture of validation and pure excitement radiating from her. The riot of people continued to protest and stand in the way of other forces at work.

"They're fighting an army... alone," Charles whispered, more to himself than to Hazel.

"Well all saw Godsend fight a hurricane, right? Are they sure they want to keep sending people after her?" Hazel replied.

"Her?" Charles asked. But was interrupted by another explosion mid-air.

Looking over, Margot had already dealt with the initial military response. The crowds only grew, feeling like they were invincible with Godsend on their side.

Margot, shooting out the tires on the last vehicle, flipped out of the way, crashing into the middle of one of the main streets. The people around her cheered her on.

"**LOOK OUT. I'M GOING FULL THROTTLE. STRAIGHT TO D.C.**" She stretched one leg of the suit back, charging up energy. The people of all different backgrounds cheered her on as she launched herself at speeds nobody could even fathom.

To the people there, it looked as if Margot disappeared. Many fell back from the sheer force behind her. Regardless they all continued cheering for justice to be brought.

Meanwhile, online, people were in a frenzy. On social media platforms, the news of Godsend's return and the declaration of martial law sent shockwaves. Hashtags like #GodsendReturns and #MartialLaw trended, with users expressing a mixture of awe and terror. "They're really sending the National Guard after Godsend? This is insane, stay safe Philly!" one user posted, while another countered, "FINALLY! Someone to stand up to Hulls! Take him down, Godsend!" All while she flew through the sky.

Margot arrived in Washington D.C. in less than a minute, a silver streak against the sky, leaving a supersonic boom in her wake that rattled windows. She descended rapidly, a blur of motion, until she hovered directly above the White House, the presidential residence suddenly in panic at her imposing presence.

"**NO MORE GAMES**." her voice, amplified by the suit's speakers, thundered across the capital, echoing off the historic buildings and the grand lawn. Tourists stopped and pointed at the sky. Secret Service agents swarmed onto the lawn, weapons drawn, their faces a mixture of confusion and grim determination.

275

Inside the Oval Office, Hulls stumbled back from the window, his face pale. "How the hell is Godsend here so fast?!" he shrieked, his composure completely shattered. "The National Guard... they were supposed to put that *thing* down!"

His secretary, equally terrified, fumbled with a desk phone. "Sir, they... they were unsuccessful. Godsend disarmed most of the units in Philadelphia."

Margot, high above, noticed the rapidly increasing security. Black SUVs screeched to a halt, dispatching more agents. Snipers positioned themselves on nearby rooftops, their scopes fixed on her. She knew they were just pawns, acting on orders. Her target was the man inside.

"**TURN YOURSELF IN**." Margot roared, her voice resonating with an unyielding force. She pointed a metallic finger directly at the White House. "**DO THAT, AND WE CAN AVOID THIS GETTING UGLY**."

The president, panicked, couldn't make out what Godsend was saying to him. "Someone ask what the *hell* he means!"

The secretary threw him a phone. "ASK!" Hulls dropped the phone, quickly picking it up off of the ground. He leaned in.

The voice of President Hulls boomed over the loudspeaker. "Calvin... no, whoever you are, why would I turn *myself* in?"

Margot kept her composure. The green, glowing bar on the Godsend helmet swished down to the bottom of the face, forming a mouth. "**I KNOW ABOUT YOUR ALLIANCE, HULLS. YOUR STRING OF CONNECTIONS**." Just this alone already terrified the sitting president.

"**HOW DARKSTONE BOUGHT UP NEARLY EVERY LARGE CORPORATION. HOW THEY DECIDED ON YOU, AN INSIDER, TO RUN OFFICE. AND HOW THEY USED ARTIFICIAL INTELLIGENCE TO GASLIGHT THE PEOPLE INTO THINKING YOU WON A FAIR ELECTION.**"

President Hulls reeled, his grip tightened as he supported himself on a desk. "I'm done with pleasantries." He held the phone up to his mouth again. "I'm not negotiating with a terrorist. You're the one who keeps asserting unelected power."

Hulls looked outside the office. With Godsend flying above, all the weapons were aimed upward. But there was a massive crowd at the gates. People were protesting his existence, demanding he resign now.

"Martial law will be in place until Godsend falls. Arrest those who interfere." Hulls angrily blurted over the intercom.

In an immediate response, the entire military staff at the white house fired upon Margot. The green, digital glow quickly reverted to her eye position. She boosted back and forth, dodging the larger ammunition as smaller ammunition bounced off the liquid-metal surface of the Godsend suit.

"**BE CAREFUL WHAT YOU WISH FOR**." Margot warned. She stopped mid-air, bringing all her limbs into a crouched position. Green energy began to gather around her in the sky like it was a black hole, causing all the continued ammunition to bounce right off of her.

A swarm of drones burst out of a military truck just as a general was signalling to cancel. "GET THOSE DRONE OUT OF THE AIR! THAT'S ATTACK IS GOING TO—"

WOOSH— The air around them pushed back like a hurricane-force wind. Green energy zig-zagged out in all directions as the majority of all electronics went offline. All the drones fell to the ground. It was an electromagnetic pulse. It silenced the city, plunging everything into a strange quiet. But that quiet was short-lived. A low hum began to emanate from within the White House complex, growing steadily louder. Emergency lights flickered on, cutting through the sudden darkness, and the ground beneath the Secret Service agents vibrated.

"Backup generators online!" a voice crackled over a revived comms unit. "All systems back up, targeting Godsend!"

Margot watched as more advanced military vehicles, previously unseen, rumbled into position. Their weapon systems were glowing with an ominous energy.

"~~WE CAN STOP THIS NOW. JUST TURN IN ONE MAN.~~" Margot boomed, her voice laced with challenge. She saw the crowd at the gates, their faces a mixture of fear and defiant awe. She couldn't let them get caught in the crossfire.

"WE WILL SHOW YOU THE POWER OF THE UNITED STATES MILITARY!" a general's voice roared over a newly activated loudspeaker. "STAND DOWN, VIGILANTE! YOU ARE OUTNUMBERED!"

Margot shot forward, intercepting the second wave of drones before they could even ascend. She moved like a blur, ripping through their metallic frames one by one before the human eye could regularly perceive it. Lasers, precise and blinding, fired at the air where she had been a moment before.

Before she could move on, she noticed a squadron of heavily armored, bipedal mechs stomped out from behind the White House. They were equipped with energy cannons, their barrels spinning up with an electronic whir.

"Are we serious right now?" Margot muttered under the mask, dropping rapidly towards the ground. She landed with a seismic shockwave, sending a ripple through the pavement. The nearest mech stumbled, its aim thrown off.

She engaged the mechs directly, standing small against their size. Regardless, she dodged a volley of explosive rounds, countering with a devastating kick that crumpled the chest plate of the lead mech. It cracked, sparks flying, before toppling over. She used its falling bulk as a launchpad, springing into the air towards another. Its cannon swiveled to track her, but she was too fast. She grabbed the barrel, twisting with impossible strength, until the weapon snapped off with a shriek of tortured metal. The mech flailed as it fell.

Meanwhile, ground troops, now armed with energy rifles, formed a perimeter. Their aim was precise, but Margot was a blur. She spun around the whole perimeter, smashing through all of their weapons. She swung by a burst of energy, reappearing behind a line of soldiers and sending their weapons skittering across the ground with a line of nano-bots from the suit.

The crowd at the gates pressed against the barriers, chanting Godsend's name, their voices were a defiant roar against the military's might. Margot saw a few attempting to scale the fence. She had to keep the fight away from them.

She shot upward, drawing the fire of the remaining drones and mechs into the open sky. Laser fire and energy blasts carved glowing paths through the air, but Margot flew right through them, seemingly untouchable. One particularly large energy blast, aimed directly at her, was destroyed in a single block.

The general, watching the battle unfold on a tactical display, slammed his fist on the console. "SHE'S TOO FAST! FOCUS FIRE! OBLITERATE HER!"

Margot braced, the bullets whizzing faster and more frequently. But it was a distraction. Behind her, she saw a jet take off. Zooming in with her suit, she could see the president and his cabinet inside. The supersonic jet boomed away.

"**RUNNING AWAY, ARE WE**?" she angrily boomed. Whipping around back to the ground, she held out both of index fingers. *BAM, BAM, BAM!* She shot through the military's gear with energy blasts right out of her fingers.

"DON'T LET HIM GET AWAY!" a civilian, attempting to climb the fence shouted. Margot saw him shout this just as the police tasered him, bringing him off of the fence.

"**I CAN'T DO THIS ALONE. ALL OF YOU**..." Margot boomed, directed at the crowd. "**FIGHT FOR THE FUTURE. ONE FOR ALL OF US**."

The crowd, empowered by Godsend's words, erupted in a deafening roar. They surged against the police lines, their collective anger a force to be reckoned with. "FIGHT FOR US, GODSEND!" a woman screamed, her voice cracking with emotion. "WE'RE WITH YOU!"

Margot, looking at the countless faces, knew what she had to do. This wasn't just for Lily, her friends, her mother, or for herself. This was for the future, for everyone. To destroy a system designed to crush them.

Margot's voice shot out through the suit, reaching every corner of the capital. "**YOUR VOICES ARE MY POWER**."

She crouched low, the suit gathering an incredible energy. The green digital streak across her face pulsed and brightened, flickering as all the possible power was gathered into her boosters. The ground beneath her cracked with immense pressure. With a sound that tore through the air like a sonic boom, Margot launched herself into the sky. She became a distant speck, leaving behind a whirlwind and a collective roar from the crowd.

Margot, in the Godsend suit, blasted through the atmosphere. Fighter jets surrounded her as she flew after the president's jet.

"**OUT OF MY WAY**," she snapped, boosting past the group.

"DON'T LET HER GET AWAY!" one of the pilots shouted through the comms. "FIRE AT WILL!"

Margot twisted, a small speck against the dark sky, as missiles streaked past her. She dodged up, down, around, and more. With one still on her tail, she flew towards the last remaining one. Flying directly up, she got the two off of her trail, and they exploded into each other. The relentless jets formed a diamond formation, attempting to box her in.

"**DON'T DO THIS**," Margot's voice boomed, full of disdain. She accelerated, leaving contrails in her wake. She then suddenly stopped midair, causing two of the jets to overshoot. Before they could correct, she jumped on one. She shot through the weapons system, causing an explosion that threw the jet off-course.

"THEY'RE TOO FAST!" a pilot yelled, his voice strained.

Another jet behind tried firing everything it had at once. Margot met the barrage head-on, bracing as the suit absorbed the impact as if it were rain. She closed the distance in an instant, smashing through the jet's right wing with a single jab. The pilot ejected with a parachute as his disabled jet plummeted to the earth.

The remaining jets scattered, their pilots too afraid to engage. They weren't fighting a person, they were fighting *Godsend*.

"**YOU CAN STILL TURN AROUND. PUT AN END TO THIS**." Margot roared, her voice echoing through the upper atmosphere. The president's jet in the distance continued its desperate flight. Her focus narrowed to the one jet. She gathered the suit's green energy, and launched herself forward. She was like a living bullet.

BOOM! The suit collided with a ballistic missile, throwing her off course. She caught herself in the air, shaking her head and observing her surroundings. More fighter jets. Even more than there were originally.

"We can do this all day. Give up," a pilot demanded, his voice projected out of the jet's cockpit.

Margot met their challenge. "**AND I CAN DO THIS FOREVER**." She burst forward, enduring more missiles. She burst through, bunching through yet another jet's wing. Turning around through the bullet barrage, she realized she was losing Hulls. His jet was getting further as the distractions piled up.

"FIRE FROM BELOW!" a pilot commanded over the comms. Margot looked down to see a giant electromagnetic cannon mounted on a military vehicle on the ground below her. She braced, knowing those traveled at the speed of light.

To the military, Godsend was enveloped by a beam of light like the sun. It appeared as if the streak of light would evaporate anything in its path. But as it faded...

"**NOT EVEN A SUNBURN**." Margot's voice was getting continually more strained. The suit was in tact, fully functional. Steam floated around, off of her from the heat of the blast.

"We can't do this. This isn't a person, it's a *monster*," one of the pilots, their voice shaky, said on the comms.

"For how long?" another pilot questioned. Most of the team was back on board. They continued their assault. They got more reinforcements.

Margot raged. The endless assault, the relentless waves of jets, the energy cannons firing from the ground. Hulls was getting away. The green glow around her suit flickered with her growing frustration.

"**YOU'RE WASTING YOUR TIME**!" she roared, her voice cracking slightly under the strain.

A squadron of stealth drones swarmed from behind her, unleashing a volley of plasma bolts. Margot spun, shooting through them while dodging the jets' barrage. The suit was holding, but the persistent impacts were grating on her.

"WE HAVE OUR ORDERS, VIGILANTE!" another authoritative voice boomed over the comms. "SURRENDER, OR BE ERADICATED!"

Margot cackled. It was a harsh, humorless sound that echoed across the atmosphere. "**THAT'S FOR ME TO TELL YOU**."

She accelerated, leaving a trail of shattered metal and sparking circuits. She shot towards the nearest fighter jet, its pilot desperately trying to evade. Margot grasped its tailfin, throwing it violently. The jet spiraled downwards, out of control.

"**THIS IS A WASTE OF TIME**!" Margot screamed, the filter on her voice almost failing under the sheer force of her anger. She was losing her lead. Hulls was getting too distant.

She gathered all her remaining energy, the green light around her intensifying to a blinding aura. The air glowed around her.

"NOW!" one of the pilots shouted. All of the remaining jets shot their energy canons at once. The force of all of them was enough to shoot Margot off in the other direction.

She spun out, completely shot in the other direction. The blast was so powerful that she couldn't regain her balance. In her spiral, she thought of only one thing: she needed to get out of this cycle. So as she rolled toward the ground, she gathered all of her energy and shot off in another random direction, so her path wouldn't line up with where they thought she went.

She crashed into a mountain, leaving a dent in the ground below her. All went quiet. She only heard her own deep breaths.

"Damnit," she scoffed, barely able to catch her breath. But her muscles sitting still for just a moment let all of the pressure relax off of them. There, lying on the mountain with nobody around for miles, she passed out.

Hours passed until Margot came to. When she did, it was past midnight. She dusted the dirt off of her metallic suit, sitting up and staring off into the sky. She attempted to get the mask of the suit to pop up, so she could look into the sky uninterrupted. But it didn't.

"Ugh, damn thing is stuck," she groaned, getting up off of the ground. Off in the distance, she saw a town. "There's only one thing left to do. Find him." Her determination was unwavering. She trudged forward despite the circumstances.

But it wasn't that straightforward. The country, unsure of what was happening, went into panic mode. Due to censorship and miscommunication, many were suddenly placed under martial law. Kids stayed home from school, and people sheltered in place. People held their breath, unsure what was going on.

The next week was a collective held breath for the people. Rumors spread of Godsend going town to town, looking for Hulls. The president's whereabouts became unknown. The continent was in disarray.

The dusty winds of Nebraska whipped through the deserted streets. A tumbleweed rolled lazily across the cracked streets. Stores were shuttered and the usual traffic was replaced by an eerie silence. It had been days since the Godsend event, and the martial law declared by President Hulls had continued on.

Outside a weathered apartment building, a woman named Sarah stood defiantly toward her landlord. Mr. Henderson, an older man with a constant angry face, gestured at the empty streets behind them.

"I don't care if the whole country's on lockdown, Sarah. Rent's due. And it's been due for three days now," Mr. Henderson grumbled.

Sarah threw her hands up. "Mr. Henderson, how am I supposed to pay you? The bank's closed, my job's closed, *everything* is closed! Nobody's getting paid!"

"That's not my problem," he retorted, crossing his arms. "I have bills to pay too. If you can't pay, then you gotta go. Simple as that."

"Go where? There's nowhere to go! The roads are blocked, the trains aren't running!" Sarah's voice rose, desperation creeping in. "This is ridiculous! We're under *martial law*!"

"And I'm upholding the law, Sarah. My law. My property, my rules," he said, stepping closer, his shadow looming over her. "Now, are you going to pay, or am I going to have to escort you out?"

Just as Mr. Henderson put his foot down, a sudden gust of wind swept through the street. Both Sarah and Mr. Henderson shielded their faces.

A metallic figure descended, landing with a soft thud that nonetheless vibrated the very ground beneath their feet. This wasn't the knight they had seen on television. The suit had been dented and battered. Burn marks and dried blood covered its limbs. The silver suit, once a beacon of hope, now carried a lasting dread.

"**WHAT SEEMS TO BE THE PROBLEM HERE**?" Godsend's question echoed through the empty streets. The metallic figure barely could stand up straight.

Mr. Henderson, phone still clutched to his ear, dropped it with a clatter. His jaw hung open, his eyes wide with a mixture of terror and disbelief.

"I'll pay later! We're okay!" Sarah shouted, nervous at the sight of Godsend.

"**NO**," Margot's voice boomed through the filter, "**THAT ISN'T RIGHT OF HIM**." She pointed a finger at him, charging up an energy blast.

Sarah stood in front of Mr. Henderson, stopping Margot from shooting their way. "We might not agree, Godsend! But you can go. Go fix this situation! Get us out of martial law!" Sarah threatened.

Margot, still fully in the battered suit, just stood there. It was as if her mind wasn't really with her. "**WILL DO. ANY WORD ON WHERE HULLS WENT?**"

Sarah narrowed her eyes. "The police station is down on the corner."

Margot didn't even understand that this was a jab at her. Sarash just wanted this 'martial law' madness to end. *Is that who Godsend is?* She thought.

"**I'LL KEEP LOOKING**," Margot, through the filter, told her. She turned, stumbling through the street. Nobody was outside. It was a ghost town.

Televisions outside displayed news broadcasts. She saw clips from this past week. Clips of her fighting soldiers on the ground near a lake. Clips of her flying through the air, smashing through drones. Clips of her running through the city, defending against vehicle ambushes. She had been beaten up, exhausted, and driven to hunger. But she just kept moving.

A news broadcaster interrupted her stumble. "In other news, Hulls is now declaring that he will have an immediate press conference in Trenton, New Jersey to address to martial law situation—"

"**THERE YOU ARE**." Without a second thought, Margot left cracks in the ground as she leapt up. Looking into the sky, she then shot herself forward. This game of cat-and-mouse had gone on too long. Trenton was her next stop.

It didn't take long until she was hovering over the city, trying to spot where he might possibly be. A giant white tent was set up in the parking lot of a stadium. Security seemed ready, but oddly sparse. At this point it didn't phase Margot. She hovered down, running as her feet hit the pavement. She walked in through the door, suddenly feeling a hand on her shoulder.

She flinched. "Margot—" a familiar voice called out. As she turned, Declan backed up. "Margot. There you are."

Bewildered, she took a look around. The tent was empty. The only people there were her old friends from Alcoholics Anonymous.

"Man you have no idea what it took to get that falsely broadcasted," Hazel laughed. Margot didn't get it.

"**WHY**?" is all she questioned, attempting to go back out the door. Amara stood by it.

"You'll have to get through me *again* if you want to leave that easily," Amara boasted, grinning at Godsend before her.

"Cat's out of the bag, Margot. Knew it was you the second you got to the town hall with Charles," Hazel told her, "Though now with you gone for so long, it wasn't hard to figure out. Heard your family ties led back to that fancy suit you got there."

"**YOU'RE WORKING FOR HULLS**?!" Margot questioned in anguish.

Owen spoke up. "Of course not. We just wanted to get you here. Ask you a few things. Like... Why'd you hide everything from us?"

"**I HAD TO. I DIDN'T WANT TO INVOLVE ANYONE ELSE**."

"But you did..." Milo timidly started, "You brought Calvin into it.

"**IT WAS AN IDEA. I GAVE HIM AN OUT IF HE WANTED IT. IT WAS HIS DECISION IN THE END**."

Amara stepped forward. "You fought with me multiple times, and here I thought I was fighting Calvin. Why didn't you just *talk* to me?"

"**I COULDN'T. I DIDN'T KNOW HOW TO. NOT LIKE YOU'D BELIEVE ME**."

"You could have at least tried, Margot. But look where we are now," Hazel interrupted, "We were on our way, but Charles has been hiding away this whole time. Security has to guard him because the whole country's a mess."

"**NONE OF YOU HAVE SEEN THE LIGHT FADE FROM PEOPLE'S EYES OVER, AND OVER AGAIN. I STILL NEED TO END THIS**."

"You realize it isn't too late, right?" Declan asked, stepping in. "We can work with you. We can work with Hazel. After this shitshow, there's no way that Hulls is getting back on stage. You exposed him, the world *knows* he's a phony."

"**HE IS BUT ONE PERSON IN A WEB OF CORRUPTION. THE ONLY WAY IS TO MAKE AN EXAMPLE. TO MAKE SURE NOBODY EVER TRIES THIS AGAIN.**"

The group collectively sighed. It was grating. Margot's mind was unreachable.

"It's not the only way." Milo stood his ground. "You can stand down. We can politically stand up to this web of corruption now. You've done enough."

"Yeah," Declan stepped in, "We can get people in on a special election. We can work on fixing what this has broken over the years. We can give the 'hallowed' people you care about so much their lives back."

"And you can finally *rest*," Amara emphasized, looking into the mask of the Godsend suit, "You look so bruised, tarnished, and broken. Isn't it time to put down the suit?"

"**HOW MANY PEOPLE WILL HAVE TO SUFFER AS WE TAKE YEARS TO FIX THIS**?" Margot's voice shakily shot back. "**HOW MANY WILL DIE? HOW MUCH WILL BE TAKEN? THIS CORRUPTION... IT NEEDS TO END NOW**!"

"Margot..." Hazel felt the pain in her voice. "Are you... crying?"

The suit whirred to life. She began to hover. "**I'M SORRY.**"

"MARGOT!" Owen shouted, "I GET IT! I'M PISSED OFF TOO! I WAS USED, AND I'M SO PISSED! BUT I KNOW I CAN'T JUST LET THAT HATE DRIVE ME FOREVER!"

"YEAH, MARGOT! LET US HELP!" Amara shouted up as the others braced themselves for the wind whipping through the air.

"THERE'S SOMEONE WHO WASN'T SAVED. SOMEONE WHO WAS EVERYTHING TO ME. I WILL NEVER LET WHAT HAPPENED TO HER HAPPEN AGAIN."

With that, she blasted upward, breaking through the tent they had set up. The group all put their arms up in case anything fell on them, but nothing of the sort happened. They all stood facing up to the sky, Margot now a speck in their vision.

Hazel tightened her grip. "Be safe..." was all she could muster out.

"Save the hallowed" repeated in Margot's head over and over again. She had to stay awake. She had to keep on fighting. She looked down upon the city, seeing that the military had caught on to her yet again.

"Prepare to engage Godsend," one of the pilots said over the comms. Military jets flew her way, sending more missiles.

"Ugh. My head hurts..." Margot muttered under the mask. She pointed her finger forward, barely able to aim it properly at this point. She shot downward at the jets, blowing up missiles on the way.

"She's creating collateral damage to the city below. We need to change our position," another pilot commented. Margot was surprised they couldn't tell that she could intercept their radio. Predicting the move, she flew downward as they flew up. Meeting them in the middle.

"**QUIT INTERFERING WITH ME!**" Margot shouted through the suit, punching through one of the aircrafts. It exploded.

"Pilots, change to defensive position," a new radio signal came through, "Air Force One is taking off from New York right now."

"**GREED INCARNATE**." Margot boomed. Her arms quivered as she continued to be fired upon. Despite all the damage, burns, and blood, she remained bulletproof.

One pilot, taking off his communications headset, asked his co-pilot, "Is this a good idea?"

"President Hulls will go overseas. We're pretty sure Godsend can't leap over oceans. Remains to be seen, though," his co-pilot responded.

But they didn't see Godsend charge at them like they had anticipated. Instead, Margot flew straight up, nearly going out of the atmosphere. There, she beamed down, headed straight for New York.

"MAYDAY! DISTRACTION FAILED! HER SUIT MUST HAVE PICKED IT UP OR SOMETHING!" one of the pilots shouted over the comms. "ENGAGING ALL FORCES NOW!"

Margot felt a surge of adrenaline, pushing through the exhaustion. She wouldn't let anything stand in her way. The jets swarmed around her, with only more on the way.

They opened fire, a blinding sea of missiles and energy blasts. It was an all-out assault, a desperate attempt to overwhelm her. Margot met it head-on. She twisted and spun, deflecting missiles with precise movements, shattering energy blasts with bursts of her own suit's power. She continued to claw and lash out at the bullet hell surrounding her, leaping miles while doing so. One missile, too close to evade, clipped her right leg. The suit barely registered the impact, but Margot felt a jolt.

"**I CANNOT BE STOPPED!**" she roared, her voice quivering with the absolute euphoric rush her body was feeling. *I'M SO CLOSE NOW!* Her mind rushed to keep on going.

She surged forward, tearing through the formation. Each leap left a trail of crippled jets. She stopped paying attention to the casualty count as the jets fell from the sky. Another exploded as she sent a focused blast of energy through its engine.

The remaining pilots were choked with fear and desperation. "She's insane! She's destroying us!" one cried over the comms. "Fall back! We can't—"

But a new voice, cold and unwavering, cut them off. "NO RETREAT. KEEP HER ENGAGED. DO NOT LET HER

REACH AIR FORCE ONE." It was Hulls, his voice laced with hatred, blaring into their radio.

Margot knew her time was short. She could see Air Force One now. It was just lifting off. She was bloodthirsty. That long awaited victory was just what she needed.

She became a blinding beacon, a star in the sky of the green, twisted energy that enveloped her. She laughed as she launched herself, the force of a hurricane on her feet. The jets behind her all fell to the ground like flies.

"MARGOT! STOP THIS MADNESS!" a new voice boomed, cutting through the chaos. It wasn't the strained cry of a frightened pilot, but a familiar voice.

Margot, mid-flight, slammed to a halt. Directly in front of her was a colossal mech suit, far more advanced than the ones she had faced before. It was a dark, intimidating machine, bearing the insignia of the U.S. government. Its arm cannons hummed with suppressed power. From a viewport on the mech's head, a face could be seen. It was detective Miller.

"GUESS I HAD TO OUT MYSELF. YOU WOULD HAVE NEVER FOUND ME." Margot gloated.

"This is the last line of defense, Margot Davis," Miller stated, his voice resonating through external speakers. "Every remaining dime, every last shred of our resources, poured into this."

"MOVE," she demanded. Nothing came of the demand. She considered going around.

Miller scoffed at the confrontation. "I may have failed to find you, Godsend. But I know what you're like. And what you're doing, Margot, this isn't you. This isn't what your friend in the hospital would have wanted."

That was too far. "EVEN MENTIONING HER IS BEYOND WHAT YOU DESERVE." Margot's voice cracked with guttural fury that sent a shiver down Miller's spine. The green digital streak on her helmet flared violently, the suit charged a terrifying power.

The air around her warped with an intense heat. Miller while in the mech got a massive warning. Her energy was spiking like it never had before. "Margot, wait! Think about—"

He didn't get to finish. Margot vanished. Not merely moved, but *disappeared* from existence. A nanosecond later, a sickening screech of metal echoed, followed by a deafening *CRACK* that tore through the sky. Margot reappeared, her arm buried elbow-deep into the mech's chest plate. She ripped upward with unimaginable force. This mech was designed to withstand ballistic missiles. It was rated to go to the bottom of the ocean. It was air tight enough for space. Regardless, sparks showered the atmosphere and alarm bells shrieked from within the mangled machine. She tore it open.

Miller screamed desperately as he saw Godsend crash through the rest of the suit, ripping it to shreds from the inside out.

The colossal machine buckled. A blinding flash erupted from its chest, followed by an explosion that ripped through the atmosphere. Shrapnel rained down, glowing red hot. The last resort that the military, and perhaps the world, had against Godsend was gone.

Margot hovered amidst the debris, chest heaving, the suit's green glow still flickering erratically. "**THAT'S WHAT YOU GET**." She looked up, desperately trying to find Air Force One. It was still in her sight.

Her rage burned away any of her exhaustion. Air Force One was flying out of range, but it was still there. She would not fail. Not now. Not when she was so close.

She gathered every last ounce of energy, every nanobot in her suit screaming under the immense strain. The green glow surrounding her shot her forward like a living dart, accelerating with impossible speed towards the presidential jet.

The air shrieked as she whistled through it, going fast enough to heat it up as she moved. The pilots of Air Force One saw a blur in their midst. But Miller was down. They accepted their fate.

The impact was cataclysmic. Margot with the Godsend suit slammed into the presidential jet's tail section. Air Force One, designed to withstand attacks, crumpled like paper under her attack. The plane went flying down with her as she took it with her, pushing it further down until the both of them crashed into a field outside of the city.

Margot, her suit more dented and dirtier than ever, stood amidst the fiery wreckage. The suit around her appeared as a metallic demon with fire dancing around it. Groaning, she pushed herself forward, stumbling through what used to be Air Force One.

The plane was a twisted, burning mess. She continued on through the debris, her mind in a wired state. As she limped through the wreckage and the bodies left behind, she only had the president on her mind.

Then she saw it. The glint of reinforced steel. A crash-proof box was out of the wreckage, largely intact. She approached it, her heavy footsteps crunching on scorched dirt. She went around the side, seeing that one of the walls was open. Inside was President Hulls. He was still alive, somehow. He had been tossed around. His nose was bleeding.

"**SO WE FINALLY MEET**." Margot exasperatedly let out, she had been staving for this moment.

Hulls could barely breathe. He was in shock, barely hanging on. He heaved. "I hope you know... I didn't have a choice."

Margot, as Godsend, stood above him still. She didn't move, watching as he clung to life. It was as if she was savoring the moment.

"Darkstone just *liked* me. I was just *friends* with a bunch of people, you maniac!" Hulls continued crawling further back into his pod. "I didn't choose to have them fake the election and get me in. I had to. I had family members who wanted this for me, and if I didn't, I wasn't sure where my life was going! If I didn't listen to them, then, they would have ruined my life..."

"**YOU SHOULD HAVE CUT THEM OFF WHEN YOU HAD THE CHANCE**."

"Abandon my family? The people I grew up with? We all have people we love but don't agree with. Just because they might have some *less humanitarian* ideas, you would abandon *family* for that?" President Hulls pleaded, his mind not entirely there either.

Margot thought back to the death of her dad. *I WISH I COULD HAVE DONE IT!* There was no reasoning with the state her mind was in. "**YES. IF THEY ARE THE ONES WHO DECEIVE AND HURT, THOSE PEOPLE NEED TO BE PUT IN THEIR PLACE. REGARDLESS OF WHO THEY ARE**."

"Ever the objective one you are, Margot," President Hulls let out a murmur. "You have me. Now what? You want to let this place fall? Let chaos ensue?" The president started to laugh hysterically. His brain was malfunctioning. "I'm not even what you want to destroy, *Godsend*."

297

"MY NAME IS NOT GODSEND. YOU KNOW THAT'S WHAT THE PEOPLE CHOSE TO CALL ME."

Hulls scoffed. "You certainly act like you were sent by God or something. But that's too bad. People all over the world will ignore what happens today. They won't learn a thing, Margot. They'll do as they please." The way he spoke was almost taunting. It got under her skin. It took the small remaining bits of sanity she had and wasted them away. Rain began to fall as the fire around them raged on.

The President saw her anger. He only wanted to toy with it at this point. "That means the end. For both of us. Go ahead, turn me in. See what'll happen."

Margot stopped. No more twitching. No more anger. The suit's light flickered as she stood above President Hulls.

She leaned in. "THEN YOU'LL MAKE A PERFECT EXAMPLE."

The very next moment, Godsend's arm plunged through the president's chest, holding his heart on the other side.

September, decades earlier. Margot stood in the bathroom of her parents' Philadelphia home.

"Come on, Margot. It'll be good for you," Margot's mom urged. "Lily's parents specifically asked for you to be there."

Margot stared at her reflection in the full-length mirror, the black dress feeling like a weight. "I don't know, Mom. I just... I don't think I can." Her voice was barely a whisper. The thought of seeing Lily's parents, of being at a ceremony dedicated to her, was a fresh stab of pain.

"She would have wanted you there," her mom continued. "You were her best friend."

The words hung in the air with heavy, unspoken grief. Margot swallowed, making sure not to cry. She smoothed down the dress, trying to steady her trembling hands. "Okay," she finally managed, the word feeling alien on her tongue. "Okay," she said again.

The drive to Jetty Beach was silent. The same sights that excited her became too heavy to bear. The beach, the hallowed end of land where Lily and Margot conquered, had become a quiet, gloomy venue. Lily's parents stood at the water's edge. The sorrow in their faces was indescribable.

Margot's stomach churned as she approached. Lily's mom, her eyes red and puffy, spotted her first. A fresh wave of tears welled up, and she rushed forward, enveloping Margot in a hug. "Margot, thank you for coming," she choked out, her voice raw with emotion.

Margot could only nod, tears silently tracing paths down her own cheeks. Lily's dad gave her a solemn pat on the shoulder.

The small gathering moved closer to the ocean. Lily's mom held a beautiful wooden box, carved with delicate seashells.

"Lily always loved the ocean," her mom began, her voice trembling but clear. "She said it was the one place where she felt truly free. Where she could breathe." A collective sniffle went through the group. "Today, we're giving her that freedom forever."

She opened the box. The ashes mixed with the saltwater. Her very soul was now imbued in that beach.

Margot stepped to the water's edge, the cool foam washing over her bare feet. She looked out at the vast expanse of the ocean, the same ocean where she and Lily had shared so many endless summers. "I promise, Lily," she whispered, her voice barely audible above the gentle crash of the waves. "I'll protect everything you found hallowed."

She stood there for hours. The tears wouldn't stop. Just moving on wasn't an option anymore. There were people out there that had a hand in this. People that made the system the way it was. People like her were crushed, pushed aside, and mistreated. It was an unforgivable sin. Margot knew that she had to etch the world with that pain. There was never another option for her in her mind.

September, 2051. The rain poured onto the streets of New York. Thousands of people stood by, looking over. Everyone wanted to see what had happened, and where the plane had crashed.

Clang, clang, clang. Metallic footsteps could be heard from over the hill. The fiery inferno in the background. Thousands of people stayed silent behind the police tape, forcing them to stay out of the area.

The crowd saw the head of Godsend. There was almost a public outcry in victory. However, people stopped their chant before it even began. There, on Godsend's right side, was the bloodied corpse of once-president, Mr. Hulls. Pupils dilated. The people stopped. The police weren't even sure what to do.

The rain was like ice. The crowds froze as Margot continued her march. *Clang, clang, clang.* The heavy footsteps marched on.

The people will love me. I saved them all. This will be my September, right Lily?

Margot's mind had detached from reality, unaware of what was going on around her as she trudged forward. It was as if she, Godsend, had no recognition that the people were even in front of her.

The people watched as she marched forward, dragging the presidential corpse with her. Behind her was a streak of blood, leading all the way back to the fiery fate of Air Force One.

Godsend, dragging the body, pressed through the caution tape. The police didn't move an inch. Nobody did. If they were to flinch, would Godsend notice them? Would Godsend take them out next?

Clang, clang, clang. Margot dragged the body of the president through the streets of New York. Not a soul moved. Cars were still. People were still. Pet owners ran away, fearing the unwanted attention.

Clang, clang, clang. Godsend walked through intersections. Through the places where people lived. Godsend brandished their ultimate achievement. There wasn't a soul that could dare threaten them anymore.

Margot pushed forward, an abhorrent mess of sleeplessness and adrenaline. There was nothing about her that was grounded anymore. But she was elated. What was this euphoric feeling? It felt disgusting.

She stopped at Wall Street. An area known to represent business. To her, a place where all evil gathered. A place where people's time was converted into the meaningless number of tradable currency. But people thought it meant something. *People were manipulated into thinking it meant something. And I have the biggest perpetrator.*

"**GO AHEAD. RUIN PEOPLE'S LIVES. MANIPULATE PEOPLE. TREAT THEM LIKE NUMBERS ON A SCREEN**," she lashed out against the world. "**BUT THIS WILL HAPPEN TO YOU**." She threw his body against the pavement. It didn't stay in one piece. The witnesses needed to grab their stomachs.

Margot's vision moved to one of those bystanders who flinched. They were crying in distress. She looked away. *But I saved you, didn't I?* She looked at her own hands. Battered. Bloodied.

"**I Th**ink... **I NEE**d som**E f**R**ES**h air..." her voice faltered, the filter breaking. Her deep breaths started to turn into rapid breathing. She attempted to get the helmet off. It wasn't coming off.

One person, willing to risk it all, walked up to Margot. She stood in front of her, a well dressed office lady. "Was it worth it, Godsend?" she asked.

"I ju**ST NEE**d... I nee**D A MINU**te... I need to breathe..." Margot continued to panic, unable to rip the suit off of herself. It was like it dug deep, sticking its own veins within hers.

"Was it worth throwing everyone's lives into disarray so you could kill the president? Even if he's a fraud... how does this help us now?" the lady cried out, "ANSWER ME!"

"**GIVE ME A MINUTE**!" Margot immediately pointed a finger toward her, prepared to shoot. She stumbled back as Margot grabbed her own arm. *I... didn't mean to do that.*

"Am I next?!" she screamed, backing up even further as Margot attempted to get the suit off of her arm.

"**NO**!" Margot shouted, "I can't get it off. I can't get **GODSEND OFF**!"

The people watched in horror as Margot clawed at her own body, the suit attempting to block her own attacks on herself.

This was supposed to be my month. I just got justice for Lily's death. I got the payback that he deserved! Her mind raced, looking back at where the president's body had been. A bloody explosion. Guts on the floor.

Was he that badly mangled? Margot thought, *Did I do that?*

"GET OFF OF ME!" Margot commanded, tearing off a chunk of the chest, and throwing it on to the ground. It attempted to jump back up, repairing itself. Margot shot it multiple times with the hand of the suit.

A police officer came to the scene. He and his pistol. "Ma'am, I'm gonna want you to back up for this one."

Margot turned to face him. He caught her in the middle of trying to strip off the armor. But it wasn't going without a fight.

"**WHAT DO YOU WANT**?" she asked. "**YOU IN WITH HULLS AS WELL**?"

The policeman gulped. "For the murder of the President of the United States..."

"No wait, I didn't mean that! It... wants me to *keep fighting!*" Margot had a hard time stopping herself.

The policeman drew his pistol, holding it so he could see down the sight. "...I hereby place you under arrest, Margot Davis."

"**SHOOT** this thing **OFF** me!" she begged, attempting to rip the suit off of her body. The policeman obliged, shooting at her. But the suit itself bounced the bullets off. It then shot back through her leg, where she hadn't ripped off yet. It just grazed the police officer.

"STOP!" she tried to stop the suit. It wouldn't. She had no choice. Gathering energy again, she jumped into the evening sky.

She flew as fast as she could. The suit both bloodied and ingrained into her. *When was the last time I stepped out of this thing?*

She continued flying, seeing Philadelphia below her now. She flew down, crashing into where her bunker had been. It was clearly raided. Parts of it were destroyed.

"COMPACT BACK INTO A DISC! NOW!" she shouted. The suit would not listen. *When did I really become Godsend?*

"You did the minute you put on the suit, Margot," a voice from behind her said. A small, young voice. Margot turned around. It was her. It was little Margot.

"What...?" Margot asked, still attempting to rip the suit off of her. She stopped, looking at her younger self. She knew now that she was losing it.

"Your friends wanted to help you. You *did* have other options..." little Margot continued, "But you weren't happy with that. Etching this pain into the world was the only one that you wanted."

"DON'T TALK TO ME LIKE YOU KNOW THAT!" Margot shouted back, sounding as if the suit had really taken her over.

304

"I *do* know that. I *am* you," little Margot asserted. "I know all of the anger you felt. I know all of the spite you felt. I know how you wanted to tear it all down. Nobody can fault you for feeling that way."

Margot grit her teeth. She didn't want this *thing* controlling her anymore. "Then why? Why did it end up like this? I never wanted to be *Godsend*!" Margot tore off another piece of the suit, "I just wanted to make a better world. A world where girls like Lily would have survived. One where the people aren't tormented by the system every damn day!"

"Is that the truth?" little Margot shot back, "Or did you just want revenge on a system that took the one person you held dear?"

The rain intensified, washing over the ruined bunker entrance. It poured over Margot's battered suit. She stood panting, clutching the mangled piece of armor in her hand, staring angrily at the apparition of her younger self.

"It's... it's not just revenge," Margot whispered, her voice failing her. She looked at the torn metal in her hand, then back at little Margot. "I wanted to protect the hallowed. Everything Lily loved."

Little Margot tilted her head, seeming to see right through her older self. "And the death of President Hulls? The detective? The military? Was that protecting the hallowed? Or was that just... satisfying your anger?"

Margot flinched, feeling exposed. "He was a symbol! A symbol of everything that took Lily from me, that took my parents. The world needed a message. They needed to *see*. If they feared something, *anything*, it would stop them from taking advantage of the people."

"So, you became what you fought against," little Margot accused. "You took lives. You instilled fear. You broke things, just like they did."

Margot stumbled back, the weight of little Margot's words crashing down on her. The suit, still clinging to her, felt heavier than ever. "No! I didn't... I had to. There was no other way. They wouldn't listen. Nothing would have changed."

"And now?" little Margot asked, stepping closer, her small hand reaching out to touch the blood-stained suit. "Is the world better, Margot? Are people safer? Or are they just... more afraid?"

Margot looked around the ruined bunker. She remembered the faces in the crowd on Wall Street, the fear, the horror. The silence. The cheers for her in Philadelphia seemed like they were just a dream.

"THIS WAS MY ONLY OPTION!" Margot shot back, the suit still not coming off. "Since you know so much, how do I get this thing *off* me already?

Suddenly, little Margot's face appeared only inches away from her own as she turned. "Stop pretending. Lily didn't do this. You did."

"GAH!" Margot was caught off-guard. She fell to the ground, hitting her tail bone in the process. She put her hand to her back, then looked back up. Little Margot was gone. But she heard footsteps approaching above.

"FREEZE, GODSEND!" Two police officers aimed from above, looking in with the rain that poured in.

"PLEASE! JUST STOP!" Margot shouted. But it was useless. They weren't responding. They were attempting to gun her down. She didn't know what else to do. Little Margot had told her to stop lying. *What did that mean?*

Margot stumbled back from the barrage of bullets. Behind her was the safe. It was the very safe she last threw her mother's cassette player in. Somehow, despite most things being taken or rummaged through, they had left that safe alone.

"FINE!" Margot cried out, a desperate plea. She grabbed the safe. She gathered energy again, zooming past the police and throwing herself back into the sky.

She flew through the sky. The rain poured as she crossed over the city. With tears in her eyes, she asked just one thing: "JUST LET ME BE FREE OF ~~GODSEND~~!"

Storm clouds littered the sky. The person many knew as *Godsend* flew through them. Margot, through the rain, saw it ahead of her. It was where the land met the sea. It was her hallowed end.

That was the beach. Jetty Beach. She hadn't been there since...

The voice of a memory played in her head. "*A horseshoe crab!*" She looked down on the beach, desperately looking for a horseshoe crab. None in sight.

Crash. The sand formed a Margot-sized pit as she landed in the sand on the Jetty.

"Lily..." Margot coughed out, getting up. The Godsend mask was half broken on her face. The place looked the same as it once did. The same waves washed up on the shore. The sand felt warm, getting through the small holes in her suit.

She remembered the days they had spent here together. How she desperately missed it. How she wanted to come back here so badly. The sand itself brought back memories. In one of them, they were adventuring.

"Lily, wait up!" Margot, much younger, cried as she chased after her friend. Lily, already by the water, scooped up a handful of wet sand, letting it sift through her fingers.

"Margot, look!" Lily exclaimed, holding up a perfect, unbroken seashell. "It's like a tiny house for a crab!"

Margot reached her, breathless. As she saw the shell, a wide grin spread on her face. "Cool! But can we find even more?"

They spent hours that day, meticulously searching the shore, each shell a treasure, each discovery a shared laugh. The sun dipped below the horizon, painting the sky

308

in hues of orange and purple. As they sat side-by-side, they gloated about how many seashells they were able to find each.

The memory faded, replaced by the reality of the stormy sky. Margot stared at the rough waves, the sand still clinging to her suit. The cold rain began to fall harder.. The weight of the suit felt heavier than ever.

"Lily," she whispered, her voice barely a croak, "I tried. I really did." She fell to her knees. Her eyes blurred with tears, the rain mixing with the saltwater on her face. Another memory surfaced, sharp and clear despite the haze of exhaustion and despair.

Margot and Lily, both teenagers, sat on the same sandy stretch of Jetty Beach. The sun was blazing, the two were freshly out of the water. Lily was tracing patterns in the sand with a stick, a frown on her face.

"You can't fix everything, Margot," Lily said, breaking the silence between them.

Margot, who had been meticulously cleaning a piece of driftwood, looked up, annoyed. "What are you talking about?"

"I'm talking about how you always try to take on the world's problems," Lily replied, the stick still in her hands as she gestured. "Like with the neighbor's dog. It's not your fault his dog ran away. Yet, you spent all day looking for it, missing out on practice."

"Someone had to," Margot retorted, defensive. "He was really upset. And I found him, didn't I?"

"That's not the point," Lily sighed, tossing her stick aside. "The point is, you don't have to carry everyone's burdens. It's too much, Margot. You're going to burn yourself out."

Margot scoffed, turning back to her driftwood. "Someone has to care, Lily. If I don't, who will?"

"But why always *you*?" Lily pressed, her voice softening slightly. "Like, you do the same thing every time I get exhausted. You notice I'm breathing differently and suddenly you start to baby me."

"Dude," Margot responded, "I can't help that. I'm worried about you."

"Margot, there's a difference between worry and babysitting. You don't need to rush to get me a bottle of water. I can do my own things."

Margot shrugged, a tight knot forming in her stomach. "I can't just stand by when things are wrong. I have to do something."

Lily looked at her friend, a worried expression on her face. "I just don't want to see you get hurt trying to save *the world*, Margot. You're going to try and protect everything, and forget all about yourself."

Margot didn't respond, ignoring her as she meticulously polishing the driftwood.

The memory shattered. *Somehow she knew back then, huh?* Margot thought. She looked up. The safe was buried in the sand in front of her. She ripped it apart with the strength of the Godsend suit, not giving it a second thought.

Inside was the cassette player. *Mom,* Margot thought. Her memories played back to her father's betrayal. How her mom entrusted everything to her, caring about her even when the rest of the world wanted to pretend she didn't exist.

"Would... you be proud...?" Margot, tears falling from her face, asked aloud. "Or... would you just be afraid?"

The cassette lay on the ground right next to where the safe was torn open. The piece of tape, decades old, somehow stayed on. It read, "On Beaches."

Margot knew this song all too well. It was with her every step of the way through her life. It was her favorite song, and one Lily said reminded her of Margot.

"I'm sorry, Lily. My ambitions, my fears... I might have used your dreams..." Margot's tears continued to flow with the rain, "...to help me move on."

She put the cassette in.

Play.

The hum of the amps first turned on. A guitar strummed, a melancholy tune. Drums kicked in, leading into the song.

As it began, all the memories of her listening to it came back.

...the days blend together...

A vibrant summer afternoon. Margot and Lily built sandcastles on the Jetty. Lily, covered in sand, giggled as a wave rushed up and flattened their moat. Margot, ever the determined one, just laughed and started digging a new trench. Lily eagerly joined in.

...when we're here in the now...

The annual town fair. Margot clutched a giant stuffed animal she'd won at the ring toss, a prize Lily had easily guided her to. Lily, with her arm linked through Margot's, dragged her towards the Ferris wheel.

"Come on, Margot! It'll be amazing! We can see the whole town from up there!" she said. Margot, hesitant but unable to resist Lily's march, allowed herself to be pulled along. As the Ferris wheel ascended, the lights of the fair twinkled below. Lily pointed out all the landmarks, her voice full of wonder, making Margot forget her fear.

311

...but it took a while to realize...

A quiet evening. The two were in Lily's bedroom. They sprawled on the floor, surrounded by textbooks and empty snack wrappers, studying for a history test. Lily, struggling with dates, threw her hands up in surrender. Margot began explaining the timeline using a series of exaggerated voices for historical figures, making Lily burst into laughter.

...that I was the happiest...

A chilly autumn evening. Margot and Lily sat bundled in blankets on a hill overlooking the city, thermos of hot chocolate between them. They were stargazing, Lily pointing out constellations she'd learned from a library book. Margot, content just to be beside her, listened while occasionally tracing imaginary lines between the stars.

...when we're on beaches.

That day. Margot pounded on the wall. Tears welled up as she relived the fresh memory of Lily's final moments. "WHERE AM I GONNA BE WITHOUT YOU, DUMBASS?!" she shouted, crying and running outside. She couldn't stay in that hospital anymore. She couldn't listen to that song right now. She knew she was afraid of death. But her friend had gone first into that fire without her.

She shouted pained noises, running through puddles throughout the beach town. She kept running, and running, and running.

"Does it not scare you?" Margot asked, looking at Lily as she looked into the horizon.

"It terrifies me."

"Me too."

"WHY?" Margot shouted, crashing into a wall on the streets of the city, "WHY DIDN'T YOU SHARE MORE WITH ME?" She pounded the wall with her fist, her tears falling to the pavement below. She saw only herself, alone. Her lips tensed up as she tried to hold in the tears coming out. She couldn't. She fell to the wet pavement, hammering the ground with her fist.

"I WOULD HAVE FORCED SOMEONE TO PAY FOR YOUR TREATMENTS! YOUR EXTRA MEDICATION! WHATEVER IT WOULD HAVE TAKEN TO SAVE YOU!" Margot desperately shouted, as if she were fighting the world itself. "I'LL GET THOSE HOSPITALS BACK! I'LL MURDER THE GUYS WHO TOOK YOUR INSURANCE FROM YOU!"

She stayed there, wailing in the rain, waiting for it to go away. The world itself became her enemy. She just wanted to burn it all to the ground.

"And... you bet," Margot sniffled, "I'll protect everything you loved. Even if it kills me."

Margot snapped back to the present, the song finishing up beside her. The drums were still crashing like the waves against the shore. She looked out to the sea, where Lily had been immortalized. She sobbed, seeing what she had done.

"I know you wouldn't have wanted revenge," Margot whispered, a pained croak coming from her throat, "I'm sorry."

Crack. The suit cracked open, exposing Margot's full head. Her arms. She was free. Turning in the sand, she looked to the horizon.

"*I just don't want to see you get hurt trying to save the world, Margot.*" The words seemed to resonate from the waves like a ghost.

"That's right, you wouldn't have wanted an apology." Margot smiled, looking out to the ocean. A small beam of sunlight peaked through, illuminating a spot on the ocean.

"I'm sorry, regardless. Guess without you I got carried away." Margot, sniffling up her tears, looked into the golden glow out at sea. "I'm ready to come join you."

Behind her, a convoy pulled up. Military personnel exited the vehicle, lining up like a firing squad. "MARGOT DAVIS! TURN YOURSELF IN OR BE MET WITH LETHAL ACTION!"

Margot ignored them, dragging herself to the sea. She barely perceived that anything was going on behind her.

"Are you sure you're ready?"

"I'm sure," Margot smiled, the track of "On Beaches" repeating in the background. The paths of tears had finally begun to dry on her face, but the song brought them right back.

Bullets went off like fireworks, going right through her. Not through Godsend, but through Margot. Her limp body fell into the ocean. Her face, half in the water, still smiled. All of that sorrow was left behind as she finally joined who she couldn't live without.

...the days blend together
when we're here in the now
but it took a while to realize
that I was the happiest
when we're on beaches.

Years had passed since the name "Godsend" was commonly on the news. Cities that had been havens for the corrupt were slowly being reclaimed. The giant towers and hidden bunkers that once housed those who profited from suffering were now silent testaments to a bygone era. The stock market took a nosedive for a few years. But as new companies with more humanitarian goals rose up, so did profits.

Education flourished, access to resources became a right, not a privilege. The change wasn't instantaneous, nor was it without its challenges, but the collective will of a people, "the hallowed," made it happen.

And through it all, a name echoed that made potential autocrats: Godsend. Nobody had ever publicly confirmed the fate of the figure who had ignited the spark of change. The mystery surrounding Godsend's end, or lack thereof, was a ghost story that haunted those who had once felt invincible.

The name "Godsend" was one of controversy. On one hand, the future that came about hinged on Godsend's existence. But if you asked anybody, they'd all agree that they wouldn't have done the same thing.

Hazel Shulz, once an honor student, was now a mayoral candidate for Philadelphia. She often spoke to President Edwin from her desk. "Sir, I can't thank you enough for the public utility bill you just helped pass. Folks here are really going to enjoy it."

Charles Edwin, now president, responded from the Oval Office phone, "Oh no problem. I like being able to help you out, Hazel. But, it also feels a little unfair. I *know* you."

Hazel laughed, sitting back on her chair. "Margot wouldn't have liked that."

"Hey! I make sure to do equal amounts with city boards everywhere!" President Edwin retorted, "But that's a throwback, huh. Margot Davis."

Hazel took a deep breath. "Her name still frustrates me. While it's not a secret that *she* was behind the whole Godsend thing, it's like people barely know. And now I *know* that information isn't being censored."

"We remember, Charles said, his voice soft. "Most remember the fear, and they remember the fight. That's why we're able to do what we're doing now, Hazel. Even if I wish that wasn't the way it happened."

Hazel nodded, looking out her office window at the bustling Philadelphia streets. The rain had stopped. People were out, living their lives. The silent battles fought and the sacrifices made were now just a memory.

"I just wish she had found another way," Hazel murmured, almost to herself. "She didn't have to... end like that."

"Perhaps not," Charles agreed, a pause on his end of the line. "But in the end, she made her choice. And we move on in the world she fought for."

The conversation shifted to city planning and upcoming legislative initiatives, but Hazel couldn't get Margot off her mind that day.

In other news, Milo just bought his first house. He had become a fashion designer, and was promoting Declan's restaurant.

"Hey!" Milo waved, getting Declan's attention from across the street. Declan raised his arm as a greeting, smiling when seeing his familiar face. He became the new owner of the restaurant he used to work at.

"About time," Declan joked, motioning Milo to follow him into his newly renovated restaurant.

"Hey! This place looks good," Milo said, gesturing to the freshly painted room.

Declan beamed. "Thanks, man. Took a lot of late nights, but it's finally feeling like my own. Amara helped with the kitchen layout, too. She's got an eye for efficiency."

"Speaking of Amara, how's she doing?" Milo asked. "Haven't seen her much since... well, everything."

Declan's smile softened. "She's good. Still teaching martial arts, but she's also started a police training program for the youth. Says it's about empowering people, not just fighting. She's really found her calling. So she only comes *here* every now and then."

"That's amazing," Milo genuinely replied. "And Owen? Last I heard, he was still tinkering."

"Oh, Owen," Declan chuckled. "He's got his own lab now, funded by the government. He's working on sustainable energy solutions. Always buried in circuits and schematics, but he's happier than I've ever seen him. Said he's finally putting his 'talents to actual good' instead of... well, you know."

The two laughed, quickly getting to taking some pictures of Milo posing for a promotional social media post.

Amara was currently at her martial arts program. "Alright, focus, everyone! Deeper stances, quicker jabs!" Amara's voice, firm yet encouraging, echoed through the brightly lit gym. A group of about fifteen kids, ranging from pre-teens to teenagers, mimicked her movements, their faces a mix of concentration and effort. She paused beside a particularly eager boy named Leo, whose punches were wild and uncontrolled. "Leo, remember what we

317

talked about," she said, gently guiding his fist. "It's not just about hitting hard. It's about precision. Intention."

Leo nodded, full of unbridled energy. "Miss Taylor, can we ever get as strong as Godsend was?" he blurted out, a hushed reverence in his voice. Several other kids stopped their movements.

"Dude, we don't talk about him," another kid tried to tell him off.

Amara stopped Leo's friend. "Godsend was... powerful," she acknowledged, choosing her words carefully. "But power alone isn't enough. Godsend fought without thinking of the consequences. We want to punch with intention, not recklessly. We want to protect, not just destroy. Every move we make, every punch we throw, has to have a purpose that serves good, not just anger."

She demonstrated a controlled jab, her movements fluid and purposeful. "Recklessness leaves a trail of broken things and unintended consequences. Intention means every strike, every block, every movement is designed to create a better outcome. To uplift, not just to tear down. Do you understand the difference?"

The kids looked at each other, some nodding slowly, processing her words. Leo watched and learned, mimicking her movements.

While Amara was teaching, Pastor Alan still had his Thursday alcoholics anonymous group going. All new people at this point. Plus, the church had been renovated, and was now "new and improved."

He cleared his throat. "Alright, everyone, settle in. Welcome, and welcome back to our Thursday evening meeting. I'm Pastor Alan." He looked around at the small circle of faces, some new, some familiar, all carrying their own silent burdens.

A chorus of "Hi, Pastor Alan" echoed around the room.

"Tonight," Pastor Alan began, his voice warm and steady, "I want to talk about forgiveness. Not just forgiving others, but forgiving ourselves. For the mistakes we've made, for the paths we've taken that led us here." He paused, his gaze thoughtful. "It's easy to hold onto anger, to replay those moments where we feel we've failed. But carrying that anger, that resentment, it's like poison. Just as drinking has become a poison to our bodies and minds..."

He never got tired of helping people and just being there for them in general. He, too, felt the effects of how the world changed after Margot Davis.

People had rebuilt, governments had changed, but many still harbored hatred toward Godsend. Owen knew that for a fact.

Owen's coworker would often talk politics with him. "I don't know about these new guys, Owen. They almost sound like Godsend apologists."

"Ah c'mon," Owen twirled away from his desk with gadgets sprawled all over it, "That was a different time. Some of us felt really passionate about the message. As much as they ended up being kind of a bad guy."

"Kind of? Godsend *killed the president* dude," Owen's coworker fired back.

"Yeah, yeah. A fraudulent one, but still one that didn't need to die. I wouldn't be an apologist either," Owen told his coworker.

"Good." His coworker left him with that, turning back to the hallway.

"Sike, I couldn't afford rent if Margot didn't freak my landlord out," Owen whispered under his breath, hoping his coworker didn't hear.

Whether or not people agreed with what happened, they accepted it and moved forward. They didn't let it define them. They didn't take the nameplate of "the hallowed." Nor did they deify any vigilante after that.

With all the tech-based billionaires like Aidan Samson unsure about their safety if they kept doing surveillance type things, they took that money and invested it in other industries. Data centers were torn down, and farming made a comeback. So did the idea of the third place. With less robots, less focus on what lies beyond the computer screen, people slowly found new trends to make money on.

Happy with the lives they led now, the old alcoholics anonymous group agreed to meet up. The location was set to be Jetty Beach. Hazel showed up a little early.

She looked down, staring off into the sea. She knew that was the place where Margot Davis met her end. She still didn't feel right about it.

"I don't like what you did..." Hazel muttered, a perplexed look on her face, "...But man, what we have now is nothing like you could imagine."

Footsteps crunched on the sand behind her, pulling Hazel from her thoughts. She turned to see Milo, impeccably dressed even for the beach, a wide smile on his face as he approached. Behind him, Owen, still looking a bit disheveled but with a genuine warmth in his eyes, waved. Declan and Amara followed, a comfortable ease in their stride as they walked towards her.

"Hazel! You got here early," Milo called out, extending an arm for a hug.

"Just wanted to get a moment to myself," Hazel replied, returning the embrace. "Glad you all made it."

Owen, Declan, and Amara stood behind Milo. They all walked up to the shore.

Owen grinned. "Wouldn't miss it. It's not every day we get the old crew back together, especially after... well, everything." He gestured vaguely at the peaceful beach around them.

Amara surveyed the scene, her eyes softening slightly. "It's strange to be here now. I know this is where... well... Margot was. Too bad not everyone knows Godsend is gone. I know my building manager would immediately charge me double."

The group laughed, a lighthearted feeling at a place with such gravity.

"Well, it's different now than it was then. The world moved on," Milo commented.

"It's less heavy," Declan added, looking out at the waves. "More... relaxing?"

Amara laughed, "Oh Declan. You could never find the words."

"Hey!" he retorted, "I just mean... Well... I'm glad we're all here. You know? We did lose a few on the way. But I'd like to think they're glad that we could be here today, together."

The group sat on the long extents of sand, beach towels and all. They talked, laughed and spent all day telling each other new stories from their personal lives. The group walked through the water as well, recounting their times with Margot in the low tide.

They remembered the laughter, the fighting, all of it. They joked about each other and how they've changed. They knew life was better now than they ever thought it was going to be, back when they all turned themselves to a group to help them wash away their personal poison. But they all escaped from their prisons, confused on whether or not they owed any of that to the person the world knew as "Godsend."

Hazel picked up a stick in the low tide. It was a stick Margot would have found familiar. "Guys..." she got everyone's attention, "This might be dumb. But whatever, just follow my lead."

Hazel went far out into the low tide, pressing the stick facing upward into the sand. Her lips wavered, trying to find the words.

"Margot, I'm sorry you never got a proper burial. I'm sorry you had to go through so much you never told us about." Hazel started to speak, her eyes pointed down at the stick as if it were a gravestone.

The others, realizing what she was doing, formed into a line behind her. They all stuck out their hands, putting them on her back as she continued. They all shared the same melancholy half-smile.

"But I hope you and your friend are happy, somewhere. Even if I don't agree with what you did," Hazel exhaled, keeping the tears in.

"But I hope you know that I don't think of Godsend when I see the way the world shines brilliantly today...

...I think of you."

-THE END

ABOUT THE AUTHOR

Justin Ferrante, also known by many nicknames (including the one on the cover), is someone who loves stories. Seeing so many good stories in the world inspired him to try and make stories of his own.

He hopes to give readers a good story to enjoy, and also wishes to produce a good story for himself. Most importantly, he aims to give readers an emotionally enriching experience through the eyes of the characters. And perhaps… give them a question to ponder.

One story read is another lifetime lived.

GODSEND

ACKNOWLEDGEMENTS

My friends, family, and all those who helped me get through life as I worked on this text, I thank you first and foremost. Any and all friends and family, far and wide, are always on my mind.

I'd like to especially thank Nelari (CursedArtistNelari) for the cover art on this. It's amazing! Glad *Deltarune* art brought us together. (Shoutout to Toby Fox?)

And a huge thanks to TakezoArt for these awesome illustrations of our central character!

And of course, the biggest thanks to my supporters who helped me make funny little movies when I was younger. Including but not limited to:
Donathon Luck
Kenneth Riles
Alex Salcedo
Alexandra Tack
Zach Leith
Justin Lordahl (+ His wonderful family)
& many more.

MARGOT DAVIS

PARTING MESSAGE

Thank you for reading **End of the Hallowed.** This Novel has been a journey for me to write, as I am sure it is one for you to read.

When creating this story, I had first come up with the ending. A single question lingered in my mind: *do the means justify the end?* And while I won't answer that for you, I will say that the contents of this novel should suffice—being some brain candy for that very question.

But the very feeling that inspired the character *Godsend* was the intrinsic human want to intervene. That feeling of wanting to do something when you see something horrible on the news. So what if there *was* a character that could do that? One with no limits that had the power to solve the problems they saw with the world? And how long would it take for that character to go from being a hero to being someone who enforces their worldview on the people around them?

I hope it was good food for thought. And also, if someone believes I am trying to glorify war or terrorism, please tell them to read the book to the end. Obviously, to you, reading the end, this is a cautionary tale—one born of mistakes and tragedies. One to make those who wish immediate harm on those they dislike to think about what they're truly asking for.

Godsend may have been able to identify the problems, but perhaps, went about it the wrong way. While the way she chose mostly worked in the end, there was certainly a less bloody way. I'll leave you with that.

-Justin Ferrante

www.ingramcontent.com/pod-product-compliance
Lightning Source LLC
Chambersburg PA
CBHW070645180626
46817CB00006B/2243